Catalyst
Book 1 in the Ronos Trilogy

Tyler Rudd Hall

Also Written by Tyler Rudd Hall

The Ronos Trilogy

Catalyst

Beacon

Eviscerate

King and Wakefield

The Death of Jonas Wakefield (Short Story)

.skinz (Short Story)

For Grandpa Steed,

Thanks for taking my mom to see *Planet of the Apes, Star Wars, Invasion of the Body Snatchers, Logan's Run*, and *Earthquake* when she was a kid.

CONTENTS

Change only happens after a shift in perspective.

Chapter 1
Flame

As the sun came up Mac Narrad learned that his random urge to get out of the house that morning had saved his life. He'd been traveling for almost a half hour and was looking for a place to turn around and head back to the city. At seven in the morning the light was not coming from the east like it always did. The inferno that came after the city-sized explosion was shedding more light than the sun that was just starting to peek over the horizon.

He was 45 miles away when the shock wave hit him. Travel on the highway instantly became chaotic. The people who noticed the explosion first either increased thrusters in fear or veered off into the dead zone running along the highway. People were awake and going about their day now. The highway was full of cars heading into the city. There wasn't enough room on the side of the road for everyone.

The highway was designed to keep traffic going. That meant that the only way to stop a vehicle was to steer to the dead zone on either shoulder of the road where the hover car's thrusters would automatically shut off. Hover cars that somehow failed while on the highway were pulled to the side by powerful magnets that sensed when large objects weren't moving or when there was some kind of obstruction.

But the explosion knocked out the power to the highway. The dead zones on either side of were already at capacity and backing up onto the highway. The power was out so the magnet's sensors were not operating. Drivers who didn't steer for the shoulder smashed into the cars that were blocking the way.

Northbound traffic was a bloody mess in a matter of

seconds. No one was looking at the traffic. They all had their eyes on the flame engulfing the city in front of them.

Mac saw the genesis of the explosion. He was looking in the rear view mirror just as it was happening. There was just one ship but it was huge—the size of a small city. Northgate wasn't a small city. It had ten million people but Mac figured the out-of-place ship probably cast a shadow over more than half of Northgate. The ship looked like the top half of an oval. The curved top was completely smooth. From where he was it looked like it was one big piece of metal, but he knew that couldn't be true and attributed it to the distance between them.

There were no military ships that looked like this. Mac didn't even have to look it up—he knew everything about the ships he worked with. But he had seen this ship before; it was the same ship that had taken her five years previously.

It dropped out of the clouds unchallenged, or at least he thought it was unchallenged. The ship was so far away it was hard to see. If the military was defending at all it would be with HAAS3s, which were impossible to see from this distance.

Mac didn't notice the highway chaos at first, either. All he could think about was his family. *How close were they to the explosion? Northgate is a big city. Is it all gone now? If only they had Imps. Then I could contact them immediately. Wait, what about Chester?* Mac logged on and tried to link with his brother-in-law but there was no way to make the connection. *Is he just not answering or have they been killed?* Next time he saw his family he was going to use this as an example for why they needed to get Imps, regardless of their age or philosophy.

Imp was short for Implant which was a computer inside the brain and eyes that could be operated by thought. It was the ultimate hands free technology and nearly everyone had one from nearly birth. Mac's parents and most of the people from his small town chose not to have Imps. They worried about the government hacking the computers in their brains. Mac had only gotten one so he could enlist, a condition required for all soldiers.

Mac used his mind to bring up the display from the tiny computer implanted in his brain. There was at least one person in Passage who had an Imp. The village was so anti-government that Mac didn't know about him until he got an Imp of his own.

"What's up, Mac?" the man said when he called.

What a stupid question. Passage was close enough to hear that explosion. The only man in Passage with an Imp obviously knew what was happening.

"I need to know for sure who attacked us," said Mac.

"This is bad."

"I know. I need to find out for sure as soon as I can. I think it's the aliens, but you have access to more information than I do."

"The news is just starting to come in. Was it all of Northgate?"

"I don't know."

"I thought you were with your family in Northgate?"

"No. I left this morning. Can you reach them?" said Mac.

"I tried as soon as it happened. I couldn't get ahold of your brother-in-law. I was just about to call you when you called me."

"Keep trying. If you hear anything, call me."

"Of course."

Mac double blinked to end the conversation, another skill that had been difficult for him to pick up. More than once he had ended a conversation prematurely just by blinking normally. He looked around at the chaos on the highway. Everyone was talking, seemingly to themselves, but they were all using Imps to try and find out what was going on.

There were groups of people standing around talking. Others were trying to help people who were hurt in the accidents. Since he knew first aid, Mac tended to a woman with a cut on her head. She didn't even notice—she just kept trying to get in touch with people she knew.

"No one is answering," she said. "What does that mean?"

"Where do they live?" asked Mac.

"In the city."

"Which part?"

"Northeast. Glover area."

Mac's family was visiting his sister who lived in the southwest. There was still hope.

The woman with the cut on her head was going to be fine. Without saying thank you, she staggered away from Mac.

There were people yelling all over the place. Everyone was facing north. The flames still burned strong. The alien ship was gone. The attack happened so quickly—one minute the citizens of Northgate were waking up from a restful night and the next they were all dead or dying. Mac scolded himself for thinking so negatively. His family was still alive. He just had to find them.

Soon people were shouting out the names of towns they had managed to reach to talk to loved ones. The nagging question was, How far north will we get before the shouting stops?

"I got Hastings!" Not impressive. They had just passed through Hastings.

"Cline!"

"Masterson!"

"Colester."

Reaching Colester was a good sign; it was only fifteen minutes outside the city. The next settlement was Duchess. But no one was shouting out that name. Mac was standing beside a man who was jumping from link to link on his Imp trying to make a connection with someone. Anyone.

"I work at a firm in Duchess. I just called everyone on my list and nothing went through. I can't get ahold of any of them."

"That doesn't mean anything bad happened there," said a cup-half-full guy. "It just means their Imps aren't working."

Everyone knew Imps only stopped working if you were dead. No one said what everyone knew, what Mac already suspected.

But he had to know for sure.

Not knowing, he couldn't do that.

Not again.

He went back to his vehicle and tried to start it. The power to the highway and the dead zone was turning on and off. Emergency power was being rerouted from somewhere but it wasn't enough to keep the highway constantly powered. Mac had been one of the first to dodge into the dead zone, but even though there was nothing blocking him from going off-road there was no way he was going to get out there on his own. He enlisted help from some of the other people around him to push the car onto the grass beside the road.

"Take me with you," said one man. "I'll pay you anything you want."

Mac flashed his military ID. "You don't want to go where I'm going."

The hover car that Mac was driving was not very luxurious. It couldn't hover more than a few feet. The higher the hover the more luxurious the vehicle. Driving off road demanded careful concentration on his part. Even though he was traveling mostly over prairie to get to the city, he had to watch for uneven terrain, trees, livestock, and mostly, roiling rivers.

He struggled to keep his mind on driving when all he

could think about was the possibility of being an orphan and never seeing Janelle Stewart again. Janelle. She had been abducted five years before and was the reason he joined the military. He still hadn't been able to find her. Mostly because he still hadn't even seen the front line of the war. It was on the edge of explored space and the military had tight control over who went. He didn't know why. His Father, Richard Narrad, said that he knew where Janelle was and that Mac would be able to see her that very day. Richard wasn't a practical joker and he understood how serious this all was. No doubt he had done some digging around on his own or hired someone to. Mac's parents had never been warm to the idea of him being in the military because the military had forced him to get an Imp.

Imps had been around for his and his parent's whole lives. The Imp was created by a communications company to replace holographic phones. Sending messages from one brain to the other was awesome at first, as most new technology is. Everyone jumped at having one. Then newer versions came out. They could reach anyone on the planet. Then they could easily record and store every conversation.

That was the first hint that things were going sideways. It was becoming a device authorities could use to orchestrate a virtual but disconnected reality, at a time when no one even knew what it meant to be disconnected. There had never been a technology that worked so well to break a human mind.

The Imp wasn't designed to be the drug of the future, but that's what it became. When people who had Imps died, the family could upload everything their dead loved one had seen and heard. People started to get lost in old memories. They became so fixated on what they had lost, that they didn't notice they were losing everything else. They became disconnected from the rest of the world.

This didn't happen to everyone but it happened often enough that it was becoming a problem. What to do with the Imp information left over after someone died was still a hotly-debated question.

Soon companies were popping up offering simulated conversations with anyone. Children and adults could get vidcalls from famous people, dead people, or that hot girl a teenager had a crush on. Cases of disconnected people skyrocketed. People couldn't stop living imaginary lives through their Imps.

Then it came out that the government could track an individual's unique Imp signature. Initially viewed as an outrageous Big Brother control method, it was justified because it cut back on crime. Laws were put in place so that only certain people would be tracked: repeat criminals, sex offenders, and such. The only way the police could track an average Joe was with a warrant from a judge. These cases were rare and only happened if you were a suspect running from the law.

That's when the Imp companies started working for the government. Once they were working for the government they became the government. It was hard to tell where the Imp company ended and the government started. People's values were changing. The world started revolving around the Imps. With Imps, people could be controlled. They knew what people wanted to hear and they lied to get them on their side.

People like Mac's grandparents who were already old and didn't want the Imp surgery considered themselves lucky. They moved their families out of the city into Passage. They taught their kids to make choices for themselves. Kids were never told, Imps are evil and the government is corrupt. The adults presented all the facts. All of the facts, not just the ones that made the Imps seem absolutely necessary to existence. And then, aware of all the pros and cons, they could decide for themselves.

Of course it was hard to keep that ideology going. Maybe Mac's grandparents were all about having their kids make choices for themselves, but Mac's mom and dad told their kids that getting an Imp was turning your life over to someone else and they were never ever to do it. That lecture was wasted on Mac.

The hover car twisted onto its side and Mac banged his head against the window. He was too busy daydreaming to realize he had come to the Matzhiwan River. The car slid down the embankment towards the water and then came to a crashing halt against some trees. Mac cursed his own stupidity.

The car and his Imp detected the accident. Alarms were going off in his head and emergency calls were being made. Mac had to think quickly to cancel both emergency calls. There were laws against going off the highway. He was in the military, but he was only a Spacer so it wasn't like he could do whatever he wanted.

He shook the shock of what happened out of his head and looked around him. The embankment wasn't too steep. If the hover car still worked, he could go back up. The hover car had stopped running. To start it, he put his hand on the center of the steering wheel. After a quick scan of his hand, the display lit back up. The engine struggled to start. After a few awkward clicks and some banging noises, it came around.

The car started hovering. The hood scraped against the tree it had run into. It wasn't in park. The thrusters were still propelling the car forward. The tree groaned as it was pushed. Frantically, Mac tried to put it in reverse, but it wasn't working. The crash had messed up the computer. The lights were flashing on and off. The car was starting and stopping on its own which transformed the car into a battering ram. It hit the tree three times. The tree teetered back and forth. There was no question it was coming down.

Mac tried to steer away from it but the car's start-and-stop sequence prevented him from getting very far and mostly made things worse. The car spun around to the other side of the towering tree, so that it fell on top of Mac. The tree collapsed the entire passenger side of the car. Glass and debris flew everywhere. Mac felt cuts on his face and arms. Sparks from the console leapt onto the tree. Its leaves ignited immediately. The car was filling with an uncomfortable amount of smoke.

Mac pushed, kicked, and rattled the driver's side door. It wouldn't budge. The leaves were burning up quickly but not quick enough to set the trunk on fire. Once a tree branch caught flame the rest of them would follow. But even if they didn't, Mac would die of smoke inhalation before anything else. The windshield was broken. That was as a good an exit as any. He cut his hand on the broken glass as he pulled himself through the opening. After falling to the ground he quickly rolled away.

His adrenaline was pumping; he needed to take advantage of this energy rush.

BOOM!

The fuel from his hover car ignited. He was far enough away that the explosion itself didn't hurt him, but he was still close enough that the force of it shot him into the air and slammed him to the ground several feet away.

That got rid of his adrenaline.

Chapter 2
Front-Line Interrogation Tactics

When Mac woke up, the sun was at its zenith. He cradled his aching head in his hands and shielded his eyes from the bright sunshine. Several hours had gone by since the crash. Squinting, he surveyed the aftermath and realized how lucky he was to be alive. The car was burned out and most of the tree was charcoal, but that was the extent of the damage. Dry grass, just waiting to be lit up, was all that stood between him and the wreckage. Had the fire spread any farther, he would have been in serious trouble.

The amount of smoke coming from the car was minimal—there should have been way more. Some kind of safety mechanism must have been activated to douse the flames. As he walked closer to the hover car, wet foam on the ground confirmed his suspicions. Chester had paid extra for a cool new safety upgrade on the family vehicle. It had saved Mac's life.

His body felt like it had just been thrown down a flight of stairs. The few steps he took were slow and cautious as he looked to see if any part of him had been injured. Beyond minor scrapes and bruises he was doing okay, just a little stiff.

He was still miles away from Northgate, had no idea if his family was alive, and now he had no way of getting there other than to walk. Knowing it was a lost cause, he tried again to call Chester on his Imp. Nothing. There was, however, a message from the offices of Major Spacer Commander Littleton—that was the third highest rank in the military. **Spacer Mac Narrad, you are to report to the command post in the Northgate recovery area immediately. Since you are visiting your family on Earth a shuttle will be sent to pick you up. Further**

orders will be presented once you arrive. Mac's vacation had just been cancelled. The time stamp on the message read 09:00—two hours ago. They would have expected a response by now. He sent a message back saying he was going to be late.

Then he contacted the only man in Passage with an Imp to get an unbiased update on what Mac had missed while he was unconscious.

"What's up?" the man asked Mac.

"I got in an accident."

"Really? You okay?"

"Yeah, I'm fine. Any updates?"

"About your family? No. No one has heard anything from them here. But there's not much people can do here other than go up to Northgate and start digging through the rubble."

"How bad is it?"

"Complete. The last reports before the military put the kibosh on media coverage said that the whole city has been destroyed. There wasn't a single building left standing. I don't know if it's true. I saw some of the pictures but it wasn't a bird's-eye view. It was from the ground on the north end, so it's possible that there are still some left."

"Any survivors?"

"I haven't heard anything yet, but there has to be."

Mac could hear an approaching shuttle. They were coming to pick him up.

"I gotta go," said Mac.

"As soon as they let people into the city, let me know what you find."

"What do you mean 'as soon as they let people in the city'?"

"No one is allowed in right now. There's all kinds of radiation or something."

Mac said good-bye and double blinked.

The aliens were crafty. He had heard this about them before. Blowing up an entire city wasn't enough for them. They also used radioactive weapons so that the survivors didn't have a chance.

The approaching shuttle was an HAAS3—not what Mac was expecting. A transport shuttle would have been more appropriate. It must have been the vehicle that was closest. Or maybe the fastest.

The shuttle landed and only one person got out, an older man with orange hair. People with orange hair don't go gray as quickly as others, but if this guy's hair were any other color it definitely would have grayed by now. He was old and skinny, but he was wearing the uniform of a major in Military Intelligence. That high rank, and the sense of urgency in his step, was enough to make Mac worried. Something was wrong.

The man pulled out his gun.

"What's going on?" asked Mac. He had his hands up.

"Name and rank?" asked Orange.

"Spacer Mac Narrad. Just got assigned to Northgate recovery but I crashed before I got there."

"What are you doing out here?"

"Avoiding the highways."

"You're a Luddite?" Orange must have done his research.

"I have an Imp."

"Get down on your knees."

Mac obliged. He didn't have a choice. Orange had the gun pointed right at his head. *What is going on? Am I being targeted as the enemy? What does this have to do with being a Luddite?*

A text message came over Mac's Imp.

Message received. Shuttle dispatched. Report to Captain Austin at base.

That meant Orange wasn't here on official business. For all Mac knew he was some zealot who stole a HAAS3 and a uniform. A disgruntled employee? The military had a fair share of those. Whenever one of them was stressed beyond their breaking point, things got ugly. It almost always ended with someone getting shot.

"What's your name?" asked Mac.

"I'll be asking the questions. What do you know about the attack?"

"I saw an alien ship. I didn't recognize the weapons, but I hear they're radioactive. I don't know more than that. Was the entire city destroyed?"

"How do you know it was alien?" asked Orange.

"I've seen it before."

"Impossible. You've never been to the front line."

"No, but I've seen people get abducted by the same kind of ship. This was an alien attack."

Orange said, "That's what everyone thinks. Except for us. This wasn't an alien attack. I don't know what it was, but right now the front runner is a Luddite conspiracy. Aren't you all opposed to government and authority?"

"If I was, would I have joined the army?"

"You would if you were a spy."

This is ridiculous. When is the other shuttle going to get here? I don't want this rogue to shoot me.

"Are you going to arrest me?"

Orange shuffled his feet. He clearly didn't have the authority, or he didn't have enough evidence. There was nothing to dispute Mac's story. Orange looked over at the burned-out hover car.

"If we find out you set that hover car on fire to destroy evidence, then I will gladly be the one to take you away. You know the penalty for treason, right? Death."

Orange put the gun away. As much as he wanted Mac to be guilty, he knew there was nothing he could do right now. Based on the way the officer was behaving, Mac guessed that the major was part of a minority of people who believed that aliens were not responsible for the attack.

They could hear the sound of a second shuttle approaching. Orange started walking away from Mac. A transport shuttle landed nearby. Of the several people on board, six spacers and a lieutenant to boss them around came over to Mac's burned-out hover car. They started taking pictures and investigating the scene. Orange looked pleased with their progress. Then another HAAS3 landed, and all three of its occupants got out.

The leader of the group walked toward Mac. He had the same type of uniform as Orange did. He was also tall and thin, but unlike Orange's round head, this new guy's head came to a distinct point in the middle of his face. It looked like he could use his own face as a can opener in a tough situation.

"Spacer Narrad, I'm Major Raymond Tysons. Please follow me."

"Where are we going?"

"No questions."

Raymond, flanked by two spacers acting as guards, led Mac to the HAAS3. Mac figured maybe Raymond had sent Orange out ahead to do some initial questioning. Mac was definitely getting a bad vibe from this newcomer.

Raymond directed Mac to the back seat and sat beside him. One of the guards stayed behind and the other got into the pilot's seat.

Mac was fighting the temptation to try to get some information out of Raymond, but he didn't think that Raymond would tell him anything. And having ordered "No questions," he might punish Mac for asking anything.

The HAAS3 lifted up. They didn't need to get very high before Mac could see the destruction of Northgate. The sky to the north was still full of smoke, and even from as far away as they were, they could still see flames all over the city. It didn't look like anything could have survived. Any hope he had that his family might still be alive was reluctantly fading. The longer he looked at the destruction, the harder it was for any degree of hope to survive. He looked away, focused on other things. Birds. He saw birds flying over the city. If there was still a chance for the birds to survive then there was still a chance for his family. He just had to believe that the only man in Passage with an Imp was wrong about the radioactive weaponry.

Mac noticed that a military base was being set up on the outskirts of the city, in a farmer's field about ten miles south of Northgate. The base was still under construction, but there were enough makeshift buildings and tents for the top officers to start organizing rescue efforts and a counter-attack.

Massive trucks brought supplies needed for erecting temporary barracks, storage shelters, and administrative offices. As soon as the wheels touched down and were locked in place, military personnel surrounded the trucks to unload them and start setting things up. Computer terminals, tables, and desks were whisked away to the five large temporary structures in the center of the base.

As the HAAS3 made its approach, Mac could see three distinct areas of the base: the command centre, the airfield, and a fenced-off area. The main area comprised the command centre and administration buildings. Here the hover trucks were unloaded and sent back for more supplies. At the airfield, a steady stream of shuttles landed and lifted off. Some shuttles were flying over the city. Mac wanted to know what they were doing and how he could get on one of them. The fenced-off area had guards at the gate and it didn't look like anyone was being allowed inside. It had its own separate landing area with a dozen shuttles at the ready. The makeshift shelters here were small and spread out. In between them and the shuttles, soldiers were lined up and getting orders from a fat man in a uniform.

As Mac's HAAS3 got closer, he could see the fat man was General Zinger, the man in charge of all military operations. Whatever was going on in the fenced-off portion of the base was a big deal. Unfortunately, Mac's shuttle landed in the main airfield.

"Come with me," said Raymond.

He led the way through the base. They were moving away from the fenced-off area and toward the big administrative buildings. The makeshift buildings, resembling square tents, were all made out of thick, metallic cloth. The cloth repelled precipitation and kept the inside temperature at a comfortable level. The steel framework was set up first and then the cloth was draped over it. The cloth's metallic qualities were so strong that even high winds would not be able to disengage it from the framework. Inside the big administration building, temporary walls were put up to cordon off the covered area into several rooms.

Mac was taken to one of these rooms. All it had in it was a chair. The rest of the building had temporary flooring, but all this room had was dirt and grass. All the fun of being outdoors without that pesky sun.

"Have a seat," said Raymond.

"Did I do something wrong?" asked Mac.

"Sit down."

Mac sat down.

"Hold out your wrist."

Mac complied, knowing full well what was coming next. Raymond wanted to snap on an Imp recorder. Under the law, no one could be cut off completely from their Imp feeds. Imp tampering was outlawed. Technology companies weren't even allowed to research that area.

But authorities didn't want prisoners or anyone privy to sensitive information to have full reign of their Imps. There was no point locking up a mob boss if he could still easily run things from his cell with his Imp. So instead of taking away their rights, authorities would slap on an Imp recorder and record everything they looked at, read, or heard over their Imp.

It was just the kind of Big Brother device that the people in Passage were worried about, but Mac knew that usually only criminals got Imp recorders. Without the wrist device, Imp users could rest assured their feeds were private. He wasn't sure how it worked, though. How this thing on his wrist could record his sensory information.

"Hold out your wrist. I won't ask again," said Raymond.

Mac held out his left wrist. The thick metal bracelet snapped shut.

"Why are you doing this? Have I been charged with something?"

"You are a person of interest in the destruction of Northgate."

"What?!"

"I'll be back later to question you," Raymond said as he walked out of the room.

Mac couldn't believe what was going on. *They think I had something to do with it? The ship—it was obviously an alien attack. No human could be blamed. Except maybe the idiots who let the ship get all the way from the fringe of space to Earth. But that wasn't my fault.*

Mac couldn't sit down, but he didn't have much room to pace. Still sore from the crash, he moved gingerly. There was no time to rest—he was suspected of killing ten million people and had to think of a way to convince them of his innocence.

The Imp recorder was a way to trick panic-stricken fools into giving over evidence. The interviewer would leave them alone for a long time and wait for the suspects to lower their guard and use their Imp to do something incriminating. Everything recorded could be used against them. Trying too hard to look innocent—sending out fake messages or looking up unsanctioned information—was just as bad. It never turned out well. The best strategy was to do absolutely nothing with your Imp, and that's what Mac did.

He was innocent, and the only way Raymond could prove otherwise was to bend the truth, fabricate evidence against Mac. Mac had nothing to hide. If it came down to it, he would turn over all his Imp feeds. Everything he had seen or looked up since he got the Imp three years ago. Then they would see he had nothing to do with it.

As he walked back and forth, Mac told himself over and over that everything was going to be okay and that they would believe him. Eventually Mac calmed himself down enough to sit again. He wondered how much time had passed. He wanted to check on his Imp, but he wasn't sure if that would imply something that could be used against him, so he just left it alone. A flashing green light in his peripheral vision indicated he was getting an incoming call, but he didn't answer. It was probably the only man in Passage with an Imp. Now was not the time to talk to him.

Mac waited.

Raymond came back in the room. Orange followed.

"Did you guys get things straightened out?" Mac asked.

"You are Spacer Mac Narrad," said Orange, ignoring Mac's question.

"Yes. What's your name?"

"Major Jace Michaels, Military Intelligence. You are twenty-one years old. Joined up three years ago. Right on your eighteenth birthday. Just couldn't wait to start serving, could you?"

Jace and Raymond laughed, but Mac didn't get the joke. Jace continued.

"Says here that you grew up in Passage. That's interesting. Not big fans of technology there. But you still joined us? Got your Imp at eighteen, never heard of anyone doing that before. You're okay with switching your allegiances, I assume."

"What are you saying?" Mac asked.

"You grew up Imp-less. You can't be trusted. You've been military for three years. Learning everything you can about us. You signed up for more classes than I've taken my whole career. Whenever you have a choice you always go for the off-world assignments. You check military records and census reports weekly—sometimes daily—and have been reprimanded for trying to access classified information twice. Once more and the military would take action against you, and knowing General Zinger, your family too."

"General Zinger wouldn't do that."

"I guess we can add sucking up to General Zinger. I look at this list and I see that you are looking for something. What is it?"

Mac knew they wouldn't believe him so he didn't say anything. The fake smiles were gone from both of their faces.

"Some files are kept confidential from the census and military records. Do you know what those are?" asked Jace.

No response.

"Troop movements. Ever been to the front? Dumb question, I know. I have your whole life right here in my hands. There is one drawback to taking all those military classes. You don't get to go on as many missions. You've never been to the front, so you might not know this, but then no one on the front knows anything. Everything has to be kept a secret. The more people who know what goes on up there, the more liabilities we have. Have you heard the stories? The aliens don't kill you. They…take you. They take you and make you talk. They turn our own people against us. Troops go missing and soon the aliens know everything about what they were going to do and then use the information against us. We are losing this war…"

Raymond interrupted with a fit of coughing. Jace backtracked.

"*If* we lose this war, it will be because we lost control of information. The reason the entire city of Northgate was destroyed was that someone knew exactly where to go to slip past our fleet. I don't need you to tell me what you were looking for on those census reports and ship manifests. Those were just rhetorical questions. Once we arrest you for treason—and the murder of ten million people—we will have full access to your Imp feed. Then we'll know everything about you. *Everything.* I just need to hear you say the words. Tell me you were the one who made all this happen. Tell me this was Luddites and not aliens."

"No," said Mac. "You don't have to arrest me to get access to my Imp feed. I'll give it to you. Everything. You'll see I had nothing to do with this. I wasn't trying to find out fleet movements or what troops were where. I was just trying to find a friend who got abducted back when the war started. You gotta believe me."

"How long have you had an Imp?" asked Jace.

"Three years."

"How long do you think it would take to plan the destruction of, not just an entire city, but a city in the middle of the most secure part of your enemy's home? That's not just something you wake up and do. Whoever did this has been planning this for at least three years. Ever since the war started."

"That's insane."

"What were you doing out there in the middle of nowhere?"

"I told you I was trying to get back to Northgate to look for my family."

"Why didn't you wait for us to come pick you up?"

"I couldn't wait. I needed to know if they were still alive. Did you find anything in my car?"

"No. Not yet."

Not until they planted something, Mac figured, *and did they really think he was involved in an alien conspiracy as a teenager?*

Raymond stepped forward, "The people are already screaming for blood. Do you understand? We don't need you to confess. Not with what we have and what we will find—" *What you'll plant,* thought Mac, "—there will be enough evidence to give you, and any family members you have that might still be alive, the death penalty. Going Impless will become illegal. We don't really need you to say anything. I personally would like to just pinpoint the blame. Just admit that you had something to do with this."

"No," said Mac, and his face exploded with pain when Raymond hit him in the face with his elbow.

"That won't change my answer," said Mac.

Another elbow. And another.

"Easy, Raymond. That's not how we do things," said Jace.

"It's how I do things," said Raymond. He landed another strike with his elbow. Mac's head snapped back so fast he thought it might just break off and roll along the ground. "If you don't like it, you can leave."

When Jace left, Mac's heart sunk.

Raymond started using his fists now. It didn't hurt as much, but it wasn't like getting hit with cotton balls either. The blows switched from Mac's face to his chest. There was nothing Mac could do. Raymond's elbow shots had rendered him defenseless. Feebly raising his arms proved useless; Mac knew if he dropped to the floor, Raymond would take his boots to him.

"It doesn't matter what you say. The truth is whatever I say it is. Once everyone finds out a Luddite did all this, they will kill all of you. Your family dies with you."

Mac already had mini HAAS3s spinning around his head. He clung to the hope that the threats to his family meant Raymond knew they were still alive.

An eternity passed before Jace came back. With him was a man that Mac had met before. This new man was severely obese. His chin hung below his neck line and his cheeks were jowly like an old man's. His girth did not slow him down, though. In Passage, he would have been called "farmer fat"—a guy who looks and sweats like he's eaten a few too many cheeseburgers but who is actually very strong. The man's name was General Zinger.

"What happened here?" asked General Zinger.

Raymond was unable to come up with a lie fast enough.

"We don't need to be doing this right now. What a mess. He had nothing to do with anything. Wash him up and give him medical treatment. Then bring him to the forward command post." Zinger pointed his mighty finger at Raymond, "He will not be harmed between here and there. You aren't on the front line anymore. This isn't how we do things here. If he gets harmed any further then multiply it by a hundred and that's what you'll get."

Mac was freed. His face was cut and bleeding in several places. His body ached all over and his legs felt like overcooked spaghetti. Raymond stared him down while Jace led him out of the room and towards the medical center.

Mac hoped he would never have to deal with Raymond again, but there was something in that pointy-faced man's eyes that said he wasn't done with his interrogation.

Chapter 3
Lynn

Lynn Ryder was at the hospital in Northgate asking if this was where her husband had been admitted. The girl at the front desk didn't even look up at her as she typed the name into the computer. The results came back. He wasn't there. Frustrated, Lynn demanded that she check again. The clerk pushed some keys, looked closely at the monitor and said the search results were the same. Lynn suspected the clerk was only humoring her—going through the motions but not actually repeating the search—but there was nothing she could do about it.

Lynn had just walked out of the building when the attack began. Something was blocking out the sun. She looked up, expecting to see cloud cover, and gasped at the sight of a massive ship. It covered almost half of the sky above her. She couldn't see its stern, because tall buildings obstructed her view. Normally no ship that large would be allowed to fly so close to the city, but since no one was trying to stop it, she told herself it had to be all right.

It wasn't all right. Missiles started launching from the ship's underbelly. Blue streaks flew through the air as the missiles rocketed toward their destinations. Every time they struck the ground or a building, an explosion followed. The flurry of destruction started slowly but quickly escalated. The number of missiles coming from the ship doubled, and then tripled, until hundreds filled the air at one time. The whole city seemed to be on fire.

An explosion near Lynn tossed her into the air, and she landed with a thud on a hover bus roof. Her head was buzzing as the world around her turned into chaos. She watched in horror as a streaking missile hammered into the hospital and cringed when she felt the heat from the ensuing explosion. The building broke apart. She swallowed hard when she thought about the hospital clerk she had just been talking to. Lynn groggily looked around. She couldn't see any buildings that had not suffered damage, and very few that could even be recognized as buildings anymore.

But the attacking ship still wasn't done. Missiles kept beating down on the already broken city. Another one hit close enough to the bus to lift it into the air with her still on the roof. She screamed as she fell off the bus and onto the sidewalk. She knew she must have injuries, but she was too full of adrenaline to feel anything. If she stayed there she was going to die. She had heard that during a tornado people were supposed to hide in basements, but missiles weren't tornados. She asked herself, *How can anyone hide from so many missiles?*

Her fear morphed into anger. *Who is doing this? Who is destroying Northgate?* She didn't know exactly what kind of ship it was, spaceships weren't her bailiwick, but her best guess was that it was neither built, nor flown, by humans.

Her husband, Scott, had been mistakenly diagnosed as clinically insane for refusing to supply ammunition to the war effort. He was thrown into the psych ward by authorities who maintained that only a crazy person would do nothing while his people were being destroyed.

Scott had said he found out the truth: that there was no war. There was no alien menace. He would be supplying ammunition to an army whose only purpose was to control the populace.

Lynn believed him. Even as she looked at the ship in the atmosphere above her, she still somehow believed him.

The ship was in the middle of its destructive onslaught. Brilliant blue lights sped away in every direction from its cannons. So many that their neon blue became the new color of the sky.

Lynn didn't know where to go, so she just started running. When the last building standing in the area was hit, the roaring wave of compressed air engulfed her again. This one threw her back the way she had come. Back towards the remains of the psychiatric hospital.

The basement floor had not been structurally destroyed, even though its interior looked like it had been mixed up in a blender. Lynn landed on a hospital bed. That would have been a fortunate coincidence had she landed full on, but she landed half on and half off. The half-off part included her head, which banged on the floor.

While the city continued to crumble around her and force waves swept through the streets picking up cars, people, and buildings like they were paper, all Lynn could think about before the blackness overtook her was that she was not alone. She passed out as a man in patient's garb walked towards her.

When she regained consciousness she heard a voice.

"You hit your head pretty hard," said an unfamiliar male voice.

The room was dark. She was on a bed. There were no pillows or blankets. The cold was getting to her. *Why is it so cold?* She took in her surroundings and remembered what had happened. The annihilation of Northgate came rushing back to her all at once. Above her, where the ceiling should have been, there were only stars. They were hard to spot, though, and not because they were competing with the city lights. They were competing with the glow from the fires. The attack had happened in the early morning, so she must have been unconscious all day. She wondered if the entire city had burned down in that time.

"Here, have some water," the man said. It was the man she had seen before she passed out. He was a patient at the hospital. She could see the name tag on his wrist, flashing *Tek Dernson.*

She sat up too fast and almost fell over again. "Easy," said Tek. "Remember, your head?"

Lynn felt her head. Her strawberry-blond hair was partially covered by a bandage. She steadied herself and drank some water.

"Thank you," she said, indicating the water and the bandage. "For everything."

"Don't thank me yet. We still have issues."

"Issues?"

Tek looked over his shoulder at the door. It led into what remained of the hallway. There was enough open space beyond the debris from a collapsed section of wall for her to see that there was no one else out there.

"We aren't the only ones who survived," said Tek. "There's another patient here who found an orderly's uniform. He's going to try and fool you into thinking he's not crazy, but he is. And he's very dangerous. He wouldn't be able to process what happened here on the best of days, so he's just reverting to what he does best. Hurting people."

Lynn didn't know if she should trust Tek. A patient in a mental institution just told her not to trust the orderly. Although the world around her was on fire, she didn't want to start doubting everything. She would stick with the orderly being the one to trust.

"My name is Tek, by the way," he said.

"I know. I saw it on your wrist," said Lynn.

Tek looked down at his wrist and then ripped the I.D. tag off.

"Where does the name *Tek* come from?" asked Lynn.

"I don't know. My parents, I guess. Isn't that where you got your name?"

"Yes."

"What is your name?"

"Lynn. What's the other guy's name?"

"His name is George Mems, but he won't go by that name in case you've heard of him. He'll come up with some orderly-sounding name. Right now he is outside trying to see if he can find a way out of here. I volunteered to stay here in case you woke up. And I'm hoping he hurts himself out there and doesn't come back."

"Are we the only survivors?"

"In the whole city? I doubt it. In this building? Yes. Maybe even in the immediate area."

Lynn drained the rest of the water. It was energizing her again. Her senses felt sharper by the time she finished. Getting off the bed, she took stock of herself. Never had she looked like a fit person, even though she had always been able to hold her own. There was some extra cushion in the back and she usually avoided form-fitting clothes just so she could more easily hide her unflattering curves, not that there were a lot of them or that they were noticeable by anyone but her.

Her left leg was the worst. There was a big cut going up the side. As she took some test steps, pain shot through that leg and up into her body. Her left pant leg was shredded. The only reason it wasn't flapping around right now was because of the bandages someone applied.

"Did you bandage me up?" asked Lynn.

"No. George did. I tried to help but he wouldn't let me. I'm not even sure your head was bleeding, but he bandaged it anyway when I told him how you fell."

Lynn reached up and felt her head. It hurt enough to tell her it was bruised, but the bandage was dry. She took it off and found no blood underneath either. Her hair was a tangled mess now. Just yesterday she had thought about cutting it short. She had always worn it long, and she thought cutting it would keep her from being recognized. Then she figured hair length didn't matter—as long as she had her Imp the authorities would be able to track her if they needed to.

She tried calling her parents on her Imp. It didn't work. She couldn't even bring up a list of contacts or a status report or anything. It felt so foreign to have a clear view of everything going on around her. There was always some little icon blocking her vision. Some little light that would eventually fade into the background, but was always still there.

Now there was nothing.

Lynn had never experienced anything like this before.

"Your Imp, is it working?" asked Lynn.

"No. Neither is George's."

Lynn was beginning to think that there was no George. Tek was, after all, a psychiatric patient. Maybe George was his imaginary friend.

"How is that possible?" Lynn asked. "There should be something there. Even an indicator it's not working. I've had that before, but what I'm seeing now, what I'm *not* seeing now, is impossible."

"Unless you get invasive surgery, but they only do that stuff in the movies."

Lynn did some practice laps around the small room to make sure her leg would work well enough to walk away from here. She kept looking at the door waiting for George to come back, but no one came.

"I'm not waiting for anyone to come back," said Lynn. "If there's as much destruction as I remember seeing, then I need to go out and find some help because it's going to take forever for help to come find me."

"And I'm coming with you. I'm done being alone with George." Tek got up and walked to the door. "Follow me. I know a way."

Lynn didn't have any choice, but she was going to keep her eyes open for a chance to ditch him.

Tek led the way out of the room. If the walls hadn't been so high they could have just pulled themselves out of the building. They were in the hospital's basement, so Lynn assumed a stairwell was the logical way out. But they didn't exist anymore. The only way out was at a spot where a damaged wall leaned at just the right angle to allow them to pull themselves up.

"I thought you said George was looking for a way out," said Lynn as they crawled up the wall.

"Not out of the hospital. You'll see what I mean when we get to the top."

And she did.

They were surrounded by rubble. There were no roads. There weren't even spaces between the piles of rubble that used to be buildings. It was just rubble. Collapsed buildings and piled-up cars. Some were on fire, some were smoldering. The area they were in had mostly office buildings that were built using few flammable materials. But nearby, something big was on fire. The glow was easy to see—even through the thick dust and darkness of night—and it cast long shadows over the rubble. The heat from the fire was making Lynn uncomfortable. More troublesome was her fear the flames might spread. She doubted she could scramble over the wreckage fast enough to keep far enough ahead of the flames. She looked around to try and determine where the closest fire was. The glow was brightest right behind them.

"Which way did he go?" asked Lynn.

"He said we needed to go away from whatever is on fire over there." Tek pointed towards the glow Lynn was worried about.

The smoke was thick but high above their heads. Even so, Lynn heard someone cough.

"Is it him?" she asked. "Should we hide?"

"It's no use. If we can hear him, then he can hear us."

From the rubble emerged a man in an orderly's uniform. Lynn was relived to find out that George wasn't a figment of Tek's imagination, but she still didn't feel safe around either of them.

Both the orderly's uniform and the patient's clothing were all white— or at least they used to be. Tek and

George were filthy dirty. Tek's patients' garb comprised a T-shirt, loose pants with no pockets, and a housecoat, but he'd had no time to grab his housecoat.

George wore white dress pants and a white button-up shirt. Neither fit him properly. He was wearing the uniform of a much taller man. The pant legs and shirt sleeves were rolled up.

"She's up!" said George.

"Yes."

George held out his grubby hand to shake. He had a goofy grin on his face as if he were genuinely glad to see her but there was a hint of anger in his eyes that warned of something dark inside the fake orderly.

"My name is Orely. It's a pleasure to formally meet you."

Lynn shook George's hand and he leaned down and kissed hers. She looked sideways at Tek who had an I-told-you-so look on his face. It was just like he said. George would have a name like an orderly. Orely the orderly.

"Did you find a way out, Orely?" asked Tek.

George didn't answer right away. He had forgotten his own fake name. With a loud "Aha!" he responded. "There is no easy way out of here but I may have found the best way to go. The trouble is I don't know where to go after that. Do either of you know the city very well?"

"No," said Lynn. "This is the first time I've been to Northgate."

"I grew up here. I know exactly where we are," said Tek.

"Then you know the quickest way out of the city?" George asked.

"Yes and no. The quickest way is back towards those flames, but we don't want to go that way. If we go forward—the way you suggest—it's about twenty blocks to the river. We could float our way out."

The sound of explosions and rubble collapsing was almost constant. But by now it was little more than background noise, and any new noises were especially noticeable.

"Do you hear that?" asked Lynn.

They all stopped and looked back, the direction George had come from.

"I don't hear anything," said Tek.

"I hear it," said George. Lynn wondered if he actually had.

"What does it sound like?"

"Breathing," said Lynn. "Really heavy breathing."

They slowly started backing away, heading towards the hospital.

The light dancing off the collapsed buildings turned every shadow into a wraith. There were so many cracks and crevasses. Whoever—or whatever—was making that breathing noise could be hiding anywhere.

The breathy sound got louder and louder. It was moving towards them.

"I can hear it now," said Tek.

From where they were standing they spotted a relatively clear path back to the hospital. It wasn't exactly shelter, it didn't even have a roof, but it was something familiar and Lynn desperately wanted to be there.

Since the whatever-it-is was moving, it had to know they were moving as well. They were being stalked. "Where are you hiding?" Lynn whispered as she scanned the ridge of the nearest rubble pile. That's when she saw it.

It looked almost human in that it had two legs, two arms, and one head, but they were all oddly shaped. The arms were longer than the legs and ended in sharp points, more like claws than hands. Possibly it was holding long knives or swords, but there was no evidence it even had hands. The head was deformed—twice the size of most humans' skulls—but from that distance, she couldn't make out any facial details. Its breath was echoing within its presumably massive mouth and protrusions jutted out at random angles from the rest of its head.

There was nothing friendly-looking about this thing.

Lynn grabbed Tek's hand and pointed out the shadowy figure. She heard his breathing quicken. George saw it too. He didn't say anything—he just ran. The thing started down the pile of what used to be a building. It was coming towards them.

No one had to yell "run." They just did. Back to the hospital. There had to be a place to hide in the basement.

As soon as they started running the thing started running as well and it was much faster than they were. Its long strides were easily closing the gap between them.

Lynn was the slowest of the three. Her injured leg was slowing them down. Every time she looked back, the thing was closer. It was wearing dark clothing, but it also looked like it had skin flaps coming off of it. She was moving too much to tell whether it was the creature's own skin or if it was skin harvested from previous hunts.

The two men had already gone down the leaning wall that served as a ramp to the basement. When she got to the hospital she jumped onto the ramp, slid down the wall and thumped to an abrupt stop at the bottom. It hurt, but there was no time to worry about that. She rolled to the side, hid under the ramp and waited. *Tek and George must have found a better place to hide. Of course they did, they had all kinds of time to explore while I was unconscious.*

The thing stopped at the top of the ramp. *What kind of weapons do you have?* Lynn wondered. If it had grenades or explosives of any kind, she knew it was all over. All she remembered seeing were the knives for hands and the elongated, skull-shaped head. She hoped that was all it had.

Lynn didn't have the luxury of time to ponder questions about where this thing came from or why it was chasing them. That this was happening right after the unidentified ship attacked the city couldn't have been a coincidence. For now, self-preservation demanded all her attention.

Lynn could hear footsteps on the ramp. Walking down. Slowly.

Lynn felt around in the darkness under the ramp for anything she could use as a weapon. A chunk of wood or a piece of rebar would have been great. Even a big piece of cement would have been helpful. There was nothing immediately around her, and she was too afraid to move to find something. If she made any kind of noise, it would be her last.

The sound of its breathing was getting to her. So deep, and the breaths were so long. What was it doing? It sounded like it was just standing there. The breathing got increasingly louder and then it just stopped. She didn't hear the whatever-it-was moving or breathing. It just stopped.

Lynn waited, barely breathing herself. Five minutes passed. Nothing. Ten minutes passed. Still nothing. Whether it was gone or not, she couldn't take this anymore. Slowly, very slowly, she slid out from under the wall. As she got to the edge she hesitated. Another step and she would be exposed. If that thing was still there, it would see her.

She closed her eyes and took three deep breaths. When she opened them again it was right there—blocking her way out!

Lynn screamed and stumbled back the other way. The thing slashed out at her with its long, sharp arms, missing her sweat-soaked skin by millimeters. Sparks shot off as its claws struck the cement wall.

"Lynn!" yelled Tek. "Lynn, where are you!"

She couldn't form words. All she could do was scream. She backed out from beneath the wall ramp and ran farther into the hospital. The thing was right behind her. One misstep and she'd be dead.

She was running down a hallway when a door flew open. There was no time to avoid it. She hit it and then fell to the floor. As she got to her knees she saw George standing there with a mischievous grin on his face. The door had a window on it. He knew she was coming. He did it on purpose.

The monster chasing her swung a blade at her, but she rolled into the room where George was. The thing followed, but hesitated. Now that it had two targets it was deciding which one to kill first.

Lynn wanted to get out of the room, but the monster was blocking her path. George panicked and charged at the door in an attempt to get out. The monster ran a blade through George's left lung. It might have been aiming for his heart, but either way he was dead. It pushed hard on the blade, and as it raised the tip in the air George's skewered body slid down the long knife.

Lynn screamed again.

This was just the scream Tek needed to find them. He pulled Lynn to the doorway and, holding a long piece of rebar, walked into the room. He saw what the monster had done to George and attacked. The rebar's tip wasn't sharp—an oversight on Tek's part—but what he lacked in brightness, he made up for in brute strength. Tek pushed with everything he had. The thing was already off balance from George's dead weight, and now it was trying to dodge Tek's rebar too. Finally the monster toppled over. All three of them fell in a heap.

Tek was the first one to get up. The thing tried to get up but couldn't. It had fallen on its other bladed arm and impaled itself. Tek backed away from the two bodies on the floor. When he hit the far wall he crumpled to the floor. His right arm was shaking uncontrollably. He clung to it with his other arm, trying to steady it.

"Are you okay?" asked Lynn. She limped over and crouched beside him. When she put her hand on his shoulder he twitched, just then realizing she was still there.

"I didn't want to do that."

"Thank you for saving me."

"I don't think you understand. I didn't..."

A loud moan came from the tangle of bodies. One of them was still alive.

Tek's arm stopped shaking as he got up to check things out. If that thing was still alive, then he was going to finish it off. Lynn didn't want to get too close, but she did want to see what in all the colonized worlds this creature was.

There were all kinds of bizarre reports about what the alien invaders looked like. No two descriptions were alike. If she survived this and got out of the city, then they could finally reveal the truth.

Tek approached the bodies. Blood was pooling on the floor. The thing was lying face down on top of George. The rebar was on the ground next to them. Tek picked it up and poked the thing. Nothing. Using the rebar he pushed the monster off of George. The look on George's face forced the air out of Lynn's lungs. It was a look of desperation. He did not want to die, but it was too late to save him.

More disturbing was the look on the thing's face. Not because it was a grotesque alien face, but because it was a human face. When Tek turned the thing over, its helmet and mask fell off. Underneath was a very normal-looking man. He had a dimpled chin. Brown hair. Brown eyes.

Lynn was still hanging back. Still not sure if they were safe. Tek started searching the man, looking for clues about his true identity. The top portion of the costume opened up. Underneath was a plain T-shirt with nothing on it to announce any military, political, or any other kind of affiliation.

"What's that sound?" asked Tek.

"I don't hear anything."

"Come closer."

Lynn took two steps forward and then she heard it: a whirring, mechanical noise. A small object attached to the helmet was spinning around.

Tek picked it up and studied it.

"There's a camera in this."

Carefully he put it down. As soon as he did he grabbed Lynn's arm, jumped away and headed for the door. He was running so fast he was practically dragging her behind him.

"Wait! What's wrong?" she asked.

"Just run!"

They bolted up the angled wall to the outside of the building and just kept running.

An explosion in the basement blasted debris into the air. Tek pulled Lynn to a safe spot under some rubble. Remnants of the hospital rained down around them.

"How did you know there was a bomb in there?" asked Lynn.

"I saw it. Right behind the camera."

"Why did they even have a camera? Who did this?"

"Whoever attacked the city left people behind to kill all the survivors. That camera and explosive was for people like us. People who fought back. They know what I look like. They will be looking for us now that we know it wasn't aliens that destroyed Northgate. It's too dangerous to let us live."

"Won't they think we died in the explosion?"

"I dropped the camera. They'll know we ran—or at least—they'll know *I* ran. I don't think they can know for sure whether or not you survived the blast."

Lynn froze. She didn't know what to do. The city around her was destroyed, and now they were being hunted. Whoever was behind all this didn't want any survivors left who might jeopardize their mission.

"We need to stick to our original plan," said Lynn. "We have to get out of the city. We have to tell people what's really going on here."

"Agreed. They might not be trying to kill all the survivors but they'll kill most of us. They'll spare just enough to provide eyewitnesses that it was the aliens who attacked."

"But they'll definitely kill anyone who finds out the truth. People like us who know it wasn't aliens."

"We need to get to the river," said Tek.

Out of habit Lynn tried to access a map of Northgate on her imp. Nothing came up. She had forgotten the Imps weren't working. Another mystery.

"You lead the way. I'm just a tourist here."

Chapter 4
Magnificent Desolation

Dr. Dalla Lana strode into the exam room and scribbled onto a chart. "So far, so good, Spacer Narrad. No broken bones, just nasty contusions. And I see here you didn't need stitches." Now that Mac's x-ray results were back and his wounds were cleaned and covered in dressings, he asked to be released.

"I'm afraid I can't do that."

"Why not? You just told me everything was fine."

"Well, yes, but we need to keep you for observation. To be sure you don't have a brain bleed. Lie down, get some rest. I'll order some more painkillers for you."

"Thanks all the same, Doc. But I have to get out of here. Where's my shirt?"

"Spacer Narrad. Lie down."

"No. I'm leaving. With or without my shirt."

"No. You're not," the doctor said, closing the door. It looked like Dr. Dalla Lana wanted to say something more aggressive, like *If you think you're leaving then you can drop dead* or something, but that's not the kind of thing doctors are supposed to say. Even military doctors keeping patients against their will. The two of them glared at each other for a moment before Mac pushed the doctor out of the way and opened the door. An alarm sounded before he made it to the nearest exit. When he got outside he was confronted by military police and a very large nurse. Mac felt a needle poke into his thigh, and suddenly he felt drowsy. "You're just being kept overnight," the nurse assured him as they strapped him to a bed and checked that his Imp recorder was still working. It didn't take him long to realize he was being swept under the rug.

Every patient in the temporary medical shelter was issued an Imp recorder. This was a government facility, the orderlies told them, and the devices were necessary to control rumors and to monitor potential security leaks to the press. Mac knew that was a lie. The government leaders controlled the press. Nothing was published without their permission. Rumors spread just as easily before Imps were invented and they would spread just as fast now.

Lying there in restraints and waiting for something to happen would have driven him crazy had it not been for Jace's visit. When he'd dropped Mac off earlier, Jace left without saying a thing. Mac's head was pulsating with pain at the time, so he couldn't remember whether Jace had been told to get him patched up or if he did it because he felt bad about the beating. When Jace came back later that night, he initially sounded like he was there to continue the questioning and not to visit someone he'd wronged.

"What happened to you?" asked Jace, pointing to the restraints.

"They didn't want me leaving and I disagreed with them."

"Well, at least you'll be happy to hear that the official report concluded the attack was carried out by aliens. So no more questioning you."

"You sound disappointed."

"I am. But not about the questioning. It's because I don't think this was an alien attack."

"It wasn't a Luddite attack either."

"Do you know there is no way to tell how many Luddites there are? So much is done on the Imps now, there's no way to keep track of the people who don't have Imps. There could be millions of Luddites out there with animosity towards—"

"Towards people that can't handle the fact that there are other points of view different from their own?"

"I was going to say people with Imps."

"Same thing," said Mac.

Mac didn't want to talk to Jace anymore. The guy still didn't trust Mac. Mac could not feel comfortable around him. He suspected he was constantly being sized up.

"I'm not one of the bad guys," said Jace.

Mac didn't say anything. He couldn't just dismiss Jace—he was the one who got General Zinger, and Zinger stopped the beating. As much as Mac appreciated that, he thought it was unusual that General Zinger acted like he knew Mac. Mac had met General Zinger only twice, once when he graduated from basic training, and once a year later when the general had called him to his office to tell Mac what a good soldier he was. Zinger added that he could see the former Luddite going places with his military career.

'I'll be keeping my eye on you,' Zinger had said.

Apparently he had meant it, but Mac hadn't believed him at the time.

Jace continued, "I just know that it wasn't aliens."

"What do you want? Why are you here?" asked Mac.

"I never meant to take the interrogation as far as Raymond did. Originally it was supposed to be just me but he's higher in the pecking order than me despite the fact we're the same rank, and he said he wanted to be there when I talked to you. I didn't know he was going to start hitting you. I came here to say I'm sorry."

"Get me out of these restraints and into the city and I'll forgive you."

"The city? Few people are being allowed in the city right now. Only certain soldiers. They get shipped out every morning but…"

"But what?"

"I got here at the very beginning of all this. I saw the base getting set up. They set up the fenced-off portion of the base first and immediately started sending shuttles full of soldiers into the city."

"So?"

"The shuttles went out full and came back empty. There are hundreds, maybe thousands, of soldiers in the city. The fenced off-area of the base is practically a ghost town now. What are they doing in Northgate?"

"Don't be so suspicious," said Mac. "It's going to take thousands more people to help with the rescue."

"But why all the secrecy?"

"It's the military. It's always like that."

"I guess. When I found out shuttles were leaving for Northgate, I tried to get a seat on one. But they wouldn't let me. 'Restricted access,' they told me."

Around this time a heavyset nurse—the one that had put her weight on Mac so they could strap him to the bed—came by and told Jace he had to leave. Mac was alone again but he couldn't sleep. The straps were driving him crazy. He couldn't relax. His family was only a few miles away, and he couldn't even get out of bed to go to the bathroom. The city was where he needed to be but he wasn't allowed to go there.

It wasn't just that he needed to know if his family was alive. He needed to know if she was there as well.

Jace came to visit for lunch. He looked flustered.

"What's up with you?" asked Mac.

"We are getting some…odd reports from the field."

"What kind of reports?"

"They are finding survivors—but they're dead."

"They aren't survivors if they're dead, Jace."

"No. No. No. They didn't die in the attack. They died after. The people who survived, some of them gathered together to try and find a way out but then something got to them. Killed them."

"Something?"

"Some of them had their throats sliced. Others had their chest ripped open."

"They didn't die of radiation?"

"I haven't seen any evidence of that."

There was no way Mac was going to lay on this hospital bed anymore. There were survivors! His family could still be alive. But now there was someone wandering around the city killing them all. He wasn't going to let that happen to his loved ones.

"Who's doing this?" asked Mac.

"*What's* doing this, you mean? No one I've talked to thinks it's human. Those aliens who attacked us either left some of their kind behind, or they unleashed a horde of monsters."

Mac rolled his eyes. He didn't believe for a second it was monsters. He was also surprised to hear Jace admit that it was an alien attack. Had he changed his mind?

"That's just what I've been hearing," said Jace.

"If the deployed soldiers aren't coming back to base, then how are these rumors starting?"

"I wondered the same thing but I can't trace the source. Everyone knows about it though."

"I need to get out of here. Use your Imp. Talk to Zinger. I need permission to go."

"Why don't you ask him?"

"I don't know how to get ahold of him," said Mac. "You knew exactly where to go when Raymond was beating the crap out of me."

"I just happened to run into him. I won't be able to do that again. There is a chain of command."

"It doesn't matter. You have to try. I need to get into the city."

"All right. I'll make some calls; see if I can get us into the city."

"Us?" asked Mac

"A few visits can't make up for what I did to you. Plus, I have an unquenchable curiosity about what's going on in Northgate."

Jace made a call, was transferred twice, and finally, to his surprise, got General Zinger's authorization to apply for a seat on a shuttle. If he and Mac wanted to be in the first wave (interesting how they didn't include the soldiers that already went into the city as the first wave) of rescuers then they needed to get to building B4. He also got permission to release Mac from medical care but no explanation as to why permission was needed to begin with. The bracelet was removed.

Mac didn't question this sudden change of heart for too long. The chaos surrounding the destruction of an entire city was going to result in the victimization of a few innocent people. He was just glad it was over and that he could finally find out where his family was. Were they huddled together looking for food to get them through another day? How easy was it to get food in a city that was rubble? What about shelter? Was there enough of a building standing to keep them safe from the elements? It was hard for Mac to think of his family in those conditions, especially the young kids, but he couldn't help it. Those thoughts forced him to move faster to get into the city.

Building B4 bordered the airfield and the restricted section of the base. As Mac and Jace walked toward it, Mac's gaze concentrated on the restricted area. There was zero movement. No one moving from building to building. No one going to get food. No one going for a run or checking equipment. There was simply no one there except for the two guards stationed outside the gate to keep people from entering.

"Why is this area restricted?" Mac asked them.

"Classified."

"What? Why?"

"Classified."

"Where are all the people?"

"Classified."

"Do you have a name?"

"Classified."

"Did you get that lisp from your Mom or your Dad?"

"Classified."

"What about the nostril burning smell and fish eyes? Did they come from one parent or were you raised by the *two* ugliest people on Earth?"

"Classified."

Mac didn't bother asking any more questions. Those goons didn't know anything. They were just told to stand there and answer *classified* to anything anyone asked them

B4 was a big hall with three offices in the back. Mac and Jace weren't the only ones who had heard the city was opening up. They joined the lineup to get into the building. The lineup chatter revealed that no one knew what was going on. Oh sure, lots of people *thought* they knew, but after the monsters that were killing survivors became ten-foot-tall beasts, each with three heads filled with razor-sharp teeth, Mac knew that this was just the rumor mill turning.

Once everyone was inside and seated, Commander Littleton spoke.

"At 0700 yesterday there was an alien attack on Northgate. We do not know at this time how they got past the orbital defenses, the scouts in our solar system, or the war cruisers at the front line. The breach has put everyone on high alert; hence the increase in security. The restricted area of the base has allowed select individuals to move into Northgate and assess the situation. The situation is this: No survivors have been found yet—not surprising, considering there aren't even any standing buildings—but we are still going to look. We have not given up."

Mac was glad to hear that they weren't giving up. He would like to have heard that they had found at least one survivor. He also wondered if Commander Littleton was going to squelch the monster rumors.

The screen behind Commander Littleton lit up. There was a map of Northgate on it. He pointed to the different areas as he spoke.

"If we are going to find survivors, it's going to be people who were outside when the attack occurred. Downtown is a write-off. No one could have survived those buildings collapsing. Shopping centers are out as well. There are major highways cutting through the city here and here. This is where our search will start."

Mac looked. One of the highways was only five blocks from where his sister lived. What would his family have been doing at seven in the morning?

"We are going in there to find survivors," said Commander Littleton.

"Why did we wait this long to start helping?" asked an angry voice from the back of the room.

"Radiation."

Commander Littleton pointed at the map. It responded to his gestures. The entire map of the city became covered in a translucent red.

"The aliens attacked with a new weapon we have not encountered before. It leaves behind powerful radiation. Yesterday we did not have the technology to survive it for very long. Since then we have developed a way to modify our current radiation suits to protect us. Yes, the radiation means there are not going to be very many survivors, but we have to look. We cannot underestimate the ingenuity of man. Especially when it comes to survival."

Commander Littleton swept his finger across the map. Half of the red disappeared. It looked like the south end of the city, favored by the wind direction, was nearly clear of radiation. But the north end was still labeled as the red zone. Mac didn't care how Commander Littleton tried to explain that. To Mac it didn't seem possible for the radiation to clear up so fast. After he found his family, he would go investigate the red zone.

"How long do you think it takes for radiation to dissipate?" Mac whispered to Jace.

"Longer than a couple of days, that's for sure."

"Let's stick together on this, okay?"

"Absolutely."

They signed up for a scouting party which allowed Mac, the soldier and pilot, and Jace, the military intelligence officer, to work together. Scouting parties were three-man groups who flew over the city to identify hazards, look for survivors and gather intelligence. Mac would pilot. The other two would keep watch.

The third man could present a problem if they decided to make a run for the red zone. He would also be an intelligence man, and he was more likely to be a hardcore military person that took everything he was told as the gospel truth. Going to the red zone meant defying orders, and that would bring hellfire and damnation.

Their assigned shuttle-mate was worse than either of them suspected.

The third scout was Major Raymond Tysons.

"The General wants my personal assessment of the devastation," he said as he climbed into the HAAS3.

Whether that was true or not remained to be seen. General Zinger had reprimanded Raymond barely twenty-four hours ago. Raymond was probably trying to redeem himself.

They hesitated for a second but followed him anyway, realizing any reluctance on their part would result in suspicion. Mac got in the pilot's seat. Directly behind him were two computer centers that scanned for life forms and mapped out areas for ground troops to move in.

The entire command deck, which was half the shuttle, was transparent. A laser and impact-proof transparent window that resembled glass, and that everyone referred to as glass, but was definitely not glass. Astro engineers had spent eight years and hundreds of millions of dollars to develop this new compound. But Mac would have flown in an open-air cockpit if that's what it took to get him home.

Unlike most people, who would play it safe while working with the superior officer who had recently abused them, Mac veered off course and made straight for his sister's house.

"What are you doing, Spacer? This is not the designated course," said Raymond.

"One little detour," said Mac

"Absolutely not. Turn this shuttle around."

Mac didn't listen. His sister's house wasn't very far away. If the usual landmarks —buildings and roads—had still been intact, he would have found it in seconds. As it was, he had to take a few minutes to compare their flight path to a map of the city.

When he was confident he had found the right spot, Mac put the shuttle down. The street was littered with burned-out hover cars, so they landed in the charred remnant of the back yard.

Raymond came flying at him. He grabbed Mac's shirt and started yelling in his face.

"You have violated the direct orders of your superior officer. I am putting you under military arrest. And when we get back to base I'm sending you right back to your Luddite family."

"That's where we are," said Mac.

"What?"

"My family. They were in that building right there. I came here to see if they're still alive."

Mac knew that it wasn't just the three of them in this conversation. There were at least two people monitoring all three of their Imp feeds. During military exercises there were always at least two people. On missions like this, there were usually more.

Going to see his family before carrying out his orders was risky. Not because he could be kicked out of the military and sent to jail—Mac didn't care about that now— but because he was banking on the likelihood that the majority of people, inside the courtroom and out, would empathize with him and forgive this slight deviation in the flight plan.

Raymond didn't say anything. He looked like he was responding to incoming messages. His grip loosened and he took a step back.

"Go get the radiation suits. You have a half hour to check things out. Then we go back to where we were assigned."

The Imps made it extremely hard to hatch schemes. Especially for low-level military people like Mac. Neither he nor Jace believed there was radiation in the city. It couldn't clear up that quickly and there would be no survivors to look for. But neither of them wanted to test their theory on himself. When the major had come on board, they knew they had found their guinea pig.

Averting his eyes from the task at hand, thus preventing anyone monitoring his feed from seeing it, Jace made a large cut in the leg of the radiation suite Raymond was going to use. He made sure to do it in a place that Raymond wouldn't see once he had the suit on.

Now Mac almost wished the military was right about the radiation.

Once they were all suited up, Mac opened the shuttle door and they walked into the desolation that was Northgate. Only one wall of Catherine and Chester's house was still standing. It was part of the living room he had sat in with his family and their framed likenesses. This wall was the only thing tall enough to obstruct their view of the neighborhood. They started their search there.

"No signs of radiation," Jace said, as he scanned the area with a portable sensor.

Raymond ignored him. "We don't have a lot of time. Get to it, Narrad."

Mac climbed over the broken walls, the collapsed roof, and the remains of furniture, as carefully as he could. He felt like he was trespassing on sacred ground. At best, his family was alive under there somewhere and he didn't want to crush them. At worst, this is where they died. This was their grave and it deserved respect.

Mac was relying on his memory of the layout of the house to help him search. Sometimes he couldn't shake the Luddite upbringing. Then he remembered he could display the house's layout on his Imp.

"I'm not getting anything, Mac," said Jace. "No heat signatures and no life signs."

"Then I need to find the bodies," said Mac.

He started picking up drywall and two-by-fours in the area that used to be the living room. That's where his family liked to congregate. It was also right by the kitchen. If there was anybody in the house they would have been in one of these rooms when the attack happened.

Every time he picked up broken pieces of the house there was just more rubble underneath to pick up. He kept hoping for hint at his family's fate. At any moment he could find out he was alone. An orphan with no brother, or sisters, or little nephew.

But that moment didn't come. No one was there.

Jace helped Mac sort through the rubble. Raymond just stood there, pointing out the time.

"Five minutes to go," he said.

"I don't think they were here," said Jace.

Mac kept lifting boards and other debris even though he thought the same thing.

"What kind of car they were driving?"

"An EL-Jay," said Mac.

Jace pointed to his left. "There's an EL-Jay shell over there. What did your parents drive?"

"An Autrik."

"Oh, wow. I didn't know they still made those," said Jace.

"They don't. My parents have had it my whole life. It keeps breaking down, but my dad keeps fixing it."

Jace walked over the rubble and onto the street to further investigate the burned-out cars.

"Two minutes!" yelled Raymond.

Mac joined Jace. There was only one car directly in front of his sister's house: The EL-Jay.

"Does your whole family fit in the Autrik?" asked Jace.

"Yes, and it's not here."

"There's still hope."

"Yes."

"Return to the hawthree. Time to go!" yelled Raymond. He didn't even wait for them to respond before he went back to the HAAS3. Mac and Jace followed closely behind him. They had no doubt Raymond had the skills to fly the shuttle and would gladly leave them behind.

Chapter 5
Survivors

When they got back to base later that night, they had to go through sensors to determine if they were exposed to radiation. Mac and Jace made sure to keep close to Raymond. Raymond got through clean. Just like everyone else. There was no radiation. The two of them gave each other knowing looks. They couldn't talk about it—Big Brother was always watching. And listening.

They could talk, though, about Mac's family.

"Where do you think they are?" asked Jace.

"I don't know. They should have all been at Catherine's. It doesn't make sense that my parents—that none of my family was there."

"So now what?"

"We go to bed. Get up in the morning and keep looking."

Mac didn't go to sleep. He lay in his bed and texted the only person left in his life who could help him.

How is the only person in Passage with an Imp doing tonight?

Been better. Some people came around. Military people. They were asking a lot of questions. Rumor is they are looking for someone to blame for this attack. Why would they blame a Luddite community?

Mac texted, **I think you know it was a cover. The official announcement here is it was an alien attack. Could be they were looking for you?**

They did try to surge me. But I've been around too long for such things.

Surges, when a suspect is overwhelmed with stimulation through their Imps. Loud noises, flashing lights. Police used it all the time to avoid chases.

But you know a way around these things, I'm assuming. Mac guessed.

Wouldn't be able to be the only Imp amongst the Luddites if I hadn't. This isn't the first time someone has come looking for me.

Have you heard from my parents? Their car wasn't there. It's possible they went home.

Sorry, but no. No one here has heard from them. People are trying to get ahold of you. They know your parents were in Northgate. Some of the neighbors wanted to hold a memorial service if...well, you know...if the entire family was dead. A lot of folks here are using your family's presumed fate as a cautionary tale. A brand new "Don't use Imps or else" story.

Do they blame me for joining up?

Not for the attack, or your family's disappearance. But your name was thrown around a bunch when the military showed up.

The only man in Passage with an Imp told Mac he needed a few minutes but would continue the text conversation shortly. So Mac waited. He had never gotten the man's whole story. For sure he was hiding, and for sure he was one of the first people to get an Imp, but beyond that, Mac knew nothing about him. After all these years the man was still extremely cautious about with whom he interacted. He and Mac never talked face to face. They only ever used their Imps, and they never used each other's real names, even though they knew them. The man lived down the street from him. For some reason the man wasn't worried about being tracked through his Imp interactions. He was always one step ahead of anyone that might be searching for him.

Mac knew being in the military meant he could be monitored at any moment. He'd explained this to the only man in Passage with an Imp but the man didn't care and Mac had never been questioned about those conversations.

As he thought about it Mac couldn't help but see the comparisons between being in the military and being under arrest. Both resulted in constant surveillance. The difference was that being monitored by the military was more of a panopticon situation. They *could* be monitoring you at any moment but you wouldn't know exactly when. When you were fitted with a recorder while under arrest everything you used your Imp for would be used against you if it went to court. Everything. The whole file was sent right to the judge.

Finding the only man in Passage with an Imp had been a complete accident. Mac had got his Imp and one of his fellow spacers gave him a "good deal" on what turned out to be a pirated and extremely short-range Imp-searching program. He had used the program at the same time he was looking at the only man in Passage with an Imp and saw a reaction that made Mac suspicious.

The only man in Passage later admitted that he wanted Mac to find out his secret so he could get inside information about how the war was going. They became fast friends.

While Mac was away his easiest connection to his family was through the only Imp in Passage. Mac had never heard him admit it, but this man loved using his Imp without anyone knowing it, and he enjoyed the connection he had with Mac.

Mac's Imp signaled an incoming text.

I'm going to send you something.

Do you need my location? Mac asked.

No. It's going to be your last resort. In case things go wrong for you in the worst way possible. I'll send it to McAllister.

The only man in Passage with an Imp disconnected before giving any more details. He knew someone might be listening. Mac had enough to go on. He lay back and, eventually, slept.

Rescue teams were starting to find survivors.

The news flooded the Imp feeds. Searchers paused to link into the feed of the soldiers who found them. Imp-to-Imp connections were usually only allowed if both parties agreed. But this was not how the military worked. If they wanted everyone to see or hear something, then everyone was patched in. Military communications officers could override the Imp feeds of anyone who failed to link up voluntarily. Having one's name on the override list could result in serious consequences.

Mac put his shuttle into auto-pilot and linked into the feed. He had been watching a series of mysterious explosions on the north end of the city, but the military feed kicked in and his view of explosions switched to a soldier on the ground. The feed panned out to show a group of ten soldiers removing debris from a subway tunnel. The subway system had been abandoned years ago, but someone must have sought it out as shelter. But why? What were they seeking shelter from? Wouldn't they want to be visible to rescuers?

The soldiers were furiously throwing rocks aside and pulling people to safety. The survivors emerged, shielding their eyes from the sun's brightness.

"Come with me," said the soldier whose feed Mac was following. The information on Mac's Imp said the soldier's name was Eric.

Eric took a glove off and grasped the hands of a mom and her four-year-old daughter. He walked them toward a medic.

"How many of you are there?" asked the mom.

"The whole military is here. You're okay."

She sat down in the back of the medic's truck. Her little girl sat on her lap. The medic knelt in from of them and asked for their names.

"I'm Shannon. This is Marina."

Eric turned away from them to go help with the others.

"Wait!" Shannon yelled.

Eric turned back. The look on Shannon's face was sheer terror. They were both afraid. Marina turned and wrapped her arms tightly around her mother's neck.

"Please! Can you stay here? I don't feel safe."

"Did you hear the part where I said, 'the whole military is here'?" Eric could have used some sensitivity training.

"They come out of nowhere. It's not safe to be alone."

Eric took a few steps closer while the medic examined Shannon. It was difficult, because Marina refused to move. He saw a bloodstain on the mom's right side, and when the medic gently untucked her shirt, everyone with an Imp saw the ugly gash.

"What happened here?"

"I was attacked. We were attacked. My husband stepped in front. The monster killed him. He tried to kill us too, but we got away and hid. I don't know where it went."

Eric looked around quickly, several times and in every direction. No monsters in the immediate area. Watching the view with Eric's head whipping back and forth was making Mac dizzy.

"Where did this happen? Did it happen here?" asked Eric.

"No. It was across the river."

"In the red zone," Mac heard Jace say from behind him.

Then the feed cut out. Mac was once again sitting at the controls of the HAAS3 flying slowly over the city. He looked back at his ginger friend. They both knew what they were going to do; they had to go to the red zone across the river. But it would be tricky with Raymond right there. They needed a good reason.

"What's the radiation protection on this shuttle?" asked Mac.

"The *Heavy Armor* part of its name would suggest it's pretty good," said Jace.

"You're not going to the red zone," said Raymond.

Mac ignored him. He was busy thinking. They knew there was no radiation—their time in the south end of the city proved that—but Mac wondered how desperate the government and military were to cover up the truth. Would they go as far as releasing radioactive material in the red zone? Was it worth the risk?

A text message sent to all military personnel flashed on Mac's Imp.

No one is to enter the red zone. This is a direct order from General Zinger.

"That solves that issue, now doesn't it. Or are you stupid enough to disobey a direct order from the highest-ranking officer in the military?" asked Raymond.

He got his answer when Mac headed straight toward the red zone. He slowed down as he flew over the river; they were almost there, and he wanted to skim the zone's edge. See if there was anything strange going on.

"Aim all the sensors north of the river. Tell me as much as you can about the red zone," said Mac.

"I'm not getting any radiation readings, if that's what you mean," said Jace.

"It's not just the radiation. You heard what that woman said. There are monsters down there," said Raymond.

"Come on now, Major. You believe in monsters?" asked Mac.

"No. But there is something down there killing people. The aliens probably left some of their soldiers behind. It's too risky to go over there."

"But we're the military. There are survivors over there. It's our job to take care of things like that. We are supposed to go into risky situations."

"It's not your call to make."

"How do…"

They all stopped talking; Jace a little after the others. All three of their Imps had simultaneously stopped working. Their vision was completely void of all obstructions—something that never happened to someone with an Imp. The Imps were being blocked. Mac noted their location, checked the shuttle's control panel. They were directly above the river, hovering just outside the red zone. Maybe moving slightly to the north, but so slowly as to be unnoticeable.

He moved the ship farther south. All of their Imps came back online.

"What was that?" asked Raymond.

"I'm trying to find out," said Jace. "There are some strong signals coming from a tower nearby." He got up and moved to the seat beside Mac. In front of them, on the north side of the river, was a small transmission tower with a tiny red light blinking on top. Obviously it had been secured to a burned-out building after the attack.

"That thing is blocking the Imps?" asked Mac.

"As far as I can tell," said Jace.

"Raymond, isn't it illegal to have Imp-blocking technology?"

"Of course," he said. "You can't even research it."

"Jace, target the tower."

"What are you doing?" Raymond shouted.

"Tower targeted," said Jace.

"Take it out," said Mac.

Before Raymond could do anything to stop it, blue lasers shot out of the HAAS3. There were no defenses on the tower. It exploded. Red hot metal mingled with the already ruined building. Mac slowly moved the shuttle closer. They had already reached the point where their Imps had stopped working before. But now that the tower was gone, so was the interference. Their Imps retained their fully functional status.

"Know anything about those towers, Raymond?" asked Mac.

"No."

Mac knew he was lying. It didn't take an expert to judge by the look on his face that he was lying. It was Mac's turn to interrogate. But he wasn't going to do it with anyone watching. He dove the shuttle straight into the red zone. As soon as he did the Imps went offline again. The entire red zone was covered in the transmission towers; the flashing red lights dotted the landscape. He jumped back and spun Raymond around in his seat.

"What are you guys hiding?"

"You are breaking a direct order from General Zinger. You're going to be court martialed and I will personally see that your family faces repercussions."

"My family might be dead. Who set up these towers?"

"I don't know."

"What have the soldiers who were flown in here been doing all this time?"

"Looking for survivors."

"How come none of them have come back to the base?"

"They have."

"They haven't. I've been watching."

"They have."

"What are they doing in the red zone?"

"They aren't in the red zone."

"Who set up the towers?"

"I told you. I don't know."

"I think you're lying."

"Then do something about it," said Raymond. "I'm your commanding officer. I order you to return to base immediately or you are no longer an officer in the military."

Mac decided he *would* do something about it, and the instant he made that decision he knew Raymond was right. Spacer Narrad was about to become civilian Narrad. This was going to make life difficult for Mac in the long run, but right now, his decision came easily.

He flew at Raymond, tackling him out of his seat and onto the floor, pinning down one arm. Raymond was so used to people doing whatever he said, Mac's lunge caught him off guard. But that lapse was short-lived. Raymond gathered his senses and struck back at Mac. With his free arm, Raymond punched Mac in the jaw and then pushed up with his other arm in an effort to free himself. It didn't work.

Mac grabbed that arm and twisted it so that Raymond was forced to roll from his back to his stomach or his arm would break. The intelligence officer kicked his legs in a futile attempt to free himself. But Mac sat on top of him, and the more Raymond struggled, the more Mac twisted on the arm he had pinned against Raymond's back. It was on the verge of breaking when the Major reluctantly admitted defeat.

"Find me something to tie him up with," said Mac.

Jace looked a little stunned at what had happened. Then he realized what Mac had already processed; they must either break away from the military and find out what was really going on, or go back to base and face the consequences. He did as Mac asked, hoping that if they ended up at a court martial they could prove that Raymond was a vindictive moron who was abusing his command. And if he and Mac collected valuable intelligence, maybe, just maybe, they wouldn't be executed or die in prison. At any rate, Jace felt like he was justified in disobeying Raymond, and he really wanted to know what was going on.

With his arm still pinned, Raymond was forced to his feet and back into his seat. Jace used cables and rope to tie Raymond's arms and legs so that he couldn't stand up or use his arms. Raymond wasn't saying a whole lot, but Mac didn't care. Of course it meant that Raymond was using his Imp—now that the tower had been destroyed that was possible—but Mac didn't regret his choices. If this is what it took to find out what happened to his family and Janelle—and what really happened to Northgate—then it was worth it.

While Raymond used his Imp, Mac got a message from someone he knew back on the Titan base. The message with it said: **Heard you got reassigned to Northgate Recovery. Have you seen this yet?** As he opened the message he received the same vid feed seven times. It was going viral. It was a live feed from a woman who was in Northgate. She was having a standoff with someone, or something. Mac had never seen anything like it before. The thing was tall, and had freakishly long arms that ended in blades. Didn't seem very practical, but neither did the skin it had hanging off of it. It had to be for show, for intimidation. As did the skull head with the matted hair. This was the monster that the survivors were talking about.

"Jace! Check this out!" Mac should have sent it right to his Imp, but being a Luddite, his first instinct was to put it on the HAAS3's monitor. "I got this from a friend and now a dozen other people. This woman is in Northgate. She's being hunted by the monster or something."

Raymond, "I said, go back to base!"

"We'll go back to base and face whatever consequences you want—after we save this girl. The video has already gone viral. Imped or not, everyone is going to see this woman. Should we tell the world Major Raymond Tysons ordered us to turn around and leave her there to die?"

Raymond seethed while a grinning Jace watched the video on the shuttle's monitor and relayed coordinates to Mac.

"Now *she's* chasing the monster. I don't understand what's going on," said Jace.

He kept narrowing down the area she was in and Mac flew in her direction, taking out towers as he went. She was in the red zone, which meant she had found out about the towers as well and disabled the block. There were so many that it was difficult to go fast and destroy them at the same time. Especially by himself. Jace fired at a few, but he was too busy watching the feed and figuring out where it was coming from. Raymond couldn't have done anything even if he wanted to. And he really didn't want to.

"She sent a text to everyone," said Jace.

"Do not read that text!" said Raymond.

"What does it say?" asked Mac.

"Do not pass along that propaganda!"

"Propaganda? She's fighting for her life down there. I'm pretty sure she doesn't have political motivations," said Jace. "The text says: 'The war is fake. I have proof. It wasn't the aliens who killed all these people and destroyed this city. Find Scott. Tell him he was right and that I love him.'"

The war is fake. It was the first time Mac had even considered it. How was it possible to fake an entire war? And why? But the more he thought about it, the more it made sense. The war was taking place so far away that, before Northgate, no one on Earth had been directly affected by it. No one knew what the aliens looked like. An impenetrable communications wall at the front line stopped information from getting through. What was the point of that? Mac had never questioned the military's need for strict secrecy. But was it really about homeland security, or was there no information because there was no war?

Even though the war was being fought far away from Earth and its colonies, millions of people were paying a Defense Tax. Patriotic citizens regularly sent supplies and homemade comforts to support the military and all the military was doing. But if the war was simply a ruse, then what was the government doing but policing the population? Were Earth's citizens being controlled by a fake war? This woman seemed to think so.

The most disturbing thought was that if the war was fake, it meant the military was responsible for the carnage. They were the ones who destroyed Northgate and killed millions of people. Mac still had trouble believing that was true, but then again, if people like Raymond were the ones making decisions, it was more than possible.

"We're close, and we need to hurry. It looks like she's hurt."

Mac started circling the area that Jace had indicated. Then there was a big explosion to his right. The fireball acted like a dirty bomb, propelling the surrounding rubble into the air. Iron beams and chunks of concrete rocketed up, out and down. The shuttle itself was assaulted by debris, but it didn't do any serious damage. The feed on the monitor showed the woman flying into the air and flipping end over end before hitting the ground.

The feed became very still. She didn't move when rubble from the explosion rained down around her. She didn't even flinch. They took small comfort in believing the monster was gone too. Unfortunately for the woman, it looked like the explosion had done what the monster couldn't.

"You're too late," said Raymond.

Chapter 6
Is It Safe?

While Mac and Jace were digging through the rubble of his sister Catherine's house, Lynn and Tek were trying to find a way to get out of the city. The river was twenty blocks to the south. A leisurely 90-minute walk two days ago. Who knew how long it would take under the new circumstances.

The city was destroyed. Its people. Its buildings. Its infrastructure. There wasn't a clear way to get to the river. Without street signs and landmarks, their only navigational aid during the day was the sun's position in the sky. At night, all they could do was guess. The river bisected the city, so as long as they went south they would eventually reach it. They scavenged for food and water as they made their way, but as one of them did that, the other kept watch.

They knew they were being hunted. When they left the hospital they had seen shadows moving in the distance. More predators had come to avenge their fallen comrade. Lynn and Tek ran as fast as they could. They never went out in the open—not that much open space even existed—which made things more difficult, but it was what they had to do.

Several hours after they left the hospital the sun was up. Exhausted, they decided to take a break. There was one rule about taking breaks: make sure no one can see you. They dug down into the rubble and found a place to rest. It looked like a cave that had conveniently formed when the building collapsed. They wouldn't be able to stand up all the way, but they would be able to lie down. Another rule they made: no talking louder than a whisper. They hadn't done much talking while they ran. Partly because they were too tired, and partly because they didn't want to be easily followed.

They climbed into the rubble cave and moved a chunk of wall over the entrance. They couldn't be seen with the naked eye, but the people hunting them likely had sensors. Lynn positioned herself between Tek and the mouth of the cave. He was a good guy and all, but he had been a patient in the looney bin. He might not be dangerous, but she still had to be careful.

The ground was mercifully flat. She lay on her back.

"How close do you think they are?" whispered Lynn.

"I have no idea. It's best to assume they are close," said Tek, also on his back.

They hadn't seen anyone since they left the hospital, just the shadows. But they knew they were being followed. Both of them felt like they were being watched the entire time they ran.

Tek's right arm started to twitch. He grabbed it to stop it.

"Are you okay?" asked Lynn.

"Yes. I can control it." He said it more to convince himself.

"Is that why you were in the hospital?"

"Yes."

"But…it was a psychiatric hospital."

"I know. No one believed how I got the tremor, or that its source is real. They think I shake my arm as an excuse for what it's done."

"How did you get it?"

"It's going to sound weird."

"That's okay."

"You won't believe me," said Tek.

"You have to tell me before I can decide if I believe you or not."

"I've seen the aliens before. I've delivered supplies to military bases for years. Until the war started, there was never any risk involved. Then I had to bring things to the front line. It's horrible out there. Our government may be corrupt, and the military can't be trusted, but that doesn't mean they should all die. And that's what's happening out there. All our soldiers are dying."

"I got this twitch when an alien touched my arm. She was trying to infect me so she could take over my body. She was killed during the attempt, but it didn't stop part of her from getting inside. There's not enough of her to take over completely, but every once and a while she tries to use my arm to do bad things."

"Tek, your arm is twitching right now. Is she trying to make you do bad things?"

"Yes."

"Do you know what she is trying to make you do?"

"No."

"Then how do you know it's bad?"

"Because it's always bad. She's the one who killed that thing last night."

"But you saved my life."

"I'm not a killer."

"Can you control it?" asked Lynn.

"For now I can. But it will get harder without my treatments."

"Treatments?"

"Shocks. While they were trying to find out what was wrong with me, they discovered electric shocks helped me gain control of my arm again. They've had to shock me once a day for almost a year."

"Shock treatments? Really?" Lynn asked. *Psychiatrists stopped administering those 40 years ago.*

"Yes."

"How long can you go without it?"

"A day, maybe a day and a half," said Tek.

"How long has it been?"

"Almost a day. They would do it just before lunch every day."

They didn't talk for a while. *Who knows if he's really telling the truth?* Lynn hated that she was becoming such a skeptic. She wanted to believe that she could help Tek. But to believe his story about the aliens, she would have to reject her husband's account of the fake war. And she wasn't about to do that. Tek had saved her life. Even if he was lying, what did he stand to gain? If she helped him find a way to get his treatments, what was the worst that could happen? He would get a little shock. That's it. She had seen firsthand a bad thing the "alien" made him do. If a little shock would help, then she had to do it.

"What were you doing in the hospital?"

"I was looking for my husband."

"Is he a patient?"

"Yes. No. He was locked up because the military doctor said he was insane, but he's not. He just didn't want to do what they said. Then they refused to tell me which hospital he was in. I've been trying to find him. On the Imp it said he was there, but that turned out to be another lie. I hope wherever he is, it's not in Northgate."

"What did they want your husband to do?"

"He was in charge of the factory that made the munitions for all the big capital ships. My husband found out..." Lynn hesitated when she realized she was about to present a conflicting idea to a mental patient with a possessed arm.

"Found out about what?"

"Found out the war isn't real."

Tek didn't answer right away.

The idea of the war being a fake wasn't new, but it wasn't popular, either because people liked to support their own fighters, or because most people on Earth just didn't care one way or the other as long as nothing changed for them. But more and more people were wondering where all the soldiers were going. Until now, Earth and its colonies had never been directly attacked. Only their ships had, and only on the fringe of explored space.

Lynn and her husband Scott started realizing that the war was being used as an excuse to control people. Anyone who did or said something the military didn't like was arrested and forced to change their ways or be publicly denounced as traitors. If they refused to cooperate, they were thrown in jail. Or worse. Scott didn't want to supply weapons to the army because he didn't think there were any aliens. If there were no aliens, then the weapons were going to be used on humans. He would not help them kill innocent civilians.

"Lynn, I know the fact that I was in a psych ward makes me hard to believe. But I know what I saw."

"I know. But I love my husband. I trust what he says…"

"He's wrong, or I would still be out there. I was delivering supplies to the front, and I saw the war with my own eyes. I was attacked. I was the only survivor."

Lynn didn't know what to say. She didn't believe he was attacked by aliens, but she wasn't about to tell him that.

"I promise I won't hurt you, Lynn. And I'll do my best to make sure you get back to your husband. Just remember that no matter what you choose to believe, don't try to convince me that what I saw didn't really happen. I know what I saw."

"After we rest, we'll try to find a way to help you get your treatments," said Lynn.

"Okay," said Tek.

"Do you know what you need?"

"A small jolt of electricity should do fine. They were also giving me some meds, but I can't remember the names at all. They weren't normal words, you know. But the shocks will get me through this until we find help."

"Okay."

"The shocks will slow the process down at least."

"Okay."

"Get some sleep."

"Okay," said Lynn.

She didn't. Not a wink. It was broad daylight outside, but dark inside the rubble cave. She lay there, eyes wide open, listening to the sound of her and Tek breathing. The only sound that disrupted it was that of his arm twitching, struggling to break free.

As bad as the city looked at night, it looked even worse during the day. They hadn't rested long. The much-needed sleep was sabotaged by anxiety. Lynn didn't know if she would ever see her husband again. She couldn't even say with confidence that she would live long enough to see the sun set.

There was no way to tell what was ahead of them or if there was anything with power nearby. If they were going to get the help that Tek said he needed, then they needed power. To scout ahead they climbed up the nearest and tallest pile of rubble.

It was not a good idea and it broke all the rules of stealth they had had set up for themselves. For several hours they were exposed. No longer crawling and climbing in between broken buildings. They were noisily trying to get to the top as fast as they could.

What they saw took their breath away.

Total devastation. Not a single building standing. Just mountains of rubble where they used to be. There were no clear roads. No trees standing. No people. No landmarks to tell them where they were. They were too far from the hospital to see it, and they weren't close enough to the river to see it either.

If it wasn't for the hundreds of fires burning throughout the city it would be a magnificent day—warm with not a cloud in the sky. It was possible the closest fire was the burning remains of the explosion from the night before, but there was no way to tell for sure.

"Lynn, get down." Tek crouched down and hid behind a chunk of cement. Lynn sat beside him.

"Look!" he said, pointing at something moving about fifty yards away.

An old man was walking in the rubble. A survivor. His clothes were dirty, his hair was flecked with ashes, and he was limping. But he was alive. Just like them, he was trying to climb a crumbled building to get a better view. When he got to the top he looked around intently, like he was trying to spot a specific place or object. When he gazed toward Lynn and Tek's hiding place, Lynn had to fight the urge to wave at him.

The man turned to his left and raised his fists in the air. He had found what he was looking for. Lynn followed his sightline and saw what the old man had been searching for. It was a light! A small red one, not too far off. It was hard to see, but as the smoke from some of the fires dissipated, the light appeared brighter. Then, she could see other lights. Small, blinking red lights, spread throughout the city.

She studied the closest one and determined that the light was attached to a transmission tower of some sort. Not one of the full-sized towers that used to populate the city; this was half that size. And it was anchored on top of the rubble. This tower—all of these towers—had been installed after the city had been destroyed.

"Oh, no," said Tek. He was still looking at the old man.

There was another dark figure climbing the rubble— one of the hunters. The old man didn't have a hope. The fake monster slit his throat before he even knew there was anything wrong.

Lynn and Tek got as low to the ground as possible. They should never have come up so high. They were exposed. The best they could do was to sit still and hope they would just blend in with the ground.

She couldn't look anymore, but Tek kept watching.

"He's searching for us. I can see him looking around for other survivors. But he doesn't know where we are. He knows we are more alert than the others, because we know we are being hunted."

"Do you see the light?"

"Yes. I see a bunch of them."

"We can use those. They're the only power source I've seen out here. It might be our only chance to shock you."

As if on cue his right arm started reaching out for Lynn. Tek pulled it back and apologized.

"How are you doing?" asked Lynn.

"I'm okay. My best guess is that we need to get to that light by sundown. If we don't then we'll have to split up. I don't want to be responsible for hurting you."

"If we split up then we should pick a place to meet after all of this is over."

"Why?"

"Because you saved my life. I owe you. Maybe there is something I can do for you," said Lynn.

"No one can help me," said Tek.

"Have you had that looked at by a biological engineer?" asked Lynn.

"No."

"Well, I am a biological engineer. Maybe I can kill the alien's cell structure, or insert a type of device you can use to control your arm, give yourself the shocks you need. Maybe even amputate and then grow you a new arm."

"You can do that?"

"Kind of. It's complicated, and still in the testing stages, but just before I left my lab they were talking about starting human testing."

"Hmm."

"I can't make any promises other than I'll try my best to help you."

"Anything is better than nothing."

The fake monster headed back down to street level, but neither Lynn nor Tek felt safe about leaving their hiding space at the top of their rubble mountain. They stayed up there for what felt like hours before carefully making their way toward the tiny red light.

They didn't talk as they crept along. At least one person was hunting them—no doubt there were more—but one was nearby. They trudged on as quietly as they could. Lynn tried to keep track of the time by looking at the sun, but the best she could do was surmise that about an hour had passed. She kept looking nervously at Tek. There was no way to know for sure if they were even going in the right direction. From street level it was impossible to see any of the lights.

Tek had to constantly hold his arm, and he kept his distance from her.

"Lynn," he finally said.

"Yes."

"I'm going to climb up here to see if I can see the light."

"Good, because I have no idea where we are."

"But when I come back down, I think you should be somewhere else."

"What?" asked Lynn.

"We need to separate."

"Can't you just keep your distance?" asked Lynn. "You said it controlled your arm, not your legs. If you just stay away from me then it should be fine."

"The thing inside me can think for itsself, Lynn. It's a living thing with cognitive abilities. It wants to hurt any human it can."

"But if it hurts you, it'll die, won't it?"

"I don't know. But it will trick you into coming close. Or it will cause a ruckus that will get the attention of whatever is hunting us. I don't know what it will do, but bad things will happen."

"Will you be able to shock yourself?"

"I don't know."

Tek started to climb.

Lynn had no other option than to leave Tek and keep walking.

She had been walking for about ten minutes when it happened. The hunter stepped in front of her and stood there. He crossed his freakishly long arms and cocked his head to one side. His fake face looked like it was made out of an animal skull. Hair burst through cracks in the bone. She knew there was a camera in there somewhere, and it was pointing right at her.

Even if she killed this guy, other hunters would come for her.

"I know you are human. You don't have to pretend anymore."

The monster raised his hands as if to say, "orders are orders." Whoever was under the mask didn't care who she was or what she knew. The fake monster, for whatever reason, was tasked with killing survivors, and that's what he was going to do.

Lynn backed away, looking around for a way to defend herself. She picked up a sharp rock she could use to stab. The monster shook his head, unable to believe that she was still going to try to defend herself.

Then the monster started running at her and she lost all willingness to stay and fight. She threw her rock and ran for her life. It hit him in the shoulder and spun him around, bringing him to one knee.

She didn't get far before she tripped and rolled onto the ground. The blow from the sharp rock wasn't enough to put the monster out of commission. He pulled out his long knife.

"Why a knife? It doesn't make sense. None of this makes sense!"

The monster shrugged again. Orders are orders. He swung back to get optimal leverage for when he stabbed Lynn through the chest. But then everything changed.

Their Imps came back on.

The monster was completely thrown off. He staggered backwards and looked skyward, searching for…what? Lynn realized the transmitters must be Imp signal blockers. How they worked or how the nearest transmitter had been turned off was beyond her. They had seen those red lights all over the city. None of the survivors would be able to use their Imps. Being hunted wasn't enough—they were purposely being cut off from the rest of the world.

Lynn started recording everything with her Imp and sending it to everyone on her contact list. It no longer mattered if she lived or died. If she got the message out then it would all be worth it. With over a thousand people on her contact list, her vid feed would be enough to start the ball rolling. The truth would come out.

While the monster was distracted she picked up another chunk of rock to hit him with, but he had already started running. Running away from her. She ran to catch up with him, all the while recording. The monster started climbing up a nearby rubble mountain. It must have been the one with the transmission tower at the top. They had been so close! Where was Tek now?

The monster wasn't too far ahead. Lynn tried throwing things at it. She needed to knock his helmet off so she could show people it was all a ruse. Even though she hit him a couple times, he didn't slow down and he didn't turn around.

She started getting all kinds of calls from friends and family. Even people she hadn't talked to in years. She ignored all the calls. Some people started texting her.

Where are you? It looks like death there.

Were you in Northgate? They said there were no survivors.

Is this the monster they've been talking about?

I thought that place was under quarantine.

Are you okay? Where's Scott?

I'm having trouble getting a solid fix on your location. If you stand still we can send someone to help.

I was trying to call you all day yesterday. I thought you were dead.

Stop chasing that thing. It's going to kill you!

I will give you $10,000 for exclusive rights to your story!!!

She had no idea who that last one was from, but they were filling up her space so she disabled incoming texts and sent out one mass text to everyone she knew.

The war is fake. I have proof. It wasn't the aliens who killed all these people and destroyed this city. Find Scott. Tell him he was right, and that I love him.

Just as she finished the text she heard a voice yelling at her from the top.

"Lynn! Get out of the way!"

She looked up. An avalanche of debris was beginning its descent. Lynn ran and leapt over chunks of concrete, broken furniture, and fallen trees. She was almost out of the avalanche's path when a rock clipped her and she fell. She scrambled behind a huge rock and grabbed a piece of metal to hold over her head. Rocks, wood, and glass showered around her. She had only been caught at the edge of the avalanche, but it still left her breathless. The deafening roar subsided as the last of the debris settled. Rubble piled on rubble. Paper, metal, wood, asphalt. A body was also thrown into the mix. The monster had been swept up in the avalanche.

Now that the monster was out of commission, she had to go and send out her proof.

She threw her make-shift helmet aside and tried to stand. The dust made her cough, and her legs weren't working properly. She was so shaken up by what had happened, her vision was blurry. Lynn froze when she heard the crunch of footsteps and sliding rocks. Someone was coming.

"Lynn!" said Tek. "Are you okay?"

"I don't know. I can't walk."

"I'm coming." More crunching and sliding of rocks as Tek moved towards her. "I found the light. It was a transmission tower of sorts. It was blocking the Imps. Tell me you got some messages out."

"Yes, I'm still recording and sending."

"Good."

"So the tower is out of commission. Does that mean you were able to shock yourself?"

Tek was right in front of her now. Her vision had cleared up enough to see him clearly.

"No. I need your help for that."

Tek had tried to tie his right arm in tight to his body, but using only one hand and his teeth, it was hard to do a good job of it. He held out his good hand to pull Lynn to her feet.

She took stock of what had happened. The monster, half-buried in rubble, wasn't moving anymore.

"Do you think it's dead?" Lynn asked.

"It's a he, remember. Just a man."

"Right."

"And yes. I think he's dead."

"Good, I need to send out some proof to everyone that this was all a lie."

She started toward the body, totally forgetting what happened the last time they killed one. Tek's right arm twitched in anticipation.

The explosion lifted Lynn and Tek off their feet. They fell back to the ground and rocks hailed down around them. She was in shock. For several seconds she just lay there in the rubble, trying to process what had happened. Tek had landed right beside Lynn. The scrap of fabric he'd used to tie his arm down was torn and fell to the ground. Against his will, his right hand started choking Lynn. She tried to scream even though there was no one around to help her.

"Lynn!"

Tek fought against his allegedly alien-infected arm. But there was nothing he could do.

"No!"

He started beating the bad arm with his good arm. He tried prying the fingers off her throat, but their grip was too strong. In desperation, as Lynn's eyes started rolling into the back of her head and she stopped struggling, he grabbed a hunk of cement and bashed his bad arm's bicep. It hurt like nothing else. On the third hit he broke the ulna. A jagged piece of the bone pierced his skin, and blood dripped onto Lynn's chest. After a couple more hits the alien inside him gave up; it had completed its task.

Tek rolled away from Lynn and started crying. He looked to see if she was breathing, but her chest remained still. It was too late. There was nothing he could do to help her.

The sound of an engine broke the silence. He looked up and saw a shuttle flying low overhead. Earth military. The shuttle landed nearby and two people came out. They knew exactly where to look. They must have been following Lynn's feed. That meant they knew that Tek had killed her.

"There they are!" the one with fire-orange hair pointed at them.

The other one led the charge. He clipped his gun back onto his belt so that he could jump over the rubble faster. The guy didn't look very old, almost too young to be in the military. He ignored Tek. All of his attention was on Lynn. As soon as he got to her he checked for breathing. Nothing. No pulse either. He started CPR.

"Jace, get your med pack!"

Jace, the ginger, holstered his gun and reached into his backpack as he ran over to his companion.

A third man staggered out of the shuttle. He was trying to untangle himself from some cords. Had he been tied up? The third man freed himself of the cord and then went back to the shuttle. He emerged again, this time with a weapon that he leveled at Jace and the other man who was trying to save Lynn.

"I'm sorry," said Tek.

"We'll worry about you later," said the man trying to save Lynn. Then he noticed the third man had his weapon out. "Not now. She's dying! We can help her!"

The man looked angry and ready to kill, but he must have been ordered to stand down because he didn't pull the trigger, yet.

"She was right. The aliens are not responsible for this," said Tek.

That got the guy's attention. He stopped helping Lynn for half a second and turned to Tek.

"Do you have proof?"

"Mac!" said Jace. "Focus. She's dying."

"The proof is roaming out there somewhere," said Tek.

All these people had to do was go find one of the fake monsters. These guys were military and they were just as confused and suspicious as he was. Maybe they were good guys. Maybe they could get to the bottom of this.

"He's going for your gun!" said the third man.

Tek looked down to see what he was talking about. Unfortunately, he was talking about Tek. His bad arm, broken and bleeding, hadn't given up. It wanted to kill one more human before it was all over. His possessed hand got a grip on Mac's gun, but a laser blast hit Tek squarely in the chest. The third man, whose name was Raymond, had fired the shot. Tek's arm, with Raymond's help, had claimed its final victim.

Chapter 7
Final Resting Place

Raymond was a trigger-happy idiot, but Mac didn't want to deal with him now; Jace was there with the med pack. Mac was still breathing into the woman's mouth and pumping blood into her heart.

"That's not going to do anything if her throat is collapsed," said Jace. He grabbed a collar and put it under her neck to help open her airway. "Try it now. I'll take over the compressions."

Because her heart had stopped, the Imp recording had ended. *If she doesn't remember to start recording again, Raymond could do whatever he wants with no consequences*, Mac thought. They worked together until Lynn's heart and lungs began working on their own. She panicked and started screaming and clawing at the thing on her neck.

"Calm down. We're here to help you," said Mac.

She wasn't listening. She kicked Mac in the chest. It didn't hurt much, but he backed away and gave her space so she could calm down. Standing up, she tore the collar off, then went back to her knees. It was helping her breathe, but she could manage well enough without it.

Finally she noticed the body of the man who had strangled her. The heavy breathing turned to sobbing. Jace felt he could move in for a comforting hug. She accepted, and cried into his shoulder.

"Listen," said Jace. "We don't have a lot of time. There aren't many people who are sympathetic to our cause."

She sniffed and looked at him, wondering how he could really be talking about this right now.

"Did you see any other survivors?" asked Mac.

"Yes, but he's dead," said Lynn.

"Where is the proof?"

"You have to find—"

Before she could finish she started screaming again. She pulled away from Mac and Jace and fell on the ground. Raymond came running from the shuttle and put restraints around her wrists. Then he fired his immobilizer at Lynn to surge her Imp feeds. She passed out. It was too much for her to take in all at once. Raymond stood over her so that neither Mac nor Jace could get close.

"You could have killed her. You're not supposed to surge people who have just been through serious trauma," said Jace.

"Neither of you have to worry about that anymore. More shuttles are on the way. You are both being transferred. Might as well forget you ever saw this girl because you're never going to see her again."

Mac hadn't started out thinking the war was fake, but as soon as that became a possibility he couldn't get the thought out of his head. The attack on Northgate had changed Mac's life forever. Why not start out with a new career too? The proof they needed to show that this war was fake, that it was the government or the military who had destroyed the city and killed millions of people, was out there somewhere. Mac needed to find it. Even if it meant going AWOL.

Raymond saw the wheels turning in Mac's mind.

"There's nowhere you can go where we can't track you," said Raymond, tapping the side of his head. "You can't run from Imps."

That wasn't true. Mac started running. He could hear Raymond cursing behind him. If Mac could get under the cover of the Imp-blocking transmission towers, he could explore the entire north side of the city to look for the proof he needed. As he ran he noticed the approaching shuttles. General Zinger would be on one of those. Mac knew not to get on his bad side. The general wasn't one to follow the rules. He just did whatever he wanted—no matter who got in his way.

Mac counted four shuttles. It would take them a while to find a place to land. There definitely wasn't enough room for all four of them to set down near Raymond and the woman. He realized he never learned what her name was. Checking up on her later was going to be difficult.

Now that she was in military custody, her fate depended on whoever did the interrogations. If it was Raymond, she was as good as dead. It also depended on the public's reaction to her video feed. If there was enough of an outcry, the military wouldn't be able to touch her without a full-blown revolution on its hands.

But that was all stuff Mac would have to look into later.

It didn't take long for his Imp to blink off. He was off the grid now. Safe. Kind of. He knew that when the shuttles landed, Raymond would send whatever spare soldiers they had to go find Mac. He hadn't forgotten about the monsters either, and would run with his gun in hand.

Even though he was free of the Imp, he used stealth to evade his pursuers. They couldn't track him as easily if he didn't follow a pattern.

How did that woman survive out here for so long? he wondered. There were no street signs to tell Mac where he was. He wouldn't be able to describe the extent of the carnage to anyone—even if he managed to get out of Northgate alive. As far as the eye could see lay piles of indistinguishable wreckage. Closer inspection revealed cement, rocks, wood, rebar, shingles, wires. Body parts mingled with broken toys and charred curtains. Homes, businesses, valued possessions, all reduced to worthless debris. Mac couldn't even tell if he was standing in a residential zone, the downtown core, or an industrial area.

He tried to distinguish where the roads were by looking for patterns created by series of charred cars. But even then it was a guessing game, because buildings had fallen onto the road and cars were thrown into buildings.

He paused for a moment to listen. Was anyone following him? It was hard to hear the subtle sound of footsteps. His heart beat heavily in his ear. Mac had to breathe deeply to calm down and listen.

Initially there was no noise, but he waited. The waiting paid off. He heard the crunch of footsteps stumbling over rubble. In this canyon of debris there was no way to tell where the noise was coming from.

"You should develop better hiding skills," said a voice right by Mac.

He jumped and flipped around. The man who snuck up had enough sense to be prepared for this and used his hand to point Mac's gun away.

"Jace!" said Mac.

"You left without saying goodbye," said Jace.

"Raymond didn't give me much of a choice."

"And you thought *I* had a choice? He thinks I'm with you on this. That we're in cahoots."

"Are we in cahoots?"

"Of course. That's why I started running right after you did, but in a different direction."

"Then how did you find me?"

"That was just a happy coincidence," Jace pointed to the top of a nearby tower. "I was up there trying to learn as much as I could when I saw you."

"I see."

"You sure didn't. You weren't even facing the right direction."

"Well, I thought someone was following me. People don't usually follow me from the front."

"Good thing I found you. We *are* being followed. There are twelve soldiers behind us right now. They aren't too far off either."

"Then let's get going," said Mac. He got up to leave, but Jace held him back.

"They sent the youngest, greenest guys I've ever seen. We should just hide in one of these cars and wait for them to pass by us. We wait here until dark. By then they should have shot themselves by accident or gone back to base. They aren't prepared for an overnight stay."

Mac thought about it. "That would give us time to rest and then move during the night."

"Exactly. Let's find a place to hide."

They looked up and down the street. There was a city hover bus. Mac decided to check it out. The small windows and big interior would make it a more comfortable hiding spot.

Inside was a grisly scene. Twenty people on board, all dead. None of them had died in the initial attack—all had been stabbed to death. Men's bodies lay crumpled in front of the women they tried to protect. But the moment the predators got on the bus, every passenger was doomed.

The murders couldn't be done quickly and cleanly with a laser blast either. Whoever did this wanted it to look horrific. Multiple wounds were inflicted with a blade of some kind. No one used swords or machetes anymore. Why go to all the trouble just to make it feel more creepy?

Mac got off the bus.

"Not in there," he said, trying not to retch.

"Over here," said Jace.

Mac trotted over to the Autrik Jace was standing beside. He couldn't help but check the plates to make sure it wasn't his parent's vehicle. It wasn't.

The Autrik was promoted as the family van of the future. That was the tag line twenty years ago when they were still popular. It sat ten people comfortably. The two of them climbed in and lay down on the floor in between rows of seats, Mac in the front and Jace in the back. A row of seats separated them. Once they were settled, there was nothing they could do but wait.

The AWOL soldiers had just nodded off when the sound of rubble crunching beneath boots woke them. The rookies sent to find them were running, trying to cover as much ground as possible. It didn't occur to them to stop and check to see if anyone was hiding, or to follow footprints in the ground, or simply to stop and listen, and Mac and Jace's Imps were blocked. Whoever sent these guys out couldn't really expect them to accomplish anything. If it hadn't been for the woman they saved, Raymond would have come himself. Lucky for Mac and Jace he wouldn't leave her alone. Not so lucky for her.

The footsteps passed, but Mac and Jace remained hidden. It would be a few more hours until sunset. Mac tried to figure out how the monsters fit into the ruse. Was it really just to start rumors? But they had killed most of the survivors, and survivors were crucial for spreading the rumors and adding credibility to them. The monsters could also be part of a plan to point the finger firmly at the aliens. It would work because no one knew what the aliens looked like.

Mac also thought of his family. Where could they be if they weren't at the house? Would he ever find them again? Were they even alive?

Mac got lost in his thoughts and memories. He started with conspiracies but they moved on to what his mind usually wandered to. His family, life in Passage, and the girl who had been taken from him.

Mac had been with Janelle the night she left—the night she was taken. He would never forget the way she looked that night. Her long blond hair, always pinned up or tied back as if she liked the length but not the hassle of taming the mess after a typical windy day in Passage. She had cloudy blue eyes that reminded him of the sky in the middle of the day. Mac would look into her eyes as often as he could. Sometimes he would forget what they were talking about.

She dated occasionally, but didn't have a steady boyfriend. No matter who she dated she always stayed friends with Mac. Janelle was older than he was. Two years older, but neither height nor age mattered to either of them. He liked to think he was mature for his age, and kids her age didn't like the same things that she did, so Janelle and Mac were a perfect match.

They were walking down a makeshift dirt road between two farmers' fields, just outside of Passage. She said she had something to show him. If she wanted Mac to be with her, then he would be there. It didn't matter why.

They walked, and the lights of Passage got smaller and smaller.

There were a lot of lights in Passage. The land around the village was flat. Blinking lights could be seen in every direction. The glow of Northgate was visible. There were moving lights from the hover cars on the highway and, in the sky, shuttles and spaceships were flying to and from Earth.

"Have you ever been off planet?" asked Mac.

"Yes, it's awesome," said Janelle. "My dad had contract work to do on Mars. At the training base they have there."

"Really? You never told me that before."

"That's where Mom died."

They walked in silence. Mac wasn't sure what to say. That was the most she had ever said about her mom before. From the town gossip he was able to put together that Janelle's father's decision to move the family to Passage had something to do with her mom's death.

"So, where are we going, anyway?" asked Mac.

"There's something I need to show you."

Mac started pulling ahead of her as they walked. He was taller. His strides were longer. She reached out and grabbed his hand to slow him down. He slowed to match her pace, but she kept holding his hand. He didn't have the courage to make the first move on his own, and if he said he was disappointed that Janelle took the initiative, he'd be lying.

Janelle looked back. The lights of the village could still be seen.

"We're almost there."

They didn't take too many more steps before she said to stop. They had just gone down a slight decline. The lights of the village couldn't be seen anymore. Neither could the lights of the highway. Even the glow of Northgate was no longer visible.

The only lights in the sky were the stars twinkling above them.

"Not even a single ship up there. How is that possible?" asked Mac.

"They are investigating reports of UFOs in the solar system. All ships have to turn off their lights or land for one hour while they look for it. My dad told me about it."

"This is incredible. I've never seen anything like this."

"No one has. There have been lights in the sky at night for hundreds of years on Earth. This is almost like time travel, isn't it?"

Mac couldn't take his eyes off the sky. It *was* like time travel. He didn't even feel like he was on Earth right now. The quietness of the world and the blackness of space felt so foreign. It was cool and frightening at the same time, though he would never admit that to anyone.

Janelle wasn't looking at the sky. She was looking right at Mac. He must have looked confused.

"Lean down," she said.

He did, and she kissed him.

Mac had never kissed anyone before. It was a dead fish kiss; Mac didn't know what to do with his lips.

It lasted for half a second. "Let's try that again." Janelle got on her tippy toes and they kissed again. Mac had never been more happy in his life, but he wasn't sure of the logistics of the kiss. He moved his lips more this time, but questions raced through his mind.

Do I put my tongue in her mouth? My mouth isn't open. Should I open it? Open my mouth and close my eyes? What about my hands…?

He decided to keep holding her hands and keep his eyes open. It was so dark out it didn't make a difference either way.

He saw it coming before she did and broke off the kiss.

"How long did you say the ships had to black out for?" asked Mac.

"One hour."

Mac had to check. Their second kiss, which would also be their last, had felt like an eternity. In a good way.

"And it just started?"

"Yes."

"I see a ship," said Mac.

"Mac, wake up."

Mac's eyes shot open. He must have been more tired than he thought. It was dark outside. Dark and quiet.

"How long was I out for?"

"I'm not sure, but you've been snoring for about an hour," said Jace.

"An hour. Why didn't you wake me up?"

"You looked tired. Plus, I was using your snores to see if they would attract anyone."

"And?"

"I think we're alone."

"Then let's go."

"I'll lead the way."

They got out of the Autrik, stretched their legs, and started marching up the garbage hill, heading for the tower at the top. Jace wanted to look at it some more. He also filled Mac in on what he knew so far.

"They aren't radio controlled, which is a good thing. That means if someone wants to turn them off then they have to go to each one and disable it. I think the plan would have been to destroy each one as they 'searched' for survivors.

"I'm not sure what their radius is, but it can't be much more than a half mile because I could see a couple dozen other lights from the one at the top here."

They got to the top of the hill. This particular mound was higher than all the other ones around it. Probably why a tower was put on it. The blinking red lights that Jace had been talking about were easy to spot in the dark. There were even more than he had originally estimated.

Jace was tinkering with the tower.

"What are you trying to do?" asked Mac.

"I'm trying to make it portable."

"Good idea. If any more are disabled, we could wander into an area where our Imps will give us away. I wish I'd known we'd need them before I started shooting at them."

Making the tower portable would eliminate the threat of being caught. Not just while they were searching the city, but also after they got out. They were going to have to stay hidden for days if they were going to blow this conspiracy open.

"What proof do you think that woman had?" asked Mac.

"I'm not sure."

"How long do you think she has before they break her?"

"She was pretty feisty. Remember the kick to your chest? And she did figure out how to survive out here with those monster things. I'll give her the benefit of the doubt."

"And how long is that?"

"A week or so. Depends on their methods of extraction."

"If we can't find our own evidence, then she'll be the one we have to go to next."

"Yeah, right, 'cause that won't be impossible."

"We have no other choice."

"That Scott guy," said Jace.

"What?"

"In her message it said to 'tell Scott he was right,' remember? Maybe he was right about the war. We could check it out."

"Yes. If worse comes to worst, we will go find one, or both, of them."

Jace was climbing the transmission tower to reach the box with the blinking light at the top. It took a while to undo the bolts holding it in place, but he managed. From his pocket he pulled out a battery. He opened the box and attached the battery.

He knocked on the outside of the box and shook it a bit to see how sturdy it was. The box was three feet long and half a foot thick with a small dish on its top, but he determined it wasn't important and threw it to the ground. It crashed and rolled all the way down to the street.

"Trying to attract more attention?" asked Mac.

"I was also seeing if it was a good idea to drop this thing down there. It's bigger than I thought. You might want to catch it."

It was dark and hard to see Jace, but Mac would manage. He got closer to the tower and held out his arms.

"Okay, I'm ready."

Jace dropped the box and Mac caught it. The box wasn't as heavy as he thought it would be. Quickly, Jace climbed down. "One of us is going to have to carry this thing. We'll go back to the cars and fashion a harness out of the safety belts. It's not too heavy, but we should still take turns."

"So this is the thing blocking the Imps?" asked Mac.

"As far as I can tell, yes. We should also keep this as further evidence. Maybe we can prove who built it."

"Good idea."

"Any suggestions about what our next move should be?"

"I think we need to find one of those monsters. They seem to be key. The woman's transmission started with one of them trying to kill her. We should start were she left off."

"How are we going to do that?"

"Well, one might find us but our guns could scare them off. I'd say our best bet is to find some survivors, blend in with them and wait for monsters to show up."

"*If* there are any survivors left," said Jace.

"What do you think her name was?" asked Jace later that night.

"What?"

"The woman we went to rescue. We can't just keep calling her 'the woman we went to rescue.' I didn't catch her name, did you?"

"No," said Mac.

"Then we need to name her. For the sake of brevity, if nothing else."

"Maybe we should call her Brevity."

"That's not a name. And she didn't look hippy enough to have a name that isn't a name."

"Then Beverly."

"Sounds like a spinster. This girl wasn't over thirty."

"How about Monica?"

"What?"

"What's wrong with Monica?"

"Do you have any daughters?" asked Jace.

"No."

"Well, when you do let your wife name the kids. I'm thinking we call the woman *Janelle*. I dated a Janelle when I was in high school, and I like remembering her."

"Not Janelle."

"Why?"

"Doesn't matter. Just not Janelle. How about Lori?"

"No."

"Megan?"

"No."

"Molly?"

"No."

"Maddy?"

No *M* names."

"Sasha?"

"No."

This went on for about an hour. It took Mac longer than he'd like to admit for him to realize that Jace wasn't particularly opposed to the names Mac was suggesting—like Chelsey, Amanda, or Carolyn—he just wanted to make noise so that people would know they were there, and talking about something as non-threatening as girls' names would help to show that they weren't dangerous. They had thought about hiding or disguising their weapons but decided it was safer to keep them holstered on their belts.

Every hour or so they would switch backpacks. At first the Imp blocker box felt light, but after an hour it got annoying. Its weight was just enough to slow them down, and the big flat area was uncomfortable against the back. If it were meant to be carried that way, then it wouldn't have been designed like that.

Jace settled on the name Gwendolyn P. Morgan for the woman they had saved. Never Gwen, or Gwendolyn, or even Mrs. Morgan. Always Gwendolyn P. Morgan. It wasn't that much shorter than "the woman we saved."

"What are the chances that anyone is even awake?" asked Jace.

"Not good. If we see anyone tonight it will probably be monsters," said Mac. "Let me ask you something."

"Go for it."

"Why are you here?"

"The same reason you are. What kind of question is that?" asked Jace.

"I'm here because my family is out here somewhere and I don't trust the military to find them or to find the real answers to what is going on here."

"I work in military intelligence. I know not to trust the military. Like I said, I'm here for the same reason you are."

"Tell me how you know?"

"Why is it so important to you?"

"I'm just making sure."

"That we're both on the right side?" asked Jace.

"Something like that," said Mac.

"Have I given you reason not to trust me?"

He hadn't, and maybe that was the most suspicious thing about Jace. Why would he go along with Mac so easily? The first time they met, Jace was convinced Mac was responsible for the attack on Northgate. And now the intelligence soldier was willing to leave the military and run off with Mac to solve the mystery themselves.

"You *did* think that I was in on the attack on Northgate," said Mac.

"I was wrong. I knew it wasn't aliens, so I just defaulted to the other group that the government doesn't trust. You used to be a Luddite," said Jace.

"What makes you think that it wasn't aliens?"

"It doesn't make strategic sense for it to be aliens. There are dozens of colonies between here and the front line of the war. Why would they bother coming all the way to Earth to destroy Northgate? I doubt it was aliens. I'm more interested in finding out who really did this so that I know who the real enemy is."

They talked about the motivation and logistics behind destroying a whole city. It would take one super weapon or a bunch of little ones. Of the two of them, only Mac had seen the attack, and from several miles away.

"The ship was alien," Mac said.

"Or made to look alien," Jace countered.

From Mac's vantage point, the attack appeared to be a series of smaller munitions that took out the entire city. That meant there was a solid trail to follow. Even the secretive military couldn't build up that much ammunition and a giant alien-looking ship without someone noticing.

Jace and Mac puzzled over why the monsters were only in the North end of the city and why the attackers came down to kill the survivors.

"Are there any government buildings in Northgate?" asked Jace.

"No. At least none that are important."

Jace grew up way south of there, near the ocean. Mac had been to Northgate several times before and knew it better than Jace did. As a kid, Mac had come here often for family vacations. It was awkward taking in the sights because none of them had Imps, and museums had virtual tour guides which were accessed only with Imps. Amusement parks were designed for people with Imps. So were sporting events and most festivals. Those were still fun without Imps, but their family would always stand out because they couldn't react to the same things everyone else did.

City parks were the best places to spend their time in the city. They were some of the few places left in the city that didn't require Imps to have fun. They would pack a lunch and play baseball or board games, but mainly these times were meant to enjoy one another's company.

The Narrads would have avoided the city altogether if their oldest daughter hadn't married an Imp person and moved to the city. They came here to be with her and her new family. Her husband was perfectly comfortable with the fact that they were Imp-less, and he never pressured his wife into getting one. He even agreed to wait until their kids were old enough to decide for themselves before they were given the Imp option.

Just as the sun was rising, Mac and Jace came to one of these parks.

Until now, Mac had no idea where in the city he was or even what direction they were going. Now he knew exactly where they were: Valentin Park.

It was his family's favorite park. They used to come here for lunch.

Then he saw the Autrik.

"No."

Mac dropped the Imp blocker on the ground and ran to his family's vehicle. They must have come here early in the morning for a breakfast picnic. Maybe they had gotten up in the morning, realized Mac wasn't there, and went to look for him at the family's favorite city park. He wanted answers, but he would probably never know—his family was dead. There were two bodies inside the Autrik. His little brother—his only brother—and his mom. Her head rested on the back of the seat. His brother was curled up on the floor behind her. Their eyes were closed. If it weren't for the blood, they would have looked like they were sleeping. He could tell from the wounds it was the monsters not the attacking ship that had killed them.

The bodies of his other family members weren't too far off. Jace found them first. He was crouched beside the twins with a confused look on his face. He reached out to brush their hair away from their faces. Mac didn't like that at all.

"Get away from them," said Mac.

"They don't even look like they're dead," said Jace.

The twins looked like they had been running away across the sports field when they were murdered. His dad was also in the field. He had died defending them.

The others, his oldest sister, her husband, and son, were in the trees. They had tried to hide. Mac couldn't believe someone would do this. His nephew was only four years old. What threat did he pose?

"Mac, I'm so sorry," said Jace.

Mac didn't say anything. He lifted his nephew's body. It was so light. So lifeless. He would put his family in a safe place where he could come back for them. They weren't meant to be in the city, even in their favorite part of the city. They needed to go home to Passage. But first, he needed to gather them together.

When he knelt next to his dad, Mac finally started freaking out. Yelling and screaming. Jace stood back and let Mac do what he needed to do. There was nothing else Jace could do; he respected Mac's earlier request to not move any of the bodies.

Jace set about making a fire. A huge one that he hoped would attract attention. He was disturbed by the discovery of the Narrad family's bodies, and building the fire was the distraction he needed.

Mac worked alone. The somber task took three hours. Mac placed the bodies in a storage shed that he had emptied out and swept clean. Once all the bodies were inside, he wrote a note and left it on his father who was lying in the middle. It said to contact Mac Narrad for arrangements to be buried in Passage. And if Mac couldn't be reached, to contact the only other man in Passage with an Imp. Except this time, Mac wrote the man's real name.

Once the door was closed, the tears stopped. Mac had to concentrate on setting things right. He was the only Narrad left.

Jace finally came over and put a hand on his shoulder. "Come with me. I have a plan."

Chapter 8
Surge

The first part of the plan was to attract attention. Jace built the fire up and then they hid and watched. Jace fed the fire two more times before they sensed another presence.

A monster, similar to the one they had seen on Lynn's video feed, strode out of the shadows. Fearlessly it strode toward the fire. Mac and Jace wondered if it had been watching from the darkness to see who had made the fire.

"The honor is all yours," whispered Jace. "Just wait for the sign."

And then they saw it.

The monster stopped walking. It shrugged its shoulders, pointed at the fire and then at other debris that might explain its cause. It appeared to be communicating with others of its kind. The portable box and the red lights blinking nearby assured them there was no way it was using an Imp, but it had a communications device all the same. Jace nodded. Mac quietly drew his gun and shot the monster in the chest. It cried out and dropped dead. Mac and Jace didn't care that the creature was in the middle of a conversation and his comrades would know that someone else was there. They just needed to use his communicator to call for a ship.

"Good shot," said Jace.

They got up and took a moment to work out the kinks that hours of crouching had caused in their legs. Unaware of the dead-man's switch that triggered an explosion to destroy evidence and witnesses, Mac and Jace trotted toward the body sprawled out near the fire. They were not close enough to be blown up by the explosion, but were momentarily airborne. Mac came down on the grass. Jace landed on the roof of the Autrik and rolled off. When they had both cleared their heads, Jace put two and two together.

"That explains the explosion in Gwendolyn P. Morgan's video feed. They must have killed that thing with the rock slide," said Jace.

"But now we have no communications device. What do we do?" said Mac.

"I'm sure another monster will come."

"If they heard that explosion, they'll assume we're dead. If we want another monster, we'll have to go to another part of the city. That'll take too long. Let's try plan B."

Plan B was to reveal themselves with the Imps, lure ships to the area, and hijack one of the ships. There was no point walking around, looking for evidence in a desolated city. They didn't even know what they were looking for. All they knew was that a now-dead man told them there was evidence of a fake war out here somewhere. Now that Mac had found his family, he didn't want to be anywhere near Northgate. The only time he planned on coming back was to get his family and then immediately go back to Passage to bury them.

For now, they had to find the two sources who had proof about the war and the attack on Northgate. One was the woman known to them as Gwendolyn P. Morgan. The other was someone she loved named Scott. Jace was going to go after Scott, and Mac was going after Gwendolyn P. Morgan. Jace had a real first name to work with, but Mac knew who had custody of the woman. Either way, finding the people who knew the truth would be easier than searching through the rubble. Especially since they didn't know what they were looking for.

Using their Imps to get found was the easiest way to get out of the city, but it was going to be under military custody. They had to be careful and quick about it. Mac went back to his hiding place while Jace went to the nearest blinking red light to rig up another Imp-blocking backpack.

"How long do we keep these activated?" asked Mac.

"Not long. And once we turn them off, we need to run like there's no tomorrow."

"Of course."

Then, as a test, they both turned off their blockers.

"Just a thought, but are you sure that they will turn back on when we want them to?"

Jace didn't look sure. "We'll find out in about ten minutes."

As soon as they switched off the Imp blockers, Mac's Imp was flooded with messages. There were several warrants out for their arrest—and from more than one governing body. He had messages from his superior officers and even one from General Zinger himself. A lot of people were looking for him and Jace.

"I just thought of something else," said Mac.

"What?"

"What if they realize we are online and they surge us?"

"Let's turn these things back on. They've had enough time." Jace frantically tried to reconnect the battery to his Imp blocker. His hands were shaking. Maybe he had been surged before and knew how uncomfortable it was. Mac had never been surged before.

Until now.

He couldn't have run even if he wanted to. Lights started flashing over his Imp and white noise blared in his ear. The noise would get loud and then soft, loud and then soft. The loud sections sounded like they were getting longer and the soft parts shorter. The lights were amazingly bright. Mac closed his eyes but that didn't help because it was coming from his Imp, not from the real world. Two seconds into the surge Mac felt sick to his stomach. It was sensory overload, the most disgustingly uncomfortable feeling that he had ever experienced.

Their enemies were closing in on them. There was nothing he could do except curl up on the grass that had been fed by the blood of his family.

Then as suddenly as it started, it stopped.

Jace was standing over him with one of the transmitters.

"How did you—didn't the surge affect you?" asked Mac.

"Of course," said Jace. He pulled Mac to his feet.

"You turned on your transmitter while being surged?"

"It's no big deal. I've had training."

"That's impossible."

"We don't have time to talk about this. Our plan is no good. We need to hide."

Mac looked around. "Follow me. I have an idea."

They each grabbed their Imp blockers. Jace had to carry his. He hadn't taken time to construct a makeshift backpack. Mac led the way to the playground. As they ran he scanned the sky. He could hear the shuttles coming but couldn't see anything yet.

There weren't a lot of places to hide. Some of the trees were still standing, but they were all on the edge of the park which was mostly devoted to sports fields, devoid of places to hide. The best cover they could find was in the playground which, strangely, was intact. Although there was a large crater near the playground made by a missile that could have been intended for the play structure.

They hid in the playground's covered twirly slide. Mac remembered when he was a kid at the playground in Passage they would try to see how many kids could fit in the slide at one time. If the kids that day were feeling cruel they would send Darren down the slide first. He was too small to hold everyone up and always ended up at the bottom of the slide with everyone on top of him. They would do that for a laugh at Darren's expense. But usually Mac would go down first and use his legs to hold himself up without going all the way to the end of the slide. When he was in place, the other kids would go down the slide until either the slide filled up or Mac's legs gave out. This time there was only one person to support on the slide, and he wouldn't be riding home with his family in the old Autrik when playtime was over. Mac went down first as always, and then used his legs to hold himself and Jace under the slide's cover. No one outside would be able to see them.

The shuttles landed, but Mac couldn't tell how many there were. The engines turned off and he could hear soldiers running and yelling. They were confused because they couldn't see any trace of Mac and Jace. It was hard to tell where the shuttles had landed.

"Poke your head out the top. See where the shuttles are," said Mac.

"Okay. Hold my transmitter."

Carefully Jace turned and climbed to the top. He peeked over the edge, looked around for a bit and then slid back down to where Mac was.

"There are four shuttles and three dozen men out there. They're anticipating a trap. Half the unit is standing by at the shuttles."

"Where are the shuttles?"

"About twenty-five yards out, twelve o'clock position."

They were so close. They just needed a way to distract them so they could make a run for it.

"Where are they looking for us?" asked Mac.

"Out in the field where we turned our Imps off. Those fools were just standing there scratching their heads."

"What type of shuttles are they flying?"

"The one closest to us is a Hawthree. The other three are transport shuttles."

That worked in their favor. Transport shuttles, even three of them, couldn't outgun an HAAS3, especially if Mac was flying it.

They heard a commander barking orders to split up to find them.

"We probably should have left sooner," said Jace.

"I know. I don't have a plan. Should we just make a run for it?"

"There's that crater in the ground between us and the shuttle. We should make for that. It will at least give us some cover. Let's take our transmitters with us when we run for it. Those guys are so reliant on their Imps, a blank screen might throw them off for a bit. I'm barely used to it myself."

"It just might work. Change the setting on your weapon, though. We don't need to kill anyone," said Mac. He knew these guys were just following orders. There was no need to kill them. Mac took out his gun and dialed it down. The lowest setting still knocked the target unconscious for several hours.

"What are the chances they will extend the same friendliness to us?" Mac asked.

"Zero. Try not to get hit."

Mac set his gun down and put the transmitter on his back. Jace would carry the other transmitter with one hand and his gun with the other. They would have just ditched that transmitter, but they'd need it after they left Northgate and separated.

"Ready?" Mac asked.

"Ready."

Mac let his leg out from under him and they wiggled down the slide. They weren't kids any more, and the transmitters they were packing didn't leave much clearance room. As Mac's feet hit the sand he hoped he wouldn't be noticed right away, but that hope was dashed when he saw two soldiers that were already at the playground. Mac shot one. Jace got the other. Other soldiers noticed. Shouts and orders. Now everyone knew where they were.

Mac and Jace just ran. Mac didn't look where he was running. He just pointed himself in the direction of the ship and ran. While he ran he picked off the targets that were closest to them.

The lack of Imp feeds did distract the soldiers long enough for Mac to shoot them, but that only worked for the people who were closest. The ones farther away were shooting non-stop, and their shots were getting closer. The Imp blockers' reach was shorter than the reach of the soldiers' guns.

Mac and Jace raced for the crater and dove in as lasers scorched the air around them. They could smell something burning. Mac grabbed handfuls of dirt to smother a small flame on his shirt sleeve.

"That was close," said Jace.

Jace had moved to the edge of the crater and was shooting at the soldiers. The crater was deep enough for them to hide in and twenty feet wide. The soldiers advanced in a wave that spanned from the twelve o'clock to five o'clock positions. The HAAS3 Mac hoped to hijack sat directly opposite of the playground at six o'clock.

Mac pulled himself along the ground to the edge of the crater to look at the shuttles. They had left guards behind, but Mac was able to take two of them out before they took cover. Other soldiers noticed, and realizing that Mac and Jace were trying to get to the shuttles, they started running back to the ships.

But what had been working against Jace and Mac before—having no cover while they ran—was now working for them. Mac was able to take out five before any of them thought to drop and crawl. That was the best they could do. Even if they had grenades, they would have to show themselves in order to throw them. If they got shot before the grenade left their hand, they would die and kill some of their buddies too. The ground between the crater and the shuttle wasn't completely flat. If the soldiers crawled, they could make their way without leaving Mac and Jace a lot to shoot at.

Mac shot two more of the soldiers that were bad army crawlers. But there were at least five more he discerned still making progress. Every time he shot at them the laser just kicked up soil and grass near them. They were going to make it to the shuttles. Mac and Jace would also have to contend with two guards laying down cover fire from behind the shuttles.

"I need help over here," said Jace.

Mac looked back at what Jace was dealing with. The soldiers were all crawling now. All the ones that Jace was in a firefight with were slowly moving towards the crater— too many to outgun. A few soldiers had positioned themselves behind the playground equipment and were peppering Jace's side of the crater with laser fire so he couldn't pick off the soldiers making their slow approach. The ground was just as uneven over there as it was near the shuttles. Mac and Jace had worked themselves into a trap.

"What we need is a grenade," said Mac.

"There are still more than twenty guys out there, all spread out. What would a grenade do?" asked Jace as they both fired from their own sides of the crater.

"We would just throw it into the biggest group of them and then make a run for the shuttle. There are only five guys over there. If we went now, we would catch them off guard. They are too focused on the shuttles. They wouldn't see us coming."

"Okay then. Let's do that," said Jace.

"What?"

"On three we run."

"Do you have a grenade or something?" asked Mac.

"Just run when I yell run and keep squeezing that trigger, okay?"

"Okay."

Jace kept his gun out but was only haphazardly shooting while he got his Imp blocker ready to throw. Now Mac understood. Blocking the Imp feed would throw them off long enough for him and Mac to get away.

Jace targeted the playground, shooting out the equipment so that it collapsed. That got rid of three guys and exposed two more that he was able to shoot. Then he started counting.

"One."

A soldier stepped around one of the transport shuttles to fire at Mac, but Mac had seen him making his move and clipped him as soon as he stepped around.

"Two."

"Three! Run!"

Jace threw the box in the air. It landed among a group crawling towards the crater, and they got so confused they stood up. Jace looked back as he ran and shot two of them in the chest. A couple more people stood up, but Mac didn't worry about them. He and Jace were closing in on the shuttles.

The five men crawling to guard the transportation hadn't been affected by the Imp feed stoppage. They kept crawling until they saw that Mac and Jace were no longer in the crater. They didn't notice in time; Mac and Jace mowed them down and then jumped into the HAAS3. Laser fire blasted against the door when it closed behind them. Mac plopped down in the pilot's seat and Jace got on the guns.

"Ramps up," said Mac.

Jace started firing. He took out the other shuttles first. The explosions knocked over several of the still-conscious soldiers. After that he just randomly fired into the field. Most of them were falling back so they didn't get hit. They ran for cover in the trees. They didn't know that Jace wasn't shooting to kill.

Mac took them into the air. They had a plan. They needed to switch shuttles as soon as they could.

"Mac!"

Mac turned just as Jace leapt from his seat to attack a soldier who had stayed behind to guard the shuttles. The spacer must have guessed they would go for the HAAS3 instead of the transport shuttles. He got a shot off, but not before Jace knocked him off balance. Instead of hitting Mac, the laser scorched the wall to his right.

Mac pulled a lever and pointed the shuttle straight up into space.

Jace and the soldier continued to struggle. Jace had dropped his weapon and wasn't wearing body armor. His blows to the soldier's helmeted head and padded torso hurt his fist. The soldier was owning him. He threw Jace against a metal cabinet and drew his gun. Jace knew he was a goner. He closed his eyes and waited for the last sound he would hear—the *bzzt* of a laser blast. When it came, he heard a thud immediately after but didn't feel the burn of a laser. The attacking soldier's dead body had fallen to the floor, not Jace.

"Thanks," said Jace.

"No sweat. Does that make us even?" asked Mac.

"I think for us to be even you would have had to stand there and watch him beat me senseless."

"Next time, then."

"Right. Let's see if there is any food on this shuttle."

"Absolutely. I'm starving."

The second part of their plan was to split up. Mac would search for Gwendolyn P. Morgan, and Jace would look for Scott. They would each need a ship, but neither could stay on the HAAS3 they hijacked. Mac entered the headings for the Earth Space Port (ESP).

The ESP was the biggest man-made structure in outer space. A close second, because of all its military traffic,

CATALYST

was the Mars Space Port (MSP). The ESP was constantly being expanded and always had a steady stream of ships landing and departing. All the spaceships were tracked. Flight controllers knew where each one was coming from and going to. Every rule had to be followed to a T or flight paths would cross and people would die. There was so much traffic that no one dared to do anything other than what they were told.

That only applied to spaceships because they were large, fast and equipped with interplanetary star drive. Mac was not flying a spaceship. He was flying a HAAS3, which were classified as shuttles even though they have more weaponry than transport shuttles do.

Shuttles didn't have an interplanetary drive so they could only effectively go short distances. Sure, they could fly to Mars, but it would take a few years.

The rules the ESP had for shuttles were much more lenient than the ones they had for spaceships. One corridor of space was designated for shuttles. Shuttle pilots using the corridor could launch or land at designated ESP pads without having to sign in. They could come and go as they pleased as long as there was room.

Pilots that flew outside of that corridor without prior consent from ESP were banned from ever landing there again. That was a life-changing ban. People always followed that rule.

Mac and Jace planned to go to the space port, steal two shuttles, and go back to Earth. Mac pushed the shuttle as fast as he could. Jace had the news playing on one of the monitors, trying to see if there was anything about them in it. There wasn't. There was a ton of stuff about the destruction of Northgate and yesterday's video feed from Gwendolyn P. Morgan, but the military had not resorted to using the media to catch Mac and Jace.

The spin on Gwendolyn P. Morgan was that she suffered from a chemical imbalance that qualified her as a

107

danger to the public. They disclosed her name—Lynn Ryder.

"Goodbye, Gwendolyn P. Morgan," said Jace.

Scott Ryder was her husband. He was in a hospital undergoing psychiatric treatment after declaring that the war was fake and refusing to supply ammunition for the military. They didn't say which hospital he was at, or even what planet he was on.

"Hopefully he wasn't in Northgate," said Jace.

Mac steered the ship around the other shuttles crowding to get to the ESP. They were leaving the atmosphere now. The sky around them was getting increasingly darker, the stars becoming brighter, more visible.

The ESP was an awkward-looking space station. When it was first built it had been beautiful, an architectural wonder. People would go just to look at it. As Earth's population grew and demanded more and more space, the people in charge of expanding ESP stopped caring about whether it looked good or not. They just needed it done.

There were all kinds of random things jutting out from the side of the space port. It resembled an exploding ball of twisted metal, an ugly man-made moon.

"I don't think we should go into the port terminal," said Mac. "Let's just steal a couple of shuttles and get out of here."

"Agreed; just follow me. I know what to do."

"You know how to steal shuttles? Shuttles don't power up unless the hand scanner recognizes the owner's, or another authorized pilot's, handprint. Right?"

"A friend of mine taught me a way around it."

"A shuttle thief?"

"I used to hang with him when we were kids. We were adrenaline junkies. I moved on to legal ways of getting my fix. Space jumps, joining the military. Stuff like that. He kept stealing things. Right now it looks like he made the better career choice."

"Let's just do this quickly before we get caught."

Jace was at the HAAS3's controls now. The land and launch (LAL) area was massive and dotted with LAL pads. The busiest areas were the ones closest to the main entrance, so he wasn't going to put the shuttle down there. Mac wasn't sure where Jace wanted to go.

Jace flew slowly and kept his eyes on what was happening below him. He moved the shuttle farther and farther away from the entrance. Open landing spaces were becoming more plentiful.

"There's our shuttle," said Jace.

He landed the stolen military shuttle six spaces away from an ugly, old-model Earth Living Shuttle (ELS). These shuttles were designed for people that weren't skilled enough to fly regular shuttles. Usually really young people or really old people. They were the Autrik of space shuttles and every bit as ugly. They had so many safety features that style and looks were not even considered. Flying an ELS was as close as a person could get to a flying box as a personal vehicle. The massive transport shuttles and ships were also very boxy, but no one judged them because they were just hauling goods from one place to another. Their pilots weren't using the transport shuttle as their main vehicle. And transport ships were at least a muted shade of gray or some other metallic color. The Earth Living Shuttles stood out thanks to their off-the-wall colors—the brighter the better. It had to do with safety. An ELS's vibrant color—assaulting to the retinas—made it easier for other pilots to see it.

"You don't think we will stand out?" asked Mac.

"In a good way. Everyone avoids these things. They assume they're being driven by bad drivers. This will keep people from getting too close and losing their Imp power. We'll be blending in by standing out," said Jace.

"Okay, so how do we steal it without the owner's handprint?"

"We don't. I saw an old lady walking this way. I think she's the one we are looking for."

"And then what?"

"We wait until she turns on the ship for us, and then we steal it."

"That won't work. Those shuttles don't start until the door is closed. It'll be locked. We won't be able to get inside. One of their many safety features. It prevents people like us from stealing them. Not that Earth Living Shuttles are in high demand," said Mac.

"There she is," Jace pointed.

The old lady walking towards the brightly-colored shuttle was very old. She used a cane and had a spine the shape of a question mark. She was too old to be driving, but there were no other people with her. Mac couldn't believe she was going to pilot the shuttle anywhere. Most likely she was just going to turn on the auto-pilot and sit back and relax.

"She's ancient."

"Yeah, this should be easy for us," said Jace.

"I kind of feel bad. What is she going to do after we take her shuttle? She'll have to walk and get help. She can hardly do that. Every step for her is only like half an inch."

"Don't feel sorry for her. Remember, she has an Imp. You are the one that is going to be in trouble."

"Me?"

"That's your shuttle. You take it to find Lynn. I'm the one with shuttle-thieving experience. I'll find another one and look for Scott."

"Why do I get the ugly one?"

"Feel free to steal any one you want, but this is going to be the easiest."

Jace got up to leave the shuttle, but something was still nagging at Mac. More so now, because Jace hadn't brought up the solution to it yet, like he wasn't even worried about it.

"What about your Imp?"asked Mac.

"What?"

"I have the only Imp blocker. What are you going to do?"

"Don't worry about it."

"We're in cahoots now. It's something I have to worry about."

Jace looked like he wanted to reveal his secrets, but something was holding him back. It dawned on Mac that, most likely, Jace didn't even have an Imp. That's why he was able to tolerate the Imp surge in Valentin Park. That's why he could reconnect the battery to his Imp blocker. Mac reached back and was ready to rip his own battery out of his Imp blocker to prove a point.

"I know you don't have an Imp. There is no way training can negate what a surge does to you. Should I disconnect my battery so you can prove me wrong?" said Mac.

"No. Don't do that," said Jace.

"Then tell me what's going on."

"I can't."

"Not reassuring."

"You have to trust me. I've been helping you this whole time. We're trying to do the same thing," said Jace.

"You've been lying to me."

"I'm helping you."

"Tell me what's going on."

"I can't. Not yet."

"This is ridiculous," said Mac.

"No. We still have a plan. You find Lynn. I find Scott. We meet up in Passage and find the proof about who is really behind the attacks on Northgate. Whether you trust me or not, we still need to do that."

Mac couldn't think of another option. True, they were both after the same thing right now, but that didn't quell the unease roiling inside him. He couldn't turn Jace over; he might break under interrogation. And Mac wasn't going to kill him. What if he was telling the truth?

"Once she opens the shuttle door, I'm going to go up and talk to her. I'll feed her some story to make her feel sorry for me," Jace said. "I'll tell her I'm from a colony. I'm new to the planet, don't have any money and I need a ride. When the shuttle starts, you walk up and block her Imp. When she starts freaking out I'll take her away to get some help. Then you sneak in and steal the shuttle."

"And you'll be just fine by yourself?" Mac asked.

"I'm very resourceful. Trust me."

Mac didn't know what to do; he wasn't sure he could trust Jace. The man who left to go talk to the old lady called himself Jace, and he claimed to be an ally, but to Mac he couldn't have been more alien.

Chapter 9
McAllister

The shuttle-stealing scheme went off without a hitch, and Mac was soon on his way in the ugly Earth Living Shuttle. Now all he needed to do was find Lynn.

The newscasts weren't the most reliable sources of information about her. The reporters were really running with the mentally unstable angle. Her whole life was being analyzed by several newsrooms. They were trying to figure out exactly where she had gotten the idea that the war wasn't real, or why she didn't love her planet enough to retract her statement, admit she was wrong. The conclusion that most of them came to was that whatever happened to her husband, who was also of the opinion that the war wasn't real, had also happened to her.

Mac didn't pay too much attention to that. Even if she had proof, the military would never share that tidbit with the media. He didn't think she was mentally unstable. He listened closely for information about where she was located now. It never got more specific than, "She's in military custody." To him that meant she wouldn't be too far from where they found her. She was probably with Zinger at the base. Mac was going to have to go back there.

He couldn't do it with an Imp.

The news was also rife with stories from survivors about monsters in the city, killing anyone who was still alive. Whatever was in the news, most people would take as the gospel truth. People would believe it really was aliens that had attacked Northgate.

First things first. Mac had to find the evidence. Then he would worry about how he was going to get it out to the masses. He hadn't been around Imps long enough to know how to easily get rid of them. Not that there was an easy way, but there had to be an easier-than-the-others way. He remembered hearing about the smiling blind people. People who had become so addicted to being plugged into the disconnected reality that it drove them mad, and they ripped their own eyes out just to escape it. It was effective, because two of the three Imp chips were in the eyes. The brain chip didn't do anything by itself. The people smile because, as the saying goes, your worst day blind is better than your best day disconnected from reality.

Mac didn't want to rip his eyes out. He didn't even want to get them surgically removed. He just wanted to get rid of his Imp. Part of the Imp was planted in the brain, but the thought of undergoing brain surgery was even worse than getting new eyes. He would find another way.

He hoped that the package the only man from Passage with an Imp had sent him might have some answers. The package was sent to McAllister. He'd go pick it up there and see if there were any answers for him.

McAllister was the town where the only man in Passage with an Imp lived before he moved to Passage. It was on the other side of the world. Far away from Northgate and Zinger. Passage was in Northern North America, and McAllister was a city in Australia. There was no reason for anyone to look for Mac there.

Mac got to McAllister easily. The shuttle Jace had chosen was old, but well maintained. It was still very fast. He landed early in the morning, perfect timing because only the early birds were up and about. He had to carry the big, funny-looking transmitter around, and the fewer eyes there were to see it, the better for Mac. He thought about trying to disguise it as a backpack, but doubted it was worth the time. No one knew what it was, or that it did something illegal. And if he disguised it, it would only look like a big, rectangular-shaped item being disguised as a backpack. It would attract more attention than it was worth. He did change out of his military clothes. He'd found some civilian clothes in the shuttle that must have belonged to the old lady's son or grandson. They were close enough to his size and didn't have any military logos or crests on them.

Mac hoped no one would catch on to what the transmitter was. He was carrying illegal technology on his back. If he got caught, there was nothing he could do to justify his actions. Everyone knew that Imp blocking was against the law. Even if he told the truth, no one would believe him.

Mac opened the door to the shuttle and walked outside. He didn't know specifically where the package was. The man had just said "McAllister." Mac took this to mean the package was waiting for him at the Post Office General.

As he walked down the street to where the building was, everyone he passed freaked out for at least a few seconds until Mac and the Imp blocker passed them and went out of range again.

"I think my Imp just stopped working!"

"What do I do?"

"Doesn't that mean you're dead?"

"I need my Imp! I need it!"

The look of relief on their faces once the Imps came back online was unnerving. People were leaning too heavily on untrustworthy technology. He'd seen and heard so much that by the time he got to the Post Office General he realized there was no way he was going to be able to go in and get his package. Not while he had this transmitter on. The person helping him would be too busy freaking out over his or her Imp malfunctioning. That, not customer service, would become the priority. He needed someone else to get it for him.

He looked around. It couldn't be just anyone. Average people on the street would question the disruption in communication. A smart person would realize it was him. A moral person would turn him into the authorities. He needed to find someone that would be grateful for the interruption.

The more time that went by the more crowded the streets became. If he was going to avoid sticking out, he'd have to duck back into the alley. That worked out for him. Mac found his man lying in the alley behind the Post Office General; the kind of guy who would be grateful to be free from an Imp.

It was easy to distinguish the reality-disconnected Imp junkies from the druggies and alcoholics. The Imp junkies just sat there. Didn't matter where they were, didn't matter what was going on around them. They sat there. The really bad ones, the homeless ones like the man in the alley, stayed plugged into their Imp worlds as much as humanly possible. They would go days without eating. Rain or sunshine, they didn't even notice the weather. The only things that mattered to them were the make-believe things in their mind.

The man was sitting, legs extended, slouched against a building. One leg was in a puddle, the other looked like it had been run over by a bike. The pool of blood under the leg was no longer liquid. It was dry, crusty. Apparently this man was about to be free of his Imp for the first time in a long time.

Mac called out to the man to see if he would respond. Nothing. He took several steps towards him. Still no indication he knew Mac was there.

The man's eyes were open but staring blankly ahead. They worked, but they couldn't see anything in the real world while he was plugged in. When Mac got close enough, the homeless man's eyes started to blink rapidly. He looked at his real surroundings for the first time in days. It didn't look like he even recognized where he was. When he looked down at his hands it didn't look like he recognized himself.

"How…" His voice was raspy. It might have been days since he visited the real world, but it had been years since he used his real voice. He had to shake the dust off.

"How…"

He started hitting the side of his head with his hand. It wasn't like the music was skipping. There was nothing wrong with his Imp. It was just being blocked.

"How… How…"

Mac went to him and grabbed his hands to stop him from hurting himself. The touch of human warmth was too much for him. The man started to cry. His tears ran freely. His voice choked and gurgled. Mac almost gagged. The man had soiled himself several times, had been sitting in it for days, not caring.

"It's okay," said Mac, patting the junkie's hands.

"How is it possible?" asked the man through the tears.

"I have something I'm not supposed to have, I guess. I thought if I helped you, you would be able to help me."

That wasn't what the man was asking, "How did I get this far?"

"I'm Mac."

"Sneed."

"Bless you."

"No, that's my name."

"Sorry."

Mac probably shouldn't have tried to get help from someone as far gone as Sneed. But he was in a rush and hadn't thought things through. He was committed now, though. He had to get that package, and he couldn't just walk away and let Sneed fall back into his fantasy prison. He helped the dirty man to his feet.

Sneed wobbled and almost fell over but Mac caught him. No explanation was given and none was needed.

"How did my Imp shut down? Is it a trick or a miracle?"

"I'll explain it to you later. Do you uh…live…nearby?"

"Yes. I'm not homeless. Although to look at me…. You want to go to my house?"

"I need your help with something, but you're going to have to shower and change your clothes first."

Sneed looked down at himself again. A whole new level of shame struck him. His pants alone were covered in so much filth that he was afraid to touch them. There was disgust in his face. The smell alone made his face scrunch in distaste. He asked, "How did I sink so low?"

"Hey, man. No judgment here. A hot shower, change of clothes, maybe some toast and a drink. You'll feel like a new man."

Sneed's house wasn't where he thought it was. He had spent so much time in a fake world that he had forgotten what was real and what was not. The two of them wandering the streets raised a lot of eyebrows. Either because Imps stopped working or because Sneed literally looked like walking garbage. Either way, a chat with local law enforcement was imminent if they didn't get inside soon.

"Let's try to keep out of sight. Take back roads and alleys to your house."

"Okay. I can't stand the snotty look people give me anyway. Despite how long I've been at this."

"Right, let's do this."

Sneed's house was as much of a mess as Sneed was. And it smelled about the same.

The living room floor was somewhere under the decomposing food, the bunched up papers, clothes, and human waste. The couch looked soggy. Mac didn't want to touch it.

Is this really worth the time I'm investing? Mac wondered. "Go get cleaned up. I'll wait for you here."

Sneed was still too out of it to get embarrassed about the state of his house. He shuffled off to his bedroom to get changed and cleaned up. Mac turned on the monitor in the living room. He switched it to the news, even though it was mostly propaganda. Well, maybe not straight-up propaganda, but there weren't too many truths about the military.

He watched mainly to kill time. On the coffee table he saw a knife. A short paring knife. It was the only thing on the table. How close was this man to being one of the smiling blind?

There weren't any noises coming from the bedroom.

"Sneed? You okay in there?"

He went to the bedroom and saw Sneed on the floor, crying again. The man was naked this time, so offering comfort was even more awkward.

"I got too far away from you. My Imp turned back on. I couldn't just leave it like that. I had to see. I had to."

"It's okay. I'll stay closer."

"Once I was in, I couldn't get out."

The disconnected, after a while they would only be able to answer one question one way. If the Imp was on, they were using it. They didn't have a choice.

"We're going to have to work on that," Mac said. "The thing I need you to do requires some distance between us."

Sneed looked terrified.

"We'll work it out. Don't worry, Sneed."

It took an hour for Sneed to get ready. He did everything slower than it would normally take someone. He wasn't used to moving muscles and lifting things. By the end of the hour his body was clean and he had on the cleanest clothes he owned. They picked up the smell of the house, but it was the best he could do. The rest of his clothes were sloshing around in the washing machine.

Mac sat Sneed down on the couch. Sneed eyed the paring knife with sad, yearning eyes.

"You sit here while I go to the other room. Just for a minute. See my watch? I'm going to time it. I'll be gone for just a minute. Then I'll be back. Do not use your Imp for that minute."

"What makes you so special?" asked Sneed.

"What?"

"Why does my Imp stop working when I'm around you?"

"Knowing would get you in trouble, and if you told the right people about me then I would get in trouble as well."

"You've given me the first taste of reality I've had in so long, I'd forgotten what it was like. I'll keep your secrets."

Mac believed him. Trusting a disconnected was risky, but they weren't dealing with money or anything of real value except to people like Sneed and Mac who didn't want anything to do with Imps. There weren't very many people left in all the worlds who didn't want Imps. If Mac helped Sneed now, he believed that Sneed would keep his secret.

"This box…" Mac said. Sneed looked at it as if noticing it for the first time…is an Imp blocker."

"Those are illegal."

"That's why I need you to keep it a secret."

"I understand."

"Okay. You ready to try this?"

"Only a minute, right?"

"Yes."

"Okay, I'm ready."

Mac took the paring knife when he left. Sneed looked relieved.

"I don't know how far this thing transmits, so just let me know when your Imp turns back on."

"Stop."

Mac was on the other side of the room, as far away from Sneed as he could get while still being in sight.

Blinking and sweating profusely, Sneed resisted the urge to use his Imp. The watch had ticked away thirty seconds.

"Can you come back now?" asked Sneed.

"It's almost time."

Sneed started rocking back and forth on the couch. Mac couldn't believe how much energy it was taking for Sneed to hold out for one minute. He looked at his watch. A minute passed, but he didn't step closer. He wanted to see how much longer Sneed could go.

The rocking got more intense. Sneed started crying. He looked so pathetic and helpless, but at the same time courageous and brave. Within the addict was a man who wanted his life back. That man had just spent two and a half minutes white knuckling into existence. Mac took a step toward him, relieving him of his pain.

"Thank you, Mac. How often are we going to do this?"

"I need you to be able to go for at least ten minutes. Maybe it can be done in five. It depends on how busy the Post Office General is."

"You...need me to pick up a package?"

"Yes."

Sneed avoided eye contact. His head lowered shamefully. He had retreated so far into his own mind that he couldn't even do a favor as simple as picking up a package.

"I used to be someone," he said. "I used to have a life. I'll do what I can to get your package, but as soon as you leave I'll go back in my made-up world."

Mac wished there was something he could do for this man, but there wasn't. Not if he wanted to save Lynn in time. The best he could do was take Sneed with him, but that was not practical; you can't be stealthy when people can smell you coming.

"Let's try it again."

They got to the post office with lots of time to spare. They waited across the street and watched to see how long the lineups were. The shortest one they timed was ten minutes. The longest was thirty-seven. The best time Sneed had so far was seven minutes.

"Do you think you can go for ten minutes?" asked Mac.

Sneed gave him a you-should-know-better look.

"Then let's wait and see if it slows down. When those lines get short, you're going in there."

"Okay," said Sneed.

They waited for another hour. Mac checked his clock. The post office would be closing in fifteen minutes. They had to go now or never.

"Just go in there for as long as you can. If you can't get the package, we'll come back tomorrow."

"It's the weekend. It's not going to be open for three days."

"Then I'll break in myself later. Point is, we have to try now. Go."

"Okay. Be right back."

Sneed said it, but took a moment to work up the courage.

"Will you walk with me across the street and wait by the door?" asked Sneed.

"Okay, let's go."

They walked quickly to the entrance, and Mac waited by the door. People coming out of the post office were causing a jam when their Imps stopped working. A crowded doorway would stop Sneed from making a quick escape. Confused, they looked at the door, the window, and each other. Mac pretended to be as confused as they were and eased his way down the street.

He looked at his watch. Three minutes.

Mac was nervous, and was sure something was wrong when seven minutes had elapsed. It would be obvious from the moment Sneed went into the building that he was an addict of some kind. After he signed on to his disconnected reality, staff would call the hospital.

It was an all-or-nothing deal with him; there was no dabbling in Imps for some. Which was too bad. It's not that Imps were evil. The problem was that people learned how to turn them into a crutch to replace having to make real decisions. At first that seemed awesome, but then they forgot how to make real decisions.

"Excuse me. Sir?" said an elderly woman.

Mac snapped around. She stood there with Sneed, who was blinking and coming back to reality. The name tag on her shirt indicated she worked at the post office.

"This fellow gave me this note."

Mac took it from her and read it:

I'm a recovering disconnected. My son is out on the street. He's a goofy-looking guy with big ears (he gets that from his mother) and a big square backpack. He is trying to help me get better by getting me to do simple, everyday things. If I look like I'm disconnected, please get the package marked for someone named PASSAGE and then take me to my son out on the street. He'll know what to do.

When he finished reading, the woman held out the package for him.

"I think it's nice what you're doing for your father. Good luck."

"Thank you," said Mac.

When she started walking away, Mac realized she hadn't freaked out about losing control of her Imp.

"You don't have an Imp, do you?" asked Mac.

"How did you know?" she asked.

"You have that look about you. Like you see the world differently. It's in your eyes," Mac lied.

"Never saw the point in getting one of those," she said.

The post office worker was a Luddite. Mac could have gotten the package a lot sooner if he had known that.

"Not exactly how we planned it, but I knew it would get done. Always have a plan B, Son." Sneed slapped Mac on the back.

Chapter 10
Disconnect

They took the package back to Sneed's house to open it. Sneed was looking better and better the longer Mac was around him. He figured Sneed really didn't like being disconnected, and the only reason he kept going back to la-la land was that he didn't feel like he had a choice anymore. But no addiction is unbeatable.

There was hope.

In the box were unusual yet familiar-looking glasses and a note.

The note read:

I hope you find this package in time. There aren't many places you can go when your Imp is marked. The moment you come back on the grid they will find you and surge you. If you do get surged I'll try to help, but remember I'm not a robot. Even I need sleep.

The glasses should be familiar to you. They are surgical glasses meant to install Imps. The truth is, it's easier to remove Imps than most people realize. It's as easy as burning them out of your eyes. People usually get hung up on the burning part I guess. Part of it could also be that the people monitoring the Imps, people like our mutual friend General Zinger, don't want people to know how easy it is to safely remove them. Fewer Imps in the world results in less control over the world.

Using them is simple. Put them on, and push the "on" button. A heads-up display will tell you what's going on.

The mechanism that holds your eyes open may cause some discomfort, but the burning smell is the worst part. I'm the one who made the adjustments to the traditional surgical glasses, so if you end up going blind you'll have me to blame. You know where I live.

After you use the glasses, keep them with you. Go find that girl, Lynn Ryder. We need the proof that she has. Don't believe for a second that aliens are responsible for your family's deaths.

I guess soon I really will be the only person in Passage with an Imp.

With deepest sympathies for your loss, I wish you good luck.

Mac showed Sneed the letter.

"Do you want to get rid of that Imp?" asked Mac.

"Yes." Sneed didn't even hesitate.

"If I do this for you, I need you to do one more thing for me."

"Anything."

"I need you to deliver a message for me. To the man who sent this to me. He lives in Passage. It's a village near Northgate."

"Northgate? That's across the world."

"It's okay. I can give you money. You just need to get there in the next week or so."

Sneed thought about it then said, "Yes. I can do that for you."

"You'll like Passage. No one there has an Imp."

"Except that one guy. What's his name?"

"You know, he never told me," Mac lied.

"How will I find him?"

"I'll tell you where he lives and what he looks like."

Getting rid of his Imp was Sneed's answer to getting his life back. Before now, Imp surgery would have been impossible. It was expensive and invasive. There was no way he could even stay offline long enough to arrange everything.

After he removed the Imp he would still be an addict psychologically, but he would have no access to his drug of choice. That was an opportunity he could not pass up.

"Test it out on me first," said Sneed. "If it doesn't work, you will be able to help me better than I would be able to help you if something were to go wrong."

"Okay. I think you're supposed to lie down."

Sneed lay down on the couch, and Mac put the glasses on him.

"Do you see the heads-up display?" asked Mac.

"No."

"Oops, forgot to turn it on." Mac pushed the only button on the glasses. "How about now?"

"Yes. It's on."

Mac couldn't see the heads-up display. All he could do was watch. There were several thin arms connected to the rim of the glasses. Two of the arms moved towards the eyes and sprayed them. Mac guessed they were spraying an anesthetic.

Sneed blinked frantically and then abruptly the blinking stopped. His eyes remained wide open, wider than Mac had ever seen them. The spray probably had something to do with that. Just in case, more tiny arms moved to hold the eyelids open.

The glasses had a red tinge to them. Now the red was getting brighter and brighter. Sneed was gripping the side of the couch, terrified. Mac could smell burning, could see smoke coming up from behind the glasses.

"What's going on?" asked Mac. "Are you okay?"

"Yes. I can't feel anything. It says it's going to burn out the Imp."

"How much longer?"

"Not much."

Ten minutes later the stench was making Mac want to vomit. The burning-eyeball smell mixed with what was already in the room was a lot to handle. There was also a small whining noise coming from the glasses. The noise got louder the further along it went, but it never got loud enough to be overpowering. Just enough to be annoying.

The whining noise stopped.

Sneed kept lying down while he read instructions on the heads-up display. Then he said, "seven," waited a minute and then got up. He took the glasses off and put them on the coffee table.

He closed his eyes for several seconds, returning moisture to them. Then he opened them again. He looked normal enough to Mac, but now it was time to see if it worked.

Mac grabbed the transmitter and walked into the other room.

"It worked!" said Sneed.

Mac ran back into the living room.

"Where's your backpack?"

The transmitter! Mac had left it in the bedroom! He turned to get back into the safety of the Imp-free zone but he didn't get there in time. The surge came and Mac fell to the ground curled up in a ball.

He tried to keep his eyes open so he could see what was going on. He tried to yell at Sneed to get out of there, but he couldn't see or hear anything. There was so much stimulation that he could barely even feel the glasses that Sneed slipped on his head.

The spray was very effective. He had clamped his eyes shut in a futile attempt to keep the debilitating flashing lights out, but the spray forced him to keep his eyes open. It was dizzying. The glasses did nothing to block the light because the input was coming right from his Imp.

His eyes continued to struggle to close but then the little arms came out from the glasses to hold his eyes open.

There must have been some instructions on the heads-up display but he couldn't see them.

As the minutes ticked by his vision became more and more red. The lights kept flashing. The white noise in his ears was cutting in and out. Then it ended altogether. The flashing lights were gone as well. He could read the heads-up display:

80%

He also noticed that Sneed was lying on top of him. Probably in an attempt to stop him from squirming.

"I'm okay," said Mac. "You can get off."

"Almost done?"

"It's at 85% now."

"Good. Do you hear the sirens?"

Mac did. They were coming for him. At least the Imp disconnected before they got there.

"They are coming for me. Maybe you should leave."

Please try not to move.

Talking was moving his face too much. Mac shut up. It was almost done It was at 98% when the door got kicked down.

"What is that smell?"

Mac recognized the voice. It was Raymond.

99%

100%

"This is my home," said Sneed. "What are you doing here?"

"That man is a fugitive. We've come to arrest him. What's on his face?"

More footsteps came into the room. Raymond had three men with him.

Surgery complete.

Please wait while we test your vision.

The glasses had not been translucent before. Now they turned translucent and Mac could see what was going on. Raymond had come into the house followed by three other men. Sneed was in front of them with his hand out trying to stop them.

Suddenly a bunch of bunnies showed up. There was one hopping on the countertop, one on the monitor in the living room, one on Sneed's outstretched hand, and one sitting lazily on Raymond's head.

How many rabbits do you see?

"Four," said Mac.

Congratulations. You may now remove the surgical glasses.

Mac did that. Everyone in the room was giving him a peculiar look. Except for Sneed who had counted seven of his own rabbits not too long ago.

"Don't mind me. Just counting rabbits," said Mac.

"Are you high?" asked Raymond. Then he realized the more important question. He pulled out his immobilizer and pointed it at Mac. Nothing happened.

"What on Earth?"

He pointed it at Sneed. Nothing happened. Mac moved closer to the group. He sensed an opportunity arising.

Sure that there was something wrong with the immobilizer, he pointed it at the closest soldier. The man went down clutching his head, and his gun tumbled to Sneed's feet. Sneed had enough sense to pick it up.

Mac acted quickly, realizing what Raymond was about to do. When he accidentally surged his own man, Mac grabbed the immobilizer from Raymond and pointed it at him.

"Go get the transmitter, Sneed," said Mac. "Leave me the gun."

Sneed handed it over and then went to the bedroom. Now Mac had a gun in one hand and an immobilizer in the other. Raymond didn't dare make a move unless Mac told him to.

With his gun, Mac prodded everyone further into the room, except for the man curled up on the floor.

"Have a seat on the couch," said Mac.

They all had disgusted looks on their faces, certain they were going to catch some disease by sitting on the couch. Sneed came back with the transmitter and all their expressions changed. The man on the floor stopped moaning and convulsing.

"Get on the couch with the others," said Mac.

"How is that possible? I don't have access to my Imp. How did you do that?" said the man as he got up and moved to the couch.

"Sneed, go check outside. See if anyone else is coming."

Raymond smiled, "You know someone will come. And soon. If the Imps aren't working, the Command will think we're dead."

"By the time this is over, you might be," said Mac.

"You're no killer."

"Why don't you tell your men what's in that box." Mac indicated the transmitter he had stolen from Northgate.

"It's alien technology. Powerful alien technology. Having it in your possession is illegal."

Mac scoffed.

"So that means these guys aren't in on your secret then, are they?" said Mac.

"I don't know what you're talking about. We've been over this before."

"You're right. New question. Where is Lynn Ryder?"

"In our custody. Soon she will be turned over to a maximum security mental hospital for the criminally insane, but for now she's with us."

"Where?"

"With us."

"Where?"

Raymond sighed, "Don't you get it? I'm not telling you."

Mac kicked the transmitter away and surged all four of them. They looked hilarious, falling over and flopping around. The first guy fell off the couch, Raymond fell on top of him, and the last two piled on top of them. They were all rolling on the ground, screaming from the overload of stimulation. They kicked up garbage and hit each other repeatedly.

Mac went over and brought the transmitter closer. They all stopped thrashing.

"Will you tell me now?"

They were still catching their breath. Mac didn't give them time to answer. He kicked the transmitter away and surged them again. Then he went over to talk to Sneed.

"Do you see anybody else coming?"

"No, are you expecting more people?"

"Eventually."

Sneed looked over at the four men twitching on the floor, "How long can you leave them like that?"

"I'm not sure. A while. I'm going to let them have it for a few minutes and then ask them again. When you are going through sensory overload you lose track of time. I want to disorient them a bit."

"Cool."

"You should go."

"What?"

"You're going to get in trouble just for being around me. Going Imp-less has given you a second chance. You should leave now. Go to Passage, but I need you to tell my friend something different. Tell him this is my plan."

Mac laid out his plan for Sneed. Both men were smiling. If the only man in Passage with an Imp was able to pull this off, and if Mac was taken where he needed to go, the plan would produce the biggest military embarrassment of all time.

Sneed didn't want to leave Mac. He looked back at the soldiers in the living room, "What about—"

"I can take care of them."

"Let me go pack some stuff."

"I'll wait until you're gone before I bring them back."

Sneed quickly packed some stuff and was ready to leave. Mac made sure to give him the surgical glasses. Sneed shook Mac's hand, but it wasn't enough. He pulled him in for a hug.

"Thank you so much."

"No problem." Mac wasn't sure what to say. He didn't set out to change this man's life. It was more of a right-place-right-time thing.

Sneed left. Mac pulled all the curtains closed to block out all the sunlight before he kicked the transmitter closer to Raymond and his men.

They were breathing even heavier now. Raymond and two other men had lost control of their bodily functions. Mac thought about pointing that out to them, but decided to save it until later. He told them all to get back on the couch. They were looking around. None of them knew how much time had passed.

"Where is Lynn Ryder?"

"I don't—"

Mac got up and went to kick the transmitter away again.

"Wait! Wait!" said one of the other men.

"What's your name?" asked Mac.

"Lieutenant Theo Ramsden."

"Do you know where Lynn Ryder is?"

"I heard Raymond talking to General Zinger. I don't know where she is now, but I know where they are going to put her."

"Don't you dare," said Raymond.

Mac pointed at the transmitter.

"They are going to take her to General Zinger's private space yacht. That's where we were going to take you too."

Mac liked what he heard. He thanked Theo and then kicked the transmitter aside. He deliberately waited half a second before pushing the button on the surge weapon. That was enough time for Raymond to do what Mac expected him to do. He leapt off the couch and tackled Mac to the ground.

"Restraints!" yelled Raymond.

Theo gave him some restraints and Mac's hands were tied up. He wasn't going anywhere.

"Didn't believe him, did ya?" said Raymond about what Theo had told him. "You should have just killed us and made a run for it. I knew you didn't have it in you."

He pushed Mac to the door while he talked his ear off.

"The thing is, we *are* taking you to General Zinger. And he does have what it takes to kill a man. You better start getting your story straight in your head. You're a prime suspect for the destruction of Northgate."

Mac couldn't help but smile. He was choosing to be an optimist about the situation. His plan had worked, and now he would be close to Lynn Ryder.

Chapter 11
Ryder Family Secrets

Everyone has secrets, and General Zinger was determined to discover what Lynn Ryder's were.

They were standing among the rubble that was Northgate. Raymond was nearby holding the immobilizer where she could see it, so she knew to be careful about what she said.

She had never been surged before that day and would do whatever she could to avoid having that awful experience again. She would keep her mouth shut about the war being fake.

Besides, she was about to talk to the biggest, most powerful man in the military. If the war was fake, he knew it. There was no point in trying to convince him about it.

"Who are you?" Zinger asked.

"My name is Lynn Ryder."

The name set something off in General Zinger's mind. *He knows about my family. He must.* She recognized the look on his face.

"No one is to harm her!" the general yelled, his abundant torso swaying back and forth as he turned to his troops. "If anything happens to her, I will personally deal with the soldiers responsible. Quietly, he asked Raymond, "Where are the other two? The ones who rescued Miss Ryder."

"*Mrs.* Ryder. I'm married," said Lynn.

Zinger considered the implications of this revelation for a moment before Raymond interrupted his thoughts.

"The other two got away. They ran further into the red zone so we couldn't track their Imps. I sent men in after them."

"If they are not found you will be stripped of your rank and assigned traffic duty at the ESP. Go find them, and don't come back until you have good news!" Zinger spoke slowly at first but got quicker and louder as he went on. Spit was flying out of his mouth. He was furious that the two men who had saved her got away.

Raymond ran off. Lynn was happy to see him leave in shame with his tail between his legs. She wasn't sure why the two men were wanted. They wore military uniforms.

Then she remembered something the ginger had said to her just before she got surged.

"There aren't many people sympathetic to our cause."

They thought the war was fake just like she did.

Zinger held out his porky hand to Lynn. She took it, and he helped her up.

"I have a lot of questions for you, Mrs. Ryder."

The questions didn't come quickly. They left the broken city behind and flew to the military base just outside the city. The base was divided into two sections—restricted and non-restricted.

The media almost made up their own camp. They weren't allowed on the base, but hundreds, possibly thousands, of reporters set up temporary shelters near the base's front entrance. It looked like a high-tech refugee camp. Lynn desperately wanted to get to those people, to get a message to her parents. They needed to know what was going on. They shared her secret as well.

When the shuttle landed, Lynn was told to stay put. Zinger left with the two men who always accompanied him. A man in uniform, Brindle, and a man who never wore a uniform and who never talked. His pointed face and widow's peak made him look angry even when he was smiling. Brindle was Zinger's gopher. "Go do this…go do that"; "yes sir, yes sir, three bags full." He was young and had a big round head with a mop of blond on top. Brindle was in amazing shape, which made his round head look even more out of place on his body.

After Zinger, Brindle, and Widow's Peak left, only one guard remained. She wouldn't be able to do anything about that. The gash in her leg started throbbing again and she realized how tired she was.

Since they left her on the shuttle, Lynn guessed she was being taken somewhere other than the base. She was right. Zinger handed over operations to the highest-ranking officer on the base, returned to the shuttle with his constant companions, and told the pilot to carry on to their next stop.

It felt like years since she had sat in a comfortable seat, one with cushions and a backrest. She knew it was probably a bad idea to fall asleep, but she couldn't help it. All the go-go-go of the last few days had drained her. She was asleep before they arrived at their destination.

She had been in her cell for a few days but she still woke up disoriented, having momentarily forgotten where she was. This day was particularly unsettling because the lights were off and she could tell she wasn't alone.

"Who's there?"

There was an unholy snarling sound. Whatever beast was watching her in the dark was slobbering with anticipation. She imagined the drool dripping down long fangs. She had to get out of there. But it was pitch black. She couldn't see a thing. Didn't matter. It was now or never. She sat up in the bed and swung her feet onto the floor. She gasped when the bed creaked loudly. The snarling was momentarily interrupted, but when the room was quiet, the snarling picked up again.

There was no way to tell how big the room was or where the door was. There was no sense in running into the dark. She walked slowly with her arms out in front of her. She decided to go in a straight line. The snarling was getting closer—she walking towards it—but the creature remained stationary. She was about to change direction when her leg hit something. She screamed.

Lynn was so scared she just wanted to run. But she tripped over whatever she had just run into. Another bed with someone in it. It was a shirtless man. He had been sleeping but was now wide awake.

"What's going on?"

"Let me go!" said Lynn.

"I'm not holding onto you."

"Let me go!"

The man just pushed her off the bed. He stomped away and flicked on a light switch. Lynn blinked several times while her eyes adjusted to the light. They were in a room with dark carpet and white walls. The beds were old. Gray-and-white striped mattresses with one lumpy pillow and a gray blanket. The man who had turned on the light was fetching his shirt from the end of the bed.

"You were sleeping when they put me in here so I kept the lights off and went to sleep too. We're lucky they gave us control of the lights. Most captors wouldn't allow that."

"I'm sorry," said Lynn. "I heard you snoring. I thought...I mean...it sounded like snarling."

The young man stuck his hand out.

"I'm Mac Narrad. You might not recognize me, but I was one of the guys that came to save you in Northgate."

She took another look at him. He was tall and well built, but didn't flaunt his ripped physique. He was young. Much younger than she was, but he appeared to have experienced much in his life. It showed in his eyes. They were much older than the rest of him. They clashed with his youthful body and brown bed-head hair.

"Saved me?" She held out her arms, indicating the room they were in.

"Um...tried to save you. We were going to stay with you, but when we found out there was evidence of the fake war out there somewhere, well, we had to go find it."

"And did you?"

"No. So we decided to find you and your husband instead."

"You know Scott? Is he all right? Where is he? Is Scott here too?"

"No. Jace—the guy I was with—went to go get your husband. I came for you."

Lynn went back and sat on her own bed. "Now what?"

Mac sat down on his bed and asked, "What evidence do you have that his war is fake?"

"Those monsters were just people dressed up. That's the only evidence I had."

"What?"

"But when you kill one, it triggers an explosion to get rid of it and any witnesses. I was almost killed by one of those two different times. If you want my evidence then you came to the wrong place. Like I said, the evidence is out in Northgate somewhere."

"So you don't actually have any evidence on you right now then."

"No."

"Great. Does your husband have any?"

"He's in a mental hospital. What do you think?"

Mac looked upset by the whole thing.

"Were you betting everything on me and Scott having what you wanted?" asked Lynn.

"Yeah."

"You should have planned that better," said Lynn.

"No kidding, eh?"

"So now what?" she asked.

"Does your Imp work?"

"No. They must have done something. Wouldn't put it past them to break the law to keep someone like me quiet. Is yours not working either?"

"I don't have one."

139

Lynn raised her eyebrows, but didn't pursue the topic. Sitting across the room from each other, and disappointed by how things had panned out so far, they sat in silence. Lynn suspected Mac had gone through a lot to get here and to find out what she knew. But what she knew wasn't helpful to him.

"You do have a plan, right?" asked Lynn.

"Yeah, I just needed you to actually know something," said Mac.

"I can still help."

"How?"

"I don't know…exactly…but I'm one of the few people who knows that it wasn't aliens who destroyed Northgate," said Lynn.

"You don't have any real evidence. For all we know it could be aliens."

"Those monsters were humans. Just like you and me."

"I know. I just want to find out who was behind the attack."

"Me too, especially if that means reuniting with my husband."

Before either of them could ask another question the doors opened. Brindle was there. He pointed at Lynn.

"The general would like to see you now."

It felt like being called to the principal's office.

"Good luck," Mac said as she left.

Despite Lynn's lack of answers, Mac still held all the right cards. There wasn't much that Zinger could do to hurt either of them. True, he would probably eventually kill both of them, but not until he asked them a ton of questions. It would take a few days before it came to that. If he and Lynn remained elusive, they could stretch it out even further. The only man in Passage with an Imp could accomplish what he needed to do if only he and Sneed had enough time.

Mac was disappointed that Lynn didn't have the answers to all his questions, yet there was something special about her. She gave off a certain energy. Besides that, in all the worlds—Earth and the others—he knew of only three people who believed the war was fake: himself, Lynn, and Scott. Jace would come around eventually, but at least he knew it wasn't aliens who destroyed Northgate. If Mac hadn't come to help Lynn, he would have one less ally. With so few perceptive people left in the worlds, they had to do whatever they could to stick together.

The fake monsters were not enough evidence to convince the masses that aliens were not responsible for the carnage at Northgate. He didn't have hard facts. He needed to find the specific people behind the attack. Right now he was trapped in this room, but when it all hit the fan he would have to act quickly. For now, he needed to stay prepared.

Brindle led Lynn down the hall, but before they turned a corner he asked to see her hand. She held it out for him and at the same time asked, "What do you need to see my hand for?"

He injected green liquid into the base of her thumb. Within seconds her vision became blurry and then disappeared altogether. She tried to walk away, but stumbling around in darkness never ended well, so she stood still.

"What did you do to me?"

"Don't worry, it's only temporary. The general has things he doesn't want you to see," said Brindle.

All she could think about was what she would do if it didn't wear off. *Will I be blind forever?*

Bindle took her arm and led her to Zinger. They went up some stairs, rode in a lift, and did some more walking. She wanted to memorize her route so that she could start planning her own, or maybe Mac's, escape. Lynn tried to keep track of lefts and rights, but there got to be too many. She was not surprised that Brindle was purposely trying to disorient her. Maybe Mac would have better luck when he was summoned to the office. She wasn't quite sure what to think of him yet. She kind of recognized him from Northgate, but that didn't mean she could trust him. He could be like Zinger and just want information. He could even be a plant. Put in her room, or cell, or whatever it is, just to gain her trust and get information out of her.

As they walked, their footsteps echoed off the walls and ceilings. Then the echoing stopped, and Lynn felt the warmth of the sun and a slight breeze on her face.

"Hold out your hand," said Brindle.

He injected her with something else. Her vision started clearing, slowly. She thought the blurred mass in front of her was a distant mountain, then she thought maybe it was a couch. When her vision fully came back she laughed to herself. It was General Zinger. He stood there waiting for her.

They were outside in a garden filled with shrubs and massive trees. No flowers. The only colors came from the green plants, the gray tile walkways, and the reddish-orange sunset. She looked into the horizon but couldn't figure out where in the world they were. The clouds were doing unnatural things as well. They looked like they were coming out of the ground. Could it be they were flying? She had never been on any craft this big and this extravagant that could fly.

"Hello, Mrs. Ryder," said General Zinger.

"Lynn."

"Are you the Ryder, or is it your husband?"

"What do you mean?"

"It doesn't matter. I looked it up." Zinger had a computer pad in his hand and was reading from it. "It's not very often, even these days, for the man to take the woman's family name when they get married."

"Did you see his last name before? Who would want to keep a surname with a silent V and two silent Ls. It's impossible to spell."

Zinger actually laughed. A booming laugh that made his whole fat face jiggle.

"That's funny. But we both know the real reason you are here."

Lynn didn't say anything.

"Your family is in charge of keeping safe an amazing power."

Lynn pretended to look confused.

"A power that can change the outcome of this war."

"This fake war?"

Now it was Zinger's turn to look confused.

"They weren't monsters. They were just people dressed up. And I know you locked my husband away because he found out the truth, not because he is mentally ill."

"How do you know it wasn't the aliens dressing up to look more menacing? Have you ever seen the aliens before? Do you know what they look like?"

"No."

"Well, I do. And for the most part, they don't look like us. But a few of them do. It could have been them who attacked us."

"What do you mean, some of them look like us? Wouldn't they all look the same?"

"You'd think so, but no. We're still trying to figure that one out. That's not what I want to talk about. I need to know where Grenor is."

"Who is Grenor?"

Zinger smiled the kind of smile an angry parent gives a child to keep himself from yelling and sending her to bed early.

"Walk with me."

They walked around the shrubs and through the garden. Zinger didn't say anything, but he was breathing heavily from the walking. He still walked fast; Lynn didn't have to slow down. Brindle and Widow's Peak were always nearby. Widow's Peak never took his eyes off Lynn.

They stepped around one last bush and came to the edge of the ship they were on. Lynn looked down. They were so high up that she couldn't tell whether they were over Europe or Asia. It should have been more windy and cold up here. She reached out and found a protective dome over this part of the ship. It let a little air in and none of the cold.

"This is my private residence," said Zinger. "There are only three people that are ever allowed to come and go from this place, and you are not one of them. Up here there is no one to save you. Up here I am the man in charge and up here people do what I tell them."

Zinger continued, "I can do whatever I want in my own house. I'm accountable to no one. Think about that while you wait in your room. The next time I call for you, I want answers."

Lynn calculated how high up she was. If she jumped, she would probably suffocate. Be dead before she hit the ground. Or maybe they were so high up that she would just float into outer space. She could see stars twinkling, even though the sun had not fully set.

"Take her back to her room."

"What did he ask you?" Mac asked when she got back.
"I don't know."
"What?"
"I mean I don't want to talk about it."
"Okay."
Lynn sat on her bed and Mac sat on his.

"We should stick together. At least until we can get you back to your husband."

"You don't even know who I am," said Lynn.

"I know you are a good person. I can't just abandon you."

"I should tell you. My husband and I don't have any physical evidence, but my husband was filling a major order for weapons and ammunition. He found out that the weapons weren't going to the front. It's possible he built the weapons that destroyed Northgate. They locked him away and put someone else in charge of filling the order when Scott refused to cooperate."

"That's fantastic."

"Excuse me?"

"Not that he got locked up. That we have a trail we can follow. We definitely need you and your husband."

"But first we have to get out of here."

"I have a plan. We…"

Lynn held a finger up to her lips, "They're probably listening. Even though we don't have Imp access."

"I know. Truth is, I don't know exactly how it will happen but I do know it will happen. Someone is coming for us. We just have to be ready for it when it happens."

"How do we get ready?"

"First we need to find out where we are."

"I know where we are. We're at Zinger's private residence. It's like a luxury space yacht. I don't know how fast it can go, or how agile it is, but I can tell you this: If we go any higher we'll be in outer space."

"Okay, good. I heard about this place when I was training on Mars. One of those stories that gets passed around but no one can ever prove. I mean, yes, they could look through a telescope and see it, but there's no way to tell if it's Zinger's."

"He said that there are only three people that can come and go from this place. Him, Brindle—the guy that escorted me to him—and some other guy whose name I don't know. He doesn't wear a uniform, so I have no idea what his job is."

"Probably a security guy of some kind. A bodyguard."

"Mac, is it okay that we're so high up? Can your friends get to us?"

"Yes. I suspected this was where they'd take me. We planned accordingly."

Lynn looked around the room for signs of surveillance equipment.

"Can we still pull this off with them expecting us to try an escape?" she asked.

"Either way, it's too late now," said Mac.

"Doesn't make me feel very confident."

"Then when we're outta here, I get to say 'I told you so.'"

The door to their cell opened. It was Mac's turn.

"Hold out your hand," said Brindle.

Mac got the blinding injection that Lynn had forgotten to tell him about. Zinger was minus a key piece of information too. The injection worked in coordination with an Imp, and Mac didn't have an Imp. He could tell it was supposed to momentarily blind him because his vision changed—like he was looking through smudged dark glasses—but he could still see.

Raymond was an idiot for not telling Zinger about Mac's Imp removal.

Mac reached out, hands slapping at Brindle's arms, shoulders, and head.

"Hold on," said Brindle. "Take it easy." Brindle caught him by the arm and led him away.

The hallways in this section were not luxurious at all. Floors, walls, ceilings—all were gray metal. Footsteps echoed off the floor; they were literally going in circles. For the third time they passed the room where Lynn was.

Then they got into an elevator. The buttons—about a dozen of them—were not labeled. Brindle pressed the second one from the top.

General Zinger's military slave must have never dealt with someone who was Imp-less. His little blinding injection must have had a hundred percent success rate before now, because he didn't even check to make sure Mac really was blind. *And they say Luddites are backward. A low-tech bandana always worked.*

The doors opened into a wide hallway. The carpet was so thick Mac could have sworn he sunk an inch into it. It was maroon and dark blue with a military crest woven in at ten foot intervals. The walls were made of mahogany. The gigantic doors at the far end of the hallway must have taken several trees to make. They led to Zinger's bedroom or his office; Mac felt sure about that.

Brindle opened a door—it was a foot thick—and obviously had a hydraulic assist mechanism because he didn't have to pull very hard. The room they entered was indeed Zinger's office. Mac struggled to resist the urge to gaze open-mouthed at the sheer size of the room. It could have been the landing bay for several HAAS3s. Zinger's office was built to impress friends and intimidate everyone else. The dark wood look extended from the hallway to this room. The high ceiling was dotted with recess lighting. The carpet maintained the maroon and blue color scheme. A massive oak desk commanded attention at the far end of the room, and a cluttered table in the middle of the room suggested some work actually got done here. Other than those pieces, and a few extra chairs against the wall, the room was empty.

Zinger sat behind the desk, and behind him a window the size of two semi-trailers stacked one on top of the other showed they were indeed in the upper atmosphere. The General was studying a desktop screen, a huge projection screen with no back. Mac could read the mirror-image letters at the top of the screen, SONOR, or from Zinger's perspective, RONOS. Mac didn't know what, or who, that was. The screen was big but Mac couldn't read any of the smaller font. He could see the picture Zinger brought up. It was a planet with vast oceans separating land masses of various sizes. It could have been Earth, but the continents didn't match up.

Another habitable planet, perhaps? He wished he could talk to Lynn about it, but he would lose the advantage of gathering information while his captors thought he was blind.

Zinger deactivated the screen and nodded at Brindle.

"Hold out your hand."

Mac did as requested. He was injected again. He felt the slight confusion of his own vision go back to normal. He made a show of his amazement over where he was now. He looked around without worrying about his reactions being seen. Standing beside him was the man who didn't wear a uniform. He had an extreme widow's peak, and he was looking very suspiciously at Mac. Did he know?

Mac smiled at him and then spoke to Zinger, "I think you put me in the wrong room. I mean, I appreciate the company...but there is way more space in here to stretch out."

"You've fallen a long way from where you started," said Zinger.

"Oh, I don't know. I was only a spacer."

"I remember you. From when you were training on Mars. I don't usually remember recruits, but I remember being told a Luddite had enlisted. I looked over your file. Was impressed with what I saw. Do you know what impressed me the most?"

Mac shook his head. He hadn't lived an impressive life.

"The fact you were willing to change who you were to do the right thing. You grew up as a Luddite, but then you got an Imp and joined the military. You saw that there was a job to be done and you did what was needed. I kept my eye on you, hoping for great things. What happened?"

"I guess I saw need for further change," said Mac.

"Too bad. Maybe we can salvage you, though. How do you plan to escape?"

"Right to the point, eh?"

"You know where we are, and you knew you were going to be here. That idiot Raymond must have told you," said Zinger.

"Actually, it was an idiot named Theo. Raymond's an idiot for different reasons."

Zinger smiled. "Either way. You found out where you were going and you made plans to escape. I want to know what those plans are."

"I don't have plans. I told a friend of mine where I was going. I'm hoping *he* has a plan."

"You sounded pretty confident when you were talking to Mrs. Ryder," said General Zinger.

"My friend is very resourceful."

"We found you. We'll find your friend. Raymond can't afford to screw up any more."

It was Mac's turn to smile. They thought this friend was Jace. That was good news for Sneed and the only man in Passage with an Imp.

"You didn't bring me here just for that, did you?"

"No. I brought you here to tell you the truth."

"Okay."

"I'm the one who destroyed Northgate. Just as you suspected."

Mac stopped smiling. His blood started boiling. Unconsciously he had already curled his hands into fists. Widow's Peak took notice and stood up. If Mac made a run at Zinger, the aide would intercept him. Mac forced himself to calm down. Zinger was a liar. He could be lying about this. Mac let him talk.

"I needed to do it to gain control of the people again. They were no longer afraid of the aliens and were no longer doing what I asked them to. I tried less devastating methods, but no one noticed. I needed a 'go big or go home' kind of message. But it won't last forever. I need your help maintaining control, Mac Narrad."

"My entire family was killed in that attack. And you expect me to help you?"

"You're not using your brain to think things through. This event, this attack has given me back control. Even Mrs. Ryder's leaked feed wasn't enough to disrupt it. But it won't last forever. Soon I will need to conduct another attack. I don't know when, but I've already got people making enough ammunition to make this attack look as insignificant as a dump in a child's pants. You can prevent that attack from happening."

"What? How?"

"Mrs. Ryder has something I need. Something that will stop this from happening. Something that can keep war from ever happening again."

Mac rolled his eyes. Even from across the room, Zinger could see it.

"She has access to power. The Ryder family is the last living family of the descendants of Grenor."

"Who's Grenor?"

"Grenor isn't a person. It's a place. A planet, to be more exact."

"Where is it? I've never heard of it."

"It would be easier for me to tell you where it isn't. I've been looking for it for a long time. That's the key Mrs. Ryder has. She knows where it is. She's been there. If she is truly a Ryder, then she was born there."

"Babies don't have good memories."

"I *know* she knows."

"And you want me to get her to say where this place is so that you can get access to power?"

"I don't have time to go into details with you right now. But I will later. I promise."

Mac had to disguise a scoff with a cough. A promise from a man who had just claimed to have killed millions of people just to control the population didn't mean a whole lot.

"Take him back," he said to Brindle. Then to Mac, "We'll leave you alone for a while. Plan your escape or whatever else you want to do, but I need that information. I'll get it one way or another. Just remember, this is the least invasive way."

Brindle had injected him again, but Zinger kept talking to Mac, goading him.

"Don't forget that your friends need a stealth shuttle to get here unnoticed. You can ask permission from me for your friends to use one since I'm the only one who can authorize their use. Also, once they get here they will need to get past the security system, and not even I know how to do that. There are five cameras in every room. There are over a hundred guards here. I'm the only person here who can open every door, so if they want to get around they will need my eye balls for the retina scanner."

"Maybe I'll just hijack this place," Mac said.

"This thing doesn't land very gracefully, so there's no point going planet side—unless you have your own continent to use as a landing pad. And there's no interplanetary drive, so you won't get very far in space before one of my people catches up to you. Face it, Narrad. You have nowhere to go."

Brindle took him a different way back to his room, but this route didn't reveal anything important.

Mac wasn't sure what was more disturbing about the conversation. The fact that Zinger thought Lynn was the key to some great, yet vague power, or that he thought that Mac's plan to escape was laughable.

"What's Grenor?" Mac asked, when he saw Lynn.
"He talked to you about that too?"
"Yeah, but he didn't cite any sources."
"That's 'cause the only source he has is a ridiculous fable passed down through the years by old spacers."
"So tell me that story."
"They say some old space explorers found a planet where the laws of time did not apply."
"What do you mean?"
"There was no way to keep time. Nothing changed. Nothing got old. Things just existed. And the planet has everything you could ever want. It's a paradise, Utopia, blah blah blah. You get the picture."
"Sure. It's the perfect place to live."
"Except for one thing. No one could leave."
"Why would they want to?"
"Exactly. They were trapped, but they didn't know they were trapped. It was so perfect they forgot what it was like not to be perfect. They were slowly losing who they were. If nothing changes, then nothing grows. But then something did change. One of the women got pregnant. The baby was able to grow up. And the explorers and their families remembered what it was like to have time and they were able to go home."
"Where does the big power come in?"
"After that, it's said, the baby and all its descendants could control time."
Mac let out a heavy sigh. He couldn't believe the ludicrous story or that Zinger believed Grenor existed. He couldn't wait to be rescued.

Chapter 12
Dead Zone

Twice a day, Lynn and Mac were separated and taken to different parts of the ship. She still wasn't allowed to see where she was going, but described in detail what she was could see between the periods of blindness. Mac recognized one of the paintings she described. It had been reported stolen over a year ago. He guessed most of the art had been stolen.

Mac was always taken to the same place. Zinger's office. Most times, before he was "given" his vision back, the general was looking at the Ronos file. Mac was never able to get close enough to see what it was. With each passing day the sweat on Zinger's brow was increasingly abundant.

The day came when Zinger did not have Ronos files open when Mac came in. He had Grenor files open, and he didn't close them before Brindle injected him.

"What's that?"

"It's all the information I've collected on Grenor. I want you to look at it. I want you to believe me," said Zinger.

As Mac walked toward the desk he felt the massive ship shudder. It hadn't done that the entire time Mac had been there. He took that as a sign. Something was about to happen. Maybe it was the only man in Passage with an Imp's way of warning Mac without tipping off everyone else.

Get it together, Mac could imagine him saying. *I'm coming for you.*

Mac picked up his pace. First things first. He had to get Lynn and himself in the same room before it all went sideways.

"Take all the time you want," said Zinger. He moved out from behind the desk so that Mac could look at the file more easily.

There were no papers on the desk. The whole desktop was a touch screen with files open. Mac just had to touch each file that he was interested in. He started at the beginning, with a file that had the earliest version of the story Lynn had told him. It was pretty close to her version.

He saw star charts and several academic papers about possible locations. Those papers appeared to be written by reputable scholars. There were also reports documenting the kinds of people who get fanatical about finding Grenor—people who crave power. One file listed several planets that could possibly be Grenor. They were all crossed out, but Mac found something familiar on the list. Ronos.

"What's this?" asked Mac, pointing it out.

"It's a planet," said Zinger.

"I've heard of all these planets, but I've never heard of Ronos."

"It's a military base. Classified to the outside worlds."

When Mac touched the word, a picture of Ronos came up. All the information was blacked out. It was the same Earth-looking planet Mac had seen in the other file.

"Why would you keep this from people? It looks just like Earth. It's the only planet that bears any resemblance to it at all," said Mac.

"Looks can be deceiving."

"Look, I'm not the one you have to convince about this. You need to show Lynn. She thinks you're insane, and she'll think I'm insane if I come to her with wild stories about secret planets and a collection of ghost stories. Why

are we always questioned separately, anyway? You should
bring her here. Show her what you have."

Zinger thought about it. "Okay. Brindle. Go get her."

Brindle left the room. Widow's Peak, as always, was
standing close to the door. Mac had never heard that man
say a word. All he did was stare, as though he was thinking
about all the ways he could kill the person he was staring
at.

"This is it, though," said Zinger. "If you want her here
to see this, I need to see some results. If you don't get me
what I want, I'll let my friend"—he indicated Widow's
Peak—"take over the information-extraction duties."

"I understand."

The ship shook again. This time everyone felt it.
Zinger and Widow's Peak looked at each other, worried.
Then it felt like the floor had given out beneath them. The
ship lurched, and all three men were thrown into the air.
Mac landed half on the chair. Zinger hit his head on the
table and went out cold. Widow's Peak managed to land,
albeit clumsily, on his feet. He looked up at Mac
suspiciously.

It was now or never. Mac was going to have to take out
Widow's Peak.

They ran at each other. Then the ship lurched again,
and they fell into each other. Widow's Peak was more
prepared for the collision. He landed with Mac's neck
between his legs. Mac wasn't even sure how that was
possible. The squeezing was cutting off his air. Mac started
throwing punches behind him. One caught Widow's Peak
in the eye. He released his leg grip enough that Mac was
able to extract himself.

There was no way Mac would be able to beat him
man-to-man. He needed a weapon. Forgetting that
Widow's Peak also had a gun, Mac ran back to the desk.
Laser blasts struck all around Mac as he dove behind the

desk. The large window behind Mac shattered and air started whistling through the office.

The wind was so fierce Mac could barely open his eyes. Crouched behind the desk, where Zinger lay unconscious, Mac poked his head out to see where Widow's Peak was. The general's bodyguard was standing in the middle of the room with his gun out and pointed at the desk. His footsteps didn't falter in the extreme wind. His eyes were just as wide and angry as they were before the window was broken. It didn't look like he was affected at all by the change. How was that possible? Mac doubted he could get up and walk without getting blown around.

Zinger started moaning. Too bad. Mac had hoped the head injury put him out for good. Widow's Peak was on the other side of the desk. Mac had only one option. He pulled out one of the desk drawers and hid under the desk.

As Widow's Peak came around the corner of the desk, Mac hurled the desk drawer at his gun hand. The wooden drawer exploded, sending shrapnel everywhere. A chuck of wood embedded itself in Widow's Peak cheek as he turned his head away from the explosion. That was what Mac was waiting for.

While Widow's Peak's attention was elsewhere, Mac struck. He kicked at the bodyguard's legs, connecting as forcefully as he could just above the guard's ankle. Widow's Peak dropped to one knee. Mac pulled out another drawer and clocked him over the head. The drawer broke in two; Widow's Peak stumbled a little, but he was still conscious.

In one final effort, Mac kicked him in the chest. Because Widow's Peak was already off balance and on one knee, the strength of the kick was too much. He rolled over on the ground and then fell out the window.

Mac took a second to gather his breath. The wind was picking up. The space yacht was falling faster. Despite the wind, Mac was able to walk out from the desk and make for the door. Before he got there, he heard someone yelling.

"Mac!"

He turned and saw Zinger propping himself up on his desk. His flabby cheeks were flapping in the wind.

"This isn't over! You can't stop me that easily!" yelled Zinger through the wind.

Mac stopped. With all the chaos of fighting Widow's Peak, he had forgotten to do something. He went back to the desk, found a computer pad and started downloading everything he could about Ronos, Grenor, and Northgate onto the pad. Zinger was still too out of it to stop him. He put up a feeble fight, but Mac pushed him aside and continued.

He couldn't fit every file on the general's computer onto the portable computer pad. He selected files that he thought were important. Grenor and Lynn were important enough to take Zinger away from Northgate, and Ronos was important enough to make him sweat.

The information finished downloading. But before he left, he had to check one more thing. He searched Zinger's entire computer for one name: Janelle Stewart.

There was one hit. It was in a document in the Ronos file, which meant he already had it on his computer pad. He would have time to look at it later. Mac ran.

As he ran out of the room, Zinger propped his massive body up again and started using the computer. He punched something into it and a giant metal sheet slid across the broken window. Mac was on the other side of the door when a metal sheet slammed down from the top of the door frame. Had he still been inside the room, he would have been trapped with Zinger. Zinger must have activated some kind of crash protocol to keep him safe while the yacht fell from the sky.

"Good luck," Mac muttered.

But he didn't really care.

The whole ship started to shake. Lights went out. He got to the elevator. It was still working, but for how long? He pushed the button to get back to the floor were Lynn was being held.

When he got off the elevator he could tell the ship was spinning slightly. He would wobble one way down the hall and then the other way. He didn't know why, but the ship was going down and they needed to get off of it.

He could hear commotion coming from the room. The door was partially ajar, but he kicked it open and charged inside. Lynn had Brindle in a headlock. His eyes rolled back into his head and he fell on the floor.

"I guess you didn't need any help this time," said Mac.

"Not this time."

The lights flashed on and off.

"Come on."

Mac grabbed her by the hand, and they ran down the hall to the elevator. They weren't able to break out into a full sprint because Lynn's leg, which had she injured at Northgate, was sore. Still, she was able to move fast enough. When they got inside, they had no idea which button to push.

"I know it's not the second from the top," said Mac.

"Oh? How do you know that?"

"Oh, because that blinding stuff didn't work on me, but I didn't tell anyone. I couldn't tell you because they were listening to our conversations."

Mac pushed the bottom button.

"While we're on the topic of secrets I've kept... I was supposed to get you to tell Zinger where Grenor was. But don't worry about that one. I wasn't really trying, and I don't even believe it's a real place. It's very possible that the general has just lost his mind."

"That would be the answer that makes the most sense."

The elevator stopped and the two of them got out. They were in the docking bay when the ship lurched one more time. Both were swept off their feet. But even worse, the ship was now in an all-out free fall and was spinning out of control.

In the docking bay, guards and crew members were trying to get out, but the last lurch sent them sliding all over the place. Mac and Lynn locked arms. If they got separated now, they might never get the chance to expose the military's corruption.

The docking bay doors opened. People nearest the doors were thrown out of the ship. Even some of the shuttles that weren't secured were shifting around.

Mac and Lynn ran to one of these shuttles.

"Grab on!" yelled Mac.

They did their best to grip the side of the shuttle. Mac moved around it to get to the front. Precious seconds ticked by. He had no idea how close to the ground they were, but they got closer by the second.

He found the door to the shuttle, got in, and pulled Lynn in behind him. He took the controls, but instead of trying to maneuver his way to the doors, he decided shooting their way out would be faster.

Mac waited until they were pushed up against a wall and let loose a volley of lasers that tore a shuttle-sized hole in the side of Zinger's luxury space yacht. The shuttle fell out of the yacht and Mac pointed its nose straight up.

Just in time, too. As the shuttle pulled away and headed for the ESP, the giant luxury ship crashed into the ocean. It hit with such force that most of it broke apart. It was possible the people on board survived, or at least some of them. Crashing into the ocean was better than exploding into the side of a mountain. Mac wondered if the only man in Passage with an Imp had done that on purpose, just in case Mac was still in there. It was a good idea, but Mac was disappointed he didn't get to see the whole thing burst into flames.

"Where are we going?" asked Lynn.

"We can lose them in the ESP."

"What?"

"Trust me, I've done it before. Is your Imp working?"

"Yes."

"Find us a ship to hide on. We need to get off-planet before they surge you."

People would be too shocked about the general's house crashing into the ocean to care much about the small shuttle that managed to escape. At least not for a few hours.

"I found someone. A friend of my father's. She is the captain of a science vessel that's scheduled for departure in an hour or so."

"You think she'll help us?"

"Yes."

"What's her name?"

"Captain Tompkins of the science vessel *Terwillegar*."

"Science vessel? Shouldn't she be Doctor Tompkins?"

"She's Captain Tompkins because she owns the *Terwillegar*."

"Okay. Let's go."

Sneed and the only man in Passage with an Imp stood on the beach. They were nowhere near Passage. They shuttled out to the coast to carry out their plan, to give Mac the best chance they could to survive the escape. The waves of the Pacific Ocean crashed around them. They had gone to a beach that was free of tourists, so no one would question the bulky equipment they had with them.

Fortunately for Mac, the two men he had asked to rescue him had occupations that demanded they think like a terrorist. Sneed was a best-selling author on multiple planets. More than one of his books dealt with terrorists. He had thought of things that the real terrorists hadn't thought of. Unfortunately, the terrorists read his books and borrowed his tactics. That was when Sneed stopped writing and disconnected into a game version of his books.

Sneed wasn't even his real name, but he was too embarrassed to say otherwise. He got the name Sneed from one of the characters in his books. It was the character he used when he was plugged in. There was part of him that wished he'd given Mac his real name when he was first brought back into the real world, but there wasn't much that could be done now.

The idea for his next book had never been published, and no one, except for the only man in Passage with an Imp, had thought of it. The basic concept was a really big dead zone that they could control. Mac's two friends created an expansive dead zone that would cause Zinger's ship to shut down and fall into the ocean when he flew through it.

They projected the dead zone weapon up into the air. Sneed was at the telescope searching the sky for the luxury space craft. When he found it, they implemented the plan. They deliberately spaced out their shots, taking the engines out one at a time. The factor they didn't consider was the need to shoot out the engines in a particular order to keep the ship balanced. They realized their mistake when the ship started tipping and spinning. So far, no shuttles had launched, and they could see people jumping or falling off the ship. Zinger's yacht was plummeting to the ocean, but they didn't believe Mac and Lynn had gotten off yet.

Seconds before it hit the water, Sneed heard an onboard explosion and the only man in Passage with an Imp pointed at a shuttle flying through a gaping hole and up into the sky. That had to be them.

"Let's pack this up," said Mac's friend from Passage.

"There is a huge wave coming this way from that thing crashing. Maybe we should leave the equipment here and let it get washed into the ocean," said Sneed.

"The military doesn't have this technology yet, or at least they haven't clued into using it as a weapon. I don't want to be responsible for giving them the idea."

"Then home we go," said Sneed. He muttered a "good luck" to the shuttle that was so small now it could hardly be seen.

Chapter 13
Terwillegar

Lynn's Imp was working again. It was odd she hadn't been surged yet. Raymond was one of the few who knew she'd been on board Zinger's yacht, but Mac could only guess at where Raymond might be now. Wherever he was, it was possible her Imp was out of range. Once they got off-planet and out into space, they would be safe. No surger or Imp had that much range. Imps were considered unwanted distractions to space explorers, so long-range capabilities weren't researched.

Lynn was able to reach Captain Tompkins by radio before the *Terwillegar* took off. She threw lab assistant coveralls at both Mac and Lynn.

"If you're coming on my ship, you better look like you belong on my ship," said Captain Tompkins.

Mac looked around for a place to change discreetly.

"No time for being shy. Just do it."

Mac was too afraid to disobey the Captain. He almost said "Yes, sir," but stopped himself just in time. Captain Melissa Tompkins was taller than Mac by three inches, and her full-bodied, fire-red hair added a few more inches. She wore tight-fitting clothes that made everyone pay attention to her, but she was as intimidating as she was beautiful.

Lynn remembered when she was a kid, her dad would say, "Mel is a brilliant scientist, and she knows how to use her brain and her beauty to get what she wants."

Captain Tompkins led her new lab assistants through the space port to the *Terwillegar*. What Lynn's dad had said about the tall redhead was true. Mac could have been on fire, and no one would have noticed. People were even turning away from the news feeds about Zinger's ship crashing into the ocean to watch her go by. The media still didn't know whose yacht it was, or they knew and weren't allowed to say. No one knew why it had crashed. People suspected another alien attack. All ships were held back until a plan was in place to determine who, or what, was responsible for the crash.

"Won't that stop us from leaving?" asked Mac, as he trotted to keep up with Captain Tompkins' lengthy strides.

"Only for a few minutes. After I drop you off, I'll go to the flight center and get special permission. They haven't denied me anything I've asked for before. I don't see why they would start now."

They walked through the public areas where people lined up to buy tickets. Others crowded around vid screens. Some waited to board their shuttles, unaware that all flights were delayed.

The trio eventually arrived at the private area of the space port where people kept their own ships. Exploration vessels, science vessels, and small private ships all left from here. When they got to the *Terwillegar's* gate, Mac was surprised that the space port authorities hadn't made it hold orbit around Earth and use cargo shuttles to pick up supplies. That was the normal procedure for larger ships. *This woman has a lot of pull around here*, Mac thought.

"The man at the door is Shand Riss," said Captain Tompkins. "He's the lead scientist on the ship. I trust him, so I told him about you. He'll get you to a safe place out of sight of the other crew members until I get back."

"Where are you going?" asked Mac.

"To get permission to leave, remember? If Shand seems a little off, don't mind him. He was raised a Luddite and doesn't have an Imp."

The *Terwillegar* was a great-looking ship. The metal it was made of was lighter than that of most other ships. It wasn't truly white, but when compared to others, it looked pearly. There were no sharp angles. It had four rounded extensions: one on the top, one on the bottom, and one on each side. The top extension had windows, so that was obviously the command deck.

The ship was big enough to need a crew of a couple hundred people. Most of the ship comprised living quarters, cafeteria, and recreation areas. Science vessels were usually out in space for months at a time. A sweet vessel like the *Terwillegar* could be out for over a year if necessary.

Mac would ask Captain Tompkins to drop them off on one of the colony worlds. He wasn't sure if Lynn had done that yet. Any colony would do, except for Mars—too much military activity on Mars.

"Hey guys," said Shand. He shook their hands and led them to their rooms. As they were walking away from the ship's ramp they heard someone calling from beneath it.

"Excuse me!"

Mac would recognize that whiny voice anywhere. It was Raymond. Had he followed them? Maybe. But if he had spotted them, he would have used his immobilizer by now. That meant Raymond didn't know they were here.

Mac pulled Shand's head close and whispered in his ear, "It's the military. They're after us. You need to hide us. Quickly."

Shand's eyes went wide. Most Luddites didn't trust the military. He opened the nearest door and pushed them inside.

"Either me or Captain Tompkins will come back for you. I'm locking this door from the outside with a pass code that only she and I know."

He left. They could still hear him on the other side of the door talking to Raymond.

"Come on up," said Shand.

Raymond's voice was too quiet to hear but as he got closer it became clearer.

"…but you didn't answer."

"I don't have an Imp."

"Really?"

"Really. Do you always carry more than one weapon with you?"

"I'm looking for someone. Two people. A man and a woman. Take me to a computer terminal. I'll show you what they look like."

"What are they supposed to have done?"

"It's part of the Northgate investigation. I can't tell you any more than that. When did you say the captain was coming back?"

"Soon. Come this way. I'll find you a terminal. We'll see if these people are on our crew."

Mac wanted to warn Shand not to do that. He shouldn't have even let Raymond onto the ship. There was no way he was leaving now if he suspected they were on this ship.

"How is Captain Tompkins' relationship with the military?" asked Mac.

"She doesn't have one. Once she finds out Raymond is on board, things are going to get really bad," said Lynn.

"Then I guess we will wait and hope it works out."

Mac didn't have much hope. A pit was forming in his stomach that told him everything was about to change. To distract himself he looked around the room they were in. It was a small room with a desk and computer terminal. A work area for whoever's office this was. There were no books on the shelf or knick-knacks on the desk, so it may not have been claimed by anyone yet.

Lynn sat in the big comfy chair behind the desk. Mac took out the computer pad he had used to download information from Zinger's computer. The first thing he wanted to do was read the information about Janelle Stewart. He did a search of her name.

Her name was featured on a full-page list of names and dates. The top of the list was labeled *Ronos Victims*. The date beside her name was the date she was taken—that day out in the field when they had their first kiss.

Mac needed to find out more about what was happening on Ronos. He couldn't understand why the military would keep it a secret. It was a beautiful planet that people could live on without building expensive domes and other life-sustaining devices.

When he opened Zinger's Ronos files he realized his mistake. He hadn't downloaded the right ones. These files were all blacked out. The only information of value that he had was the planet's location. If he wanted to learn why Janelle's name was on that list, he would have to fly to Ronos and do it himself.

Mac thought about reading the Grenor data, but he wasn't in the mood for Zinger's crazy space fantasies. Instead he went to see what Lynn was looking at on the computer terminal.

"They have footage of the attack," she said.

The video was taken from a location much closer to the action than Mac had been. The ship's image was clear. Any doubt about this being the ship that had taken Janelle was gone. It was the same ship.

Longer than it was wide, and not very tall, as it passed over Passage it filled the entire sky. The top had a smooth, curved shape. The bottom was flat, but had moving parts jutting out from underneath. It reminded Mac of a beetle. He could picture it landing and skittering across the landscape.

A spotlight shone from underneath the ship. Its beam rested on a tree close to where Mac and Janelle were standing. The tree shivered, and then all of its branches pointed straight up.

As the light moved across the ground, the grass it passed over stood straight on end and rocks shifted slightly. Janelle gripped Mac's hand. Neither of them thought to run before it was too late.

The light engulfed Mac and Janelle. Their hair stood straight up, and their clothes behaved as if gravity ceased to exist. Janelle's shirt was tucked in, but Mac kept having to pull his down so he could see. In the process, Janelle's hand slipped from his grasp.

Then the light started pulsing. Waves of increasingly brighter light extended from the ship toward Earth. As each wave hit, Mac and Janelle lifted off the ground. Higher and higher. Janelle was screaming by this time. She was lighter than Mac, so she rose higher than he did. They reached for each other, but they were too far apart. The light was too bright for them to see anything above them, but they could see the ground far below them.

When they got closer to the ship, long robotic arms came down and grabbed Mac by the leg, preventing him from getting any closer. It was clear what they wanted. Only her, not him.

Janelle screamed for him as she was pulled up into the ship, to the source of the light. Once she was inside the light turned off. Mac would have fallen, but the robot arm held him in place. Another light turned on and Mac was flung into it. Instead of taking him up into the ship, it lowered him to the ground. He landed on his stomach and spat out a mouthful of grass. When he turned over, the ship was already gone.

He hadn't seen her since.

But he would never stop searching for her.

The abductions were the first acts of the war. Mac might consider the war a fake, but the ship in the video he was watching was real. The gargantuan metal beetle was attacking Northgate. From its belly, thousands of white-hot eruptions sent a steady stream of blue missiles streaking downward, destroying the city. The feed Lynn was watching was from the World Wide News Network. Their analysts had watched the video over and over and were now posting the facts they had accumulated:

Over 522,000 missiles fired.

Spread out to cause maximum damage.

Attack went on for fifteen minutes, thirty-two seconds.

Ship's origin and destination—unknown.

After repeatedly studying the video, even military analysts could not explain how the aliens that terrorized the survivors got to the surface undetected.

"I've seen that ship before," said Mac.

"You said you saw the attack."

"I know, but before that. When I was a kid. A friend of mine was abducted and taken away in that ship. Or a ship just like it."

"Those abductions just before the war started?"

"Yes. I was taken up too, but I guess they didn't want me."

The video of the attack was the only factual reporting on the news. Everything else was just a spin. Mac stopped watching after that segment was done. Lynn kept watching. She thought it was funny how they were spinning her as a mentally deranged person.

Five minutes later they felt the entire ship shift. They were about to launch. What did that mean? Raymond would not have left quietly. If he was gone, he must have been carried off unconscious. But there was no way he would leave if he was sure Mac and Lynn were on that ship.

What felt like an eternity had only been an hour. The door to their room beeped and opened. Shand came inside.

"Sorry it took so long. We weren't able to get rid of Raymond. We tried telling him that we would be out here for over six months, but he didn't listen to us."

"What does he plan to do?" asked Mac.

"Search the ship. He knows your dad used to be friends with Captain Tompkins. As soon as she boarded he refused to let her out of his sight. She sent me here to find a better hiding spot for you guys."

"A better idea would be getting Raymond off this ship," said Mac.

"We know, but we can't do that. He's too highly ranked in the military for us to mess around with. He told us to go to Mars, and that's what she told him we were doing. But I saw her punch in the coordinates. I don't know where we're going, but it sure ain't Mars."

Mac reached for his computer pad to get the coordinates for Ronos. As long as they were off course, they might as well go somewhere interesting.

"Can you plot a course here without him noticing?" Mac showed him the Ronos file.

"Yes. That actually works better for us. We were supposed to go to the Nelson Nebula to gather data—we stopped there briefly a year or so ago and got some unexpected readings—and this Ronos place is closer to the Nelson Nebula than Mars is. Of course I'll have to confirm with the captain. But if we change coordinates, how do we handle Raymond?"

"How long will it take to get to Ronos?"

"A few days."

"We need to talk to the Captain."

"She told me to move you to her office. Raymond just finished searching there. You might have to stay in that room. If he gets close then we'll move you again."

Shand ushered them into the hallway and led the way to Tompkins' office. He insisted they hurry because he wasn't sure where Raymond was.

"I'm sorry," said Lynn.

"For what?" asked Shand.

"For making life complicated for you guys. I just didn't know who else to call. I didn't know Raymond would be so close to finding us."

"Life is always complicated with Captain Tompkins. This is hardly the worst that we've been through."

Suddenly Lynn collapsed. It happened so fast Mac assumed she tripped, but then she started thrashing around wildly with her eyes squeezed shut. A surge. Raymond was trying to flush them out. Lynn started screaming.

"Mac, help me!"

"Grab her!" said Shand.

Shand grabbed her legs while Mac awkwardly cradled her back with one hand and tried to cover her mouth with the other. It wasn't silencing her at all. Her screams echoed down the hallway. She thrashed around so much that they dropped her twice.

"How far are we?" asked Mac.

"Her office is right around the corner," said Shand.

"Is it sound proof?"

"I don't know, but it's got to be better than staying out here with her screaming in the hallway."

Either way, it didn't matter. As soon as they got to the office the surge ended. Wherever Raymond was, he couldn't have heard the screams. Lynn was exhausted. They put her down in one of the chairs facing the desk. She was breathing heavily and her cheeks were wet with tears.

"I was hoping I wouldn't have to go through that again."

The captain's office was a lot more humble than Zinger's. The carpet was stained, the pictures that hung on the wall were cheap knock-offs, the desk was lopsided— the front left leg was held up by a thin, hardcover book— and the only window was a small one right behind the desk. The stars within its frame passed by slowly. The room wasn't much bigger than the one they had just come from, but there were more chairs in this one. Mac figured it doubled as a meeting room.

"It's okay, Lynn," said Mac. "I think if he knew we were here, he wouldn't have turned the surge off."

"He might turn it back on again," said Lynn.

"Yeah, he might."

Shand said, "We'll just keep track of him and make sure there is a lot of space between him and you two so he can't hear anything. Wait here for now. I'm going to go check things out and see where the captain is."

They were alone for at least another hour before Captain Tompkins came back in.

"Sorry, that took longer than I expected. Raymond is crawling through maintenance shafts right now looking for you guys. So what are your plans?"

"What are your plans with Raymond? Can't you just orchestrate an accident?" asked Mac.

"To get rid of him? Of course we can, but he is recording everything with his Imp. He's storing it on our Imp network. As soon as we dock again, dead or alive his feed is going to automatically link up. If military communications staff sees him snooping around our ship, asking a ton of questions, and then 'accidentally' dying, they might get suspicious. We would face serious consequences. Unless you know how to modify Imp networks, then we need to think of something else," said Captain Tompkins.

"Did Shand ask you about the course change?" asked Mac.

"Yes, and I approve of the general direction, but our charts don't show the planet you guys are looking for."

"It's the home of a secret military base. Someone I know may have been taken there. I need to find her."

"You're both going?"

Lynn nodded, but Mac said, "No."

"What?" Lynn stood up quickly. She was still dizzy, so Shand helped her sit back down.

"I have no plan once we get there. I didn't go through all the trouble of helping you escape to have you die on some remote planet. I'll get Raymond off your hands. Once

I'm down there, probably as Raymond's prisoner, you will stay with Captain Tompkins and become part of their research team," said Mac.

"But I thought we were supposed to meet Scott back on Earth," said Lynn.

"I know. I'm sorry. I'll send a message to my friend and let him know that we—that you—are going to be late."

"But I can't just—"

"Finding out what really happened at Northgate is going to take time. Once you and your husband are safe you will have time to think up a strategy for exposing the truth about the war and you'll have time to gather evidence."

"Truth about the war?" asked Captain Tompkins.

"We think it's fake. That's why Raymond wants us," said Lynn.

"At least that was the initial reason. Since then I have deserted the military, stolen military equipment, illegally removed my own Imp, and most recently, helped crash the general's luxury space yacht into the ocean," said Mac.

"I haven't heard anything about a space yacht crashing," said Captain Tompkins.

"I think it was an off-the-books kind of space yacht, so they need to think up a cover story first," said Mac.

"You guys leave a path of destruction behind you," said Tompkins.

"Worried?"

"Not yet. We've been through hairier things than this. Let's just get to Ronos and see what happens."

"What's your plan for Raymond 'til then?"

"Don't worry about it. I'm sure I can keep one guy occupied for a few days. I think it's best if we try to delay your next encounter with him."

It was almost two days later when Mac and Lynn noticed it. The ship seemed wobbly. They were no longer in Tompkins' office. They had been moved four times—the last one brought them close to the cafeteria. Mac's stomach was growling, but dinner would have to wait. They weren't in charge of their own schedule at the moment. Right now they were in a meeting room just off the command deck. Mac spent most of his time with his ear pressed against the door. He liked to know what was going on, and the ship's unusual motion made him nervous. On the other side of the door he could hear chatter about a pull of some kind, but he had no idea what that meant.

Lynn stood behind Mac and spoke softly. "What are they talking about?"

"I can't tell. I think something might be going wrong."

As if on cue, the ship jerked forward. Lynn fell into Mac and his face banged into the door. The people on the command deck must have heard it, because an announcement came over the ship's intercom.

"Will Captain Tompkins please report to the command deck. That's Captain Tompkins to the command deck, please." Mac recognized the voice as Shand Riss.

"What do you think it is?" asked Lynn.

"I'm not sure," said Mac.

They both pressed against the door, strained to hear what was going on. They heard another door open and then Tompkins' voice. They also heard Raymond's whining. Now they couldn't just slip in for a quick update. Shand's voice echoed all over the ship again.

"Prepare for another jolt. We are testing an anomaly."

They braced themselves this time, so there was no awkward falling or face smashing. But there was a flurry of discussion on the other side of the door. Now, with so many people talking, it was even harder to tell what was going on. Soon the captain's overpowering voice rang out,

"Ronos is a military base! How could you not know what's going on there?"

"Uh oh," said Lynn.

"Yeah," Mac agreed, "I think the time for hiding is over."

Raymond replied, but they couldn't understand what he said. Mac and Lynn stepped back quickly as the door opened.

The command deck was a domed room encircled with windows. The center of the command deck was the control console where all the information in the science vessel was gathered. Crew members, crowded around the console, tried to understand what was happening. Captain Tompkins, the tallest of the crowd, looked like she was losing patience. Mac couldn't see Raymond in the crowd, but he could hear him.

"I have served in the military for over twenty years. I am in General Zinger's inner circle. And I'm telling you there is no military base on this planet. It's not on your star charts, and it's not on mine either."

"Mac, could you explain things to him?" asked Captain Tompkins.

The crowd divided to clear a sight path between Raymond and Mac. If Raymond hadn't been standing on the opposite side of the control console, he would have leapt at Mac. Even so, he tried to force his way through the crowd to get to Mac. Captain Tompkins held him in place with her massive hand. The puny Raymond didn't have a chance.

She kept a grip on Raymond's shoulder and led him around the control console. The break in the pandemonium, to see who the new people on the command deck were, was over now. Engineers and technicians were shouting to each other across the room and running back and forth between terminals. Four information analysts with computer pads followed Captain Tompkins around and fed her updated data while she led Raymond away from the throng to talk to Mac and Lynn.

"Let's worry about the real issues before we start bashing each other's heads in," she said.

"I'm the one who told Captain Tompkins about the base on Ronos," said Mac.

"We can't just take your word for it. You're a deserter, and before that you weren't cleared for any classified material. How could you know about it when I don't?" said Raymond.

"I got the information directly from Zinger."

Mac held out the computer pad he had stolen. Raymond studied it for a moment and then scoffed.

"This is nothing. It's all blacked out. You have a list of names and a location. He could have just been playing mind games with you," said Raymond.

"If we're still on course we'll find out soon enough whether Ronos is real or not," said Mac.

"And it's not like we can get out now anyway," Shand said from near the control console. He had been listening in on the conversation.

Mac was confused. Captain Tompkins filled him in on what was happening.

"You remember what Shand told you about the Nelson Nebula? He might have been a bit too vague about the 'unexpected readings' we got on our last trip. What we experienced was a pull. Very slight. We could hardly even feel it. But we were training a new pilot on our way home and he asked why the thrust indicator gauge was jumpy. We thought it was a computer glitch, but it wasn't. An external force was tugging at us. We assumed it was something in the Nebula, but didn't have time to investigate. Our reverse thrusters managed to get us out of its grip. Yesterday we started experiencing that same pull again. The pull's reach caught us off guard. Apparently we got too close to its source."

"And the rear thrusters…" Mac said.

"Aren't doing the job this time. The closer we get to its source, the more powerful it becomes."

Shand didn't mince words. "The reality is—we can't get out of the pull. We're going wherever it's taking us."

"Where is it taking us?" asked Mac.

Shand waved him over to the control console. He showed them on a map where they were and where they were being pulled to.

"We are either being pulled to Ronos for a landing, or we are going to crash right into it," he said.

"And there's no way to stop?"

"Not that we know of. But we'll figure something out. We have the engineers working on it now. I don't suppose you guys have any expertise in this."

"I'm just a soldier," said Mac.

"And a Luddite," Raymond sneered.

Captain Tompkins smacked Raymond on the back of the head.

"The lead scientist on this ship is also what you would call a Luddite so watch your mouth."

"You can't just hit me like that!"

"My ship. My rules," said Captain Tompkins. "Do you have any way to help us, Lynn?"

"I'm a biological engineer. I don't know what I could do."

Mac didn't know that. He wondered how a biological engineer and a factory manager got together. But now wasn't the time to ask, and he wasn't sure he wanted to listen to a love story anyway.

"You two got us into this mess. Did you not know this was going to happen?" said Captain Tompkins.

"Sorry, no. We've never been to Ronos. We're just following a lead," said Mac.

"You two are going to have to do better than that for endangering my ship and my crew."

"This could potentially kill all of us, Raymond. Are you telling the truth when you say there is no military base on Ronos?" said Mac.

"As far as I know there isn't even a planet named Ronos. It's just a big empty space," Raymond replied.

"Can we agree to put aside our differences while we try to figure out how to stay alive? I promise that once it's all over, I'll go with you to the base."

"There is no base."

"Then I'll just go with you to that big empty space."

"None of that matters if we crash into the planet," said Captain Tompkins. "We will keep trying to break free."

Mac and Lynn were relieved they didn't need to hide any more. They hovered around the control console and watched everyone work. The crew knew their ship best, so Mac and Lynn didn't offer suggestions.

Even at a dead stop, with the engines not putting out any thrust, the ship was still moving. If they veered away from the direction they were being pulled in, they were drawn back into it. The only progress that they could make was to throw the engines in reverse and fire them on full power. Even then the *Terwillegar* barely moved backwards, and they would run out of fuel before they made any significant progress.

"Is there anything nearby we can latch onto?" asked Captain Tompkins.

"No, the closest thing out there is Ronos," said Shand.

"If we made ourselves heavier, than we could slow it down," said a crew member Mac didn't know.

Captain Tompkins rolled her eyes, "If you can think of a way to do that, go for it. Personally I'm for just getting it over with."

She increased the ship's speed. In a few minutes they would find out if the ship was going to crash or not. It didn't take long for a planet to come into view.

"Looks like Ronos is real, Raymond," said Mac.

Raymond didn't say anything.

"Are we slowing down?" asked Lynn.

"No," said Shand.

The planet was getting bigger and bigger. At the speed they were going the *Terwillegar* would crash and burn instantly. At least the planet was real. Mac was glad he would have this small victory just before he died. As the planet got bigger Captain Tompkins had the pilot turn the ship's engine off so that they would just drift when the pull stopped, if it ever stopped.

"What about escape pods?" asked Mac.

"We launched one. It's trailing behind us, caught in the same pull," said Captain Tompkins.

"We're slowing down!" said Shand.

There was a collective sigh of relief. The ship slowed down and whatever was pulling them held them in orbit around Ronos. The planet engulfed half of the viewing area of the command deck. Its similarities to Earth creeped Mac out. Why would anyone keep this beautiful planet a secret?

The continent they were facing looked like a thick horseshoe. The landmass had desert at one end which turned into rocky brown mountains. The other side of these mountains was green. That green went around the rest of the horseshoe and was only broken up by another mountain range that ran along the outside of the horseshoe curve.

"Is there anything down there?" asked Mac. "Can you see the base?"

"We need to determine what is pulling us in," said Captain Tompkins.

Shand was busy at the controls of a nearby computer terminal. He passed on the results of his search to the control console in the middle of the room.

"I can answer both of your questions with the same answer. The base, or at least the only group of manmade objects as far as I can tell, is the source of the pull."

"Maybe they couldn't build anywhere else. We have no idea what it's like down on the surface," said Captain Tompkins.

While they were talking Raymond walked over to a communications console and was sending out a message, "This is Major Raymond Tysons, the military authority on the ship *Terwillegar*. Please respond."

"What are you doing? You have no authority to do that," said Captain Tompkins.

She took two steps toward Raymond, but he held out his gun. He was done playing around. If the people on the surface were allies, then he held all the cards. The ship wasn't going anywhere until the pull was shut down.

"I'm going to the planet's surface, and I'm taking the Luddite and the girl with me," said Raymond.

"Absolutely not," said Captain Tompkins.

Raymond didn't hesitate. He shot Shand in the head. His body slumped over the control console. His face was burned beyond recognition, and the putrid smell filled everyone's nostrils.

"You…" Captain Tompkins took another step toward Raymond. He shot another crew member. The entire crew screamed out, but no one dared move. Raymond was heartless. He had no problem killing Tompkins' crew members one by one to get what he wanted. Captain Tompkins valued her crew more than she valued the daughter of an old friend and some stranger.

"Take a shuttle and get out of here," she said.

Raymond pointed the gun at Mac and Lynn and ordered them to walk to the docking bay. Lynn looked completely lost. She felt responsible for the murders that just happened and cursed herself for calling on Tompkins to help her. If she hadn't gotten on the ship, none of this would have happened.

"Melissa, I am so sorry. If I had any idea this would happen—"

"Quit blubbering and move along," Raymond barked.

Captain Tompkins offered Lynn a comforting smile as she left the command deck.

Mac didn't think it was Lynn's fault. Every bad thing that happened was due to Raymond and Zinger's direct actions. The fault was all theirs. They were the ones who destroyed lives. They were the reason he and Lynn were being marched to the docking bay at gunpoint.

The shuttle they got on was an older model. Who knew why Raymond chose it. The guy was an idiot. Mac wanted to point out that his choice was old and poorly made, but he wasn't sure if he could do it without using the word idiot, and Raymond was still the man with the gun.

They went through a side door that opened into the control room. The room could accommodate four people. The front two seats were for the pilot and co-pilot. The other two had computer terminals but no flight controls. Raymond sat in the co-pilot's seat and made Mac fly.

The control room occupied the forward section of the ship. The rear section was a cargo room, slightly bigger than the control room. Mac didn't know what was back there, but usually on a ship like this it had a few spare parts, emergency gear, and empty cargo bins. The back wall of the cargo room was one big door that slid to the side so large items could be loaded and unloaded. When it was open, the shuttle appeared to be missing a wall. They made sure it was closed before they took off.

The control room housed a dangerous goods compartment in a back corner, adjacent to the cargo room door. The compartment was small but solidly built out of titanium. Two people could stand inside it, but they would be so close together that it would be awkward if they weren't really good friends.

"Take us down to the base," said Raymond.

Just as he spoke, the ship bucked.

"What did you do?" he demanded.

"I didn't do anything. It was the *Terwillegar*." said Mac.

Mac knew the feeling though. The ship was under attack. He sent a request for the bay doors to open. Captain Tompkins accepted and opened them. She didn't have a choice. If she didn't open them, Mac would be forced to shoot his way out.

The shuttle left the *Terwillegar* and flew into a war zone.

Five HAAS3s were attacking the *Terwillegar*. He knew now, without a doubt, that Ronos was a military base. Only the military flew the HAAS3. He also knew that five ships was overkill. The *Terwillegar* was a science vessel. It didn't have enough weapons to defend itself.

Mac weaved through the attacking ships and made for the planet. It was pointless, though. He knew as soon as they were finished attacking the science ship, they would come after the shuttle. Maybe sooner.

No weapons fire came from the *Terwillegar*. It was totally helpless. Raymond was smiling. How could he not see the situation for what it really was? Was he really that blinded by military camaraderie that he didn't know he was a target as well? There was a reason this base was kept top secret, even from the mighty Major Raymond Tysons.

One of the attack shuttles veered off and headed toward them as they rushed to Ronos. They weren't even in the atmosphere yet when the first laser blast struck.

"What are they doing?" asked Raymond.

He reached for the communicator and tried to send out a message.

"You are firing on a shuttle with a military officer on board!" he said.

The shots continued to rain down. Mac tried to evade them but more hit than didn't. They wouldn't last much longer.

"I'm transporting two very important prisoners. I'm under orders from General Zinger to—"

He was cut off by a laser strike that took out communications. Dropping Zinger's name didn't help. The attack continued.

"What can we do?" asked Lynn.

Looking back at the *Terwillegar,* they saw her hull start to fracture. Twisted metal, small objects, men and women streamed out the gaping hole. The ship was done for. The attackers didn't let up until the whole science vessel burst into one giant fireball. Lynn had to look away.

Now it was their turn. They had entered the atmosphere, and five shuttles attacked them instead of just one. They had no safe place to go. Originally the plan had been to go to the base, but that's where the attackers were from.

"I have an idea," said Mac.

He waited for the next laser blast to hit them and then threw the shuttle into a tailspin. The g-force pinned all three of them to their seats. Everything became a blur. It was hard to even open their eyes.

"Are you crazy?" Raymond mouthed.

Mac peered at the computer to see if his ruse worked.

It had. All five attack shuttles were returning to the base. They thought they had delivered a killing blow to the shuttle. Mac waited until the attack shuttles landed before he tried to pull them out of the downward spin. He struggled to pull up on the control stick. There was no way he was going to be able to pull them out of this deadly spin. The fake out had become a reality.

"Raymond, I'm going to need your help," said Mac. "Can you grab your control stick?"

Raymond reached. At first his hand didn't get more than two inches off the arm rest. He was such a skinny punk it was amazing he hadn't snapped in half when Mac put them in the tailspin. When he tried again he was able to put both hands on the co-pilot control stick. Together they pulled and tried to right the course they were on.

It wasn't working. They were falling closer and closer to the ground. Mac didn't even know where they were anymore. They could be falling right into the base for all he knew.

The sky was changing from white to light blue to darker blue as they got lower and lower. In seconds they would be a ball of flame, and then, nothing. Just like the people on the *Terwillegar*. They would all be dead, and no one would know what had happened to them. Jace and Scott would be waiting for Mac and Lynn on Earth, but they would never come.

Mac couldn't give up. He used every bit of energy he had to pull at the stick. He looked over and saw Raymond doing the same. Neither of them gave up. Not when they fell past the mountains, not when they fell past the foothills. Not even when they were below the trees.

Just then the ship righted itself and came out of the tailspin. But it wasn't in time. The shuttle slammed into the ground. They had leveled it out enough that they didn't burst into flames and die on impact, but the initial contact with the ground destroyed the engine and launched the shuttle through the air. It skipped across the foothills like a rock over choppy water until it found a weak spot in a rocky hillside.

The shuttle punched through the side of the hill and everything went black.

Chapter 14
Ronos

Mac was the first one to wake up. He coughed, and squinted through a window, but he couldn't see much in the darkness. He figured he'd been unconscious for a few hours—that explained the darkness—but not the purple-tinged light in a starless sky. He shook his head and rubbed his eyes. Out the window he could see rocks. A lot of rocks. Then it dawned on him—they were underground.

He remembered the tailspin, needing Raymond's help to pull the shuttle's nose up, approaching a hill, and...that was all. They must have punched into an old mineshaft or a cave system of some sort. As far as he could tell they had landed level. The nose of the shuttle was a little higher than the stern but not at an extreme angle.

He took stock of himself. There was no blood gushing and he could move both arms and legs. Raymond was still out cold. Dried blood covered a cut above his eye, and a goose egg had formed where his head hit the console. Mac grinned. *No big deal, Raymond. You don't use your head much anyway.* It was probably the least important part of his body. Right up there with his vocal cords.

The immobilizer was at his feet. Mac picked it up, but it wouldn't even turn on. It probably fell from Raymond's hand and clattered all over during the crash.

Mac undid his safety harness and stumbled back to talk to Lynn and see if she was okay.

Mac crouched by her side. "Hey, Lynn." He held her hand as he spoke. It was disturbingly cold. "Lynn?" He leaned in closer and put a finger on her neck. She had a pulse, and she was breathing. Maybe she was just one of those people who always had cold hands and feet.

She looked pretty beat up before the crash, so he wasn't sure which injuries were new and which ones were from before.

"Lynn? Are you okay?"

Slowly her eyelids fluttered open. Her eyes grew wide when she remembered what had happened.

"They're dead, aren't they?" she asked.

"Probably," said Mac.

"They're dead, and it's all my fault. I shouldn't have gone to them. You shouldn't have brought them here."

"We couldn't have known this would happen."

"We were going to a secret military base. What did you think would happen?"

"I didn't think that far ahead."

"That's your problem. You never think. You just act and everyone around you gets killed. You never think about the consequences. This is your fault. You're blinded by ridiculous goals. Secret bases? Rescuing fair maidens? What are we doing here? We should be back on Earth. I should be with Scott. I should be with my husband, but I'm stuck with you and Raymond and I don't even know what's going on anymore."

"We crashed," said Mac.

"Crashed? Where?"

"I don't know. In a cave, I think. We're on Ronos, remember?"

"Yes, I remember." Lynn pointed at Raymond slumped in his chair. "Is he…"

"I don't know. I haven't checked yet. Are you okay? I can't tell which injuries are new ones."

Lynn did the same self-diagnosis that Mac had done and came to the same conclusion.

"I'm fine, Mac. The odd bump and bruise, but nothing to worry about."

While Mac went to check on Raymond, she tried to get a closer look at where they were.

"Okay, add 'uncomfortably stiff' to the list of things not to worry about," said Lynn as she tried the door, but either it was jammed or they were so close to a rocky wall that the door couldn't open.

Her attempt to check out their surroundings failed, so she moved on to taking stock of the vessel's supplies. The dangerous goods compartment held some basic, yet important scientific equipment. None of it was dangerous. She recognized some items from when she went to school. They might be useful to collect and analyze small samples from this mystery planet. She would take a closer look later.

"He's okay," said Mac. "Or at least he's breathing."

Mac noticed a strange hissing noise. He looked around to find the source, but it sounded like it was coming from everywhere.

"Do you hear that?" he asked.

"Yes," said Lynn.

"Yes," said a very groggy Raymond. "What is it? Where are we?"

He winced as he touched the bump on his head. His eyes filled with fear when he saw the purple ambiance in the rocks.

"Holy crap. Is that gas?"

Mac looked out the front window. The purple did look like it was a gas. Denser areas were a deeper purple color than the lower density areas were. He found that the closer he leaned to the glass, the louder the hissing got. He made a quick sweep of the entire control room and found that he could hear the hissing noise against every wall except the one leading to the cargo area.

"I think the hissing is coming from that purple gas," said Mac.

"Is it eating at the ship?" asked Raymond.

The glass on the front of the shuttle was changing color. It was becoming less and less transparent. It was turning purple. Was the gas burning it?

Before he could stop her, Lynn walked to the front of the shuttle. She leaned in close to get a better look at the glass. Then she reached out with her hand to touch it. As soon as her finger touched the glass it was burned. She screamed in pain and moved back. She wiped her finger on the pilot's seat where Mac had sat. Small wisps of smoke came from the chair.

"Let me look at it," said Mac.

He grabbed her finger and held it up to his face. It had burned her almost instantly. Whatever she had picked up on her finger was still burning on the chair. If she hadn't wiped it off right away it would be burning its way down to her bone.

"That gas is eating its way inside the ship," said Mac.

"We need to get out of here," said Raymond. He undid his seatbelt and stood up slowly.

"We are surrounded by that gas. I already listened by all the walls in here," said Mac.

"Yeah, but what about the back?" said Raymond.

Raymond got out of his seat and opened the door to the cargo area of the shuttle. Mac followed behind him. Once he was at the far outside wall, Raymond put his head close to the wall, listening. But Mac didn't need to get that close to realize they were surrounded. There was no way they were getting out of the shuttle without being burned alive.

The lights start flickering. How long did they have before the power went out?

A siren wailed. The door between the cargo room and the control room slid down trapping Mac and Raymond in the cargo room. The ship had gone into lockdown. The safety system detected a dangerous substance on the outside, and now it was trying to protect the people inside. It had done the opposite. They were trapped.

"Try the locks on the door," said Raymond.

Mac tried even though he knew they wouldn't budge. After a few minutes Raymond believed him as well. They didn't bother trying to open the door leading out of the shuttle. What was the point? At best, it would open and the whole room would be flooded with the purple gas and they would die.

"Lynn? Are you okay?" Mac yelled at the door.

He could hear a muffled response. He moved along the wall connecting the two rooms until it became clearer.

"I'm in here!" Lynn was yelling over and over.

"We hear you. Are you okay?" Mac asked through the wall.

"Yes, but I'm trapped in the dangerous goods compartment. Open the door and let me out."

"We can't."

"Why not?"

"Because we're trapped in the cargo bay."

"What?"

"I think the ship went on lockdown. It sensed a threat outside. All the doors are locked now."

"There has to be an override," said Lynn.

"There probably is in the control room, but none of us are in there. Do you see a manual release in your compartment?"

"Nothing obvious, but I'll keep looking."

"Okay, I know for sure I saw one on the outside of your door. We'll try to get to you."

Raymond was walking around with a large wrench touching the walls to see how long it took for the wrench to burn. It was almost as instant as the damage to Lynn's finger.

"This stuff burns fast. Do you see how the walls are looking slightly purple?" said Raymond.

Mac looked but he couldn't tell the difference. If there was one, it wasn't very strong. Yet.

"We don't have a lot of time," said Raymond.

"Let's see what we have hanging around here."

They rummaged through the three cargo room containers and found a large replacement battery, old rags, more hand tools and a couple of expired food rations.

"Doesn't matter that they are expired. If we die, it won't be from starvation," said Mac.

They checked the storage closets. Two space suits hung from a rack. How long would they last against the gas? The entire time they were searching, the hissing sound of the gas eating away at the outside of the shuttle persisted. It was enough to drive a man crazy.

"Do we have anything that will help us escape?" asked Raymond.

The best they had were the tools. Mac might be able to open the door with them. He started to work on the lock which was nearest to Lynn so they could still talk through the wall.

"How's it going in there?" asked Mac.

"Good. A little cramped. I wish I could sit down, but at least I'm still alive to complain about it."

"I'm trying to pick the lock or override the lockdown."

After a few minutes he realized the whole endeavor was useless. He didn't have the right tools to do this. He needed a computer. It didn't matter what he did; he wouldn't be able to open the door separating them.

Raymond was already lying down on the floor. His idea of doing nothing hadn't worked either.

"I don't know if I can get this door open," Mac said to Lynn.

"What are we going to do?"

"Is there anything where you are that can help us?" asked Mac.

"I don't think so, but I'll look again."

"There's no computer terminal?"

"Definitely not."

A few more minutes of thinking yielded no results. Mac sat with his back against the interior wall opposite the dangerous goods compartment. He tossed the battery in the air, caught it, tossed it again, caught it... He had no idea what to do. He told Lynn as much.

"So all we can do is wait?" she asked.

"I guess so. You're going to last longer than we do. You're in the middle of the ship. I don't think any of the walls of the dangerous goods compartment touch the outside of the ship. The gas won't reach you until the rest of the ship is breached."

"That's not as comforting as you'd think."

"Sorry."

"Me too," said Lynn.

"What for?"

"For what I said earlier. For saying this was all your fault."

"No, you were right. I just didn't have enough time to think of a better plan. Coming here was a mistake," said Mac.

"I was right there with you. I know you did the best with what you had. If we have anyone to blame it's Zinger and the third member of our group."

"Yeah."

"I'm sorry about your family," said Lynn.

"I'm sorry I didn't bring you back to your husband," said Mac.

All they could do was wait. All Mac could do was think about what brought him to this place. Hadn't his parents warned him something like this would happen if he signed up for the military?

"You're just going to end up dying on some planet no one has ever heard of for reasons you don't even know!" his dad had shouted at him when Mac broke the news.

He was right. It killed him to think he was going to die not knowing whether the war was a fabrication or not. He decided he would at least see how much Raymond knew about the subject.

"Hey, Raymond?" Mac said.

"What?" he said.

"You know we are going to die, right?"

"Thanks for reminding me."

"I have a question for you."

"What?"

"Is the war fake?"

"What?"

"My question isn't just 'was it really aliens who attacked Northgate?' but was there ever a war to begin with?"

"Of course they did and of course there is."

"We are going to die. There's no reason to lie anymore."

"I know. I'm not lying," said Raymond.

"Zinger told me he authorized the attack on Northgate."

"Then he lied to you!" yelled Raymond. "I've been to the front line. The space station I was on was destroyed by them. I've seen them with my own eyes. I should be dead right now, but the general saved me. If he told you that he was the one responsible, then he was just trying to manipulate you. The war is real. A Luddite like you wouldn't know any better."

This close to death and Raymond still felt the need to be antagonistic. Mac didn't understand it.

"What do the aliens look like?" asked Mac.

"The ones I saw looked like us."

"The ones you saw?"

"Different people saw different things that day. But I saw aliens that look just like you and me."

That fit with what Zinger had told Mac. Was it possible they were telling the truth? If so, Mac's dying from burning purple gas on a secret military planet was worse than useless—he was dying trying to do the wrong thing. More than ever he wanted to know if Zinger and Raymond were telling him the truth.

They didn't agree on everything. Raymond insisted the attack was perpetrated by aliens, yet Zinger admitted to orchestrating the whole thing himself. *Who is the bigger liar?*

Raymond was still lying on his back.

"The ceiling is a darker purple than the rest of the room," he said.

Mac looked up. He was right. While the intensity of the purple hue on the walls could be argued, the color of the ceiling was undeniable darker. The hissing was getting louder as well.

"Mac?" said Lynn.

"Yeah?"

"Talk to me, please. I'm going loopy trapped in here alone."

"What do you want me to talk about?"

"Talk about anything."

"Raymond thinks the war is real. He said he's been to the front line. That he's seen the aliens. He says they look just like us, or at least some of them do."

"Really? Do you believe him?"

Mac looked over to see if Raymond was listening. Lynn's voice was soft even to Mac, so he doubted Raymond could hear her.

"No, I don't."

"Me either. Tek said the same thing, but he was a mental patient."

"Zinger admitted to me that he was the one behind the attacks on Northgate."

"Did he give any evidence?"

"No. He just said he needed to do it because people were losing focus on what really matters. That he was doing it to unite the people again so they could defeat the alien invaders."

"Sounds like flag-waving rhetoric to me."

"Yeah. I hear ya."

"Mac, we've just got to get out of here."

"I know."

"Let's talk about something else. Why did you join the military?"

"I'm looking for someone."

"What? Really?"

"Yeah. I knew she was out there somewhere, but I also knew my parents couldn't afford the price of a ticket to get me off Earth. Joining the military was the only option. Plus, she was one of the people abducted at the beginning of the war, so I was sure it was aliens who had done it. I signed up wanting to be sent to the front line, but it didn't work out that way."

"Where did they send you?" Lynn asked.

"I was in charge of protecting convoys between Earth and Mars. Nothing ever happened. I heard about soldiers being sent to the front line, but never anyone I actually knew. The only time we fired weapons was when other humans tried to steal military supplies. I found out later they were just starving colonists."

"Did you find your girl?"

Mac thought it was funny the way she called her *your girl*. Janelle would have liked that.

"No, I didn't find her. For the longest time I couldn't find any evidence she even existed. After she was taken, all records of her existence were erased. I couldn't even find her family; they moved after she was taken. The only evidence I ever found was a list in Zinger's office that had her name on it and linked her to this planet."

"So you think she's on that base?"

"I don't know. But I had to come and check."

Lynn didn't say anything.

"I'm sorry I got you into this," said Mac.

"It's not over yet."

She said that like she had an ace in the hole, but Mac had no idea what it could be. Lynn had a positive outlook on a hopeless situation.

It was all about perspective, and right now Raymond was the only one who had any. He had rolled onto his right side and was staring at the wall. That's when he noticed it—something so obvious they almost missed it.

"Mac! Mac!"

"What?" Mac went over to where Raymond was.

Raymond had jumped up and grabbed the wrench. He walked toward a wall.

"Look," he pointed with the wrench. "Purple. Not purple."

He was touching the wrench to an obviously purple section of the wall. Both of them could hear the hissing and see the smoke coming off where it made contact. Then he lowered the wrench. Two feet off the floor, the wall wasn't purple. He touched the wrench to it. No hissing.

"There's a two foot space where there is no gas. The gas must be lighter than the air," said Raymond. "If we can get out of the shuttle, then we can crawl out of this cave."

Mac hadn't even thought about what they would do after they got out of the cave. Once they got past this gas, they still had to go spelunking. Who knew how far down they were. Then they had to get to the base and steal a ship just to get off the planet. Forget the fact that the soldiers at the base would probably just shoot them on sight.

"But how are we going to open the door?" asked Mac.

Raymond took out his gun.

"What are you doing?" Drawn guns made Mac nervous. Especially when he didn't have one of his own.

"If we shoot the battery while it is taped to the lock, we can destroy the lock and push the door open. We should be okay if we are already lying on the ground when we open the door. It slides to the left."

"How long have you've known about this battery thing?"

"The whole time."

"Why didn't you say anything? We could have gotten to Lynn."

"No, we would have just gotten to the control room of a broken ship. That would have accomplished nothing. I didn't tell you because I knew you would waste our only opportunity to get out of here."

"You do not have an opportunity here. We are in a cave. The ground isn't flat. If the gas is lighter than air sooner or later you will have to climb through the gas to get out."

"It's better than waiting here to die."

"We can't abandon Lynn."

"Maybe you can't. But I can. I don't need you to come with me. I'm leaving with or without you."

"Not without the battery," Mac said. He held it out within an inch of the purple wall. He told Raymond to put the gun down or he would destroy their only way out. Mac held his breath, waiting for Raymond's response. Raymond lowered the gun, but Mac forgot that he was holding a second weapon. Raymond bent down, and placed the gun gently on the floor. Mac was still exhaling when Raymond sprang up and threw the wrench at him. The wrench hit Mac in the head. He fell and dropped the battery.

Raymond picked it up and went to the cargo bay door. The lock recessed a few inches into the wall. The battery easily fit in the space. Shooting it with the gun would cause a big enough explosion to destroy the lock. Mac could see that now. If only he had seen it before. His head was ringing with pain, but he still had it together enough to realize that Raymond was forgetting one very important detail. A space suit.

If they were going to crawl out of there then they needed all the protection they could get. Just like Mac hadn't figured out the battery, Raymond hadn't figured out the space suits. Mac pretended to be in more pain than he was. Hopefully Raymond would crawl out of there and forget all about them. Then Mac could put a suit on and see if there was some way to save Lynn.

Raymond got down on the ground and shot the battery. The explosion tore open the lock. There was nothing holding the door back. He rolled over closer to the door and started pushing and kicking at it to get it to slide open.

The first kick only moved it an inch. The second kick opened it enough so that gas started seeping into the room. It was collecting at the ceiling of the shuttle and slowly moving down as more gas entered the room. Mac was sure Raymond had made a deadly mistake. Within minutes the gas would overtake the entire room.

Mac rolled onto his stomach and army crawled to the storage lockers. The gas wasn't so full that he couldn't walk without being burned but he didn't want to take any chances. He needed to get the space suits. He pulled both of them down and started putting one on. The helmets fell off the top shelf when he pulled the suits down and rolled on the ground. One went far enough for Raymond to notice it. He was ready to crawl out the door when he saw the extra protection that Mac had.

"Give me the space suit," said Raymond.

"There are only two. What will Lynn wear?"

"That's Lynn's problem."

Mac had the suits and he wasn't going to give one to Raymond over Lynn. He had to act fast—Raymond still had a gun and, knowing Raymond, he was dumb enough to shoot a hole in the very thing he needed for protection against the gas. Mac scrambled to his feet. The gas was only a few inches from the top of his head now and getting lower every second. He advanced toward Raymond.

Mac tackled him and knocked the air out of Raymond's lungs. While he was incapacitated, Mac went for the gun. Raymond recovered enough to swat the gun away from Mac's grip. It flew out of the shuttle and out of sight.

"Give me that suit!" Raymond lashed out. He punched Mac in the face twice before Mac was able to kick him away. If only he had thought to put the helmet on first. They rolled away from each other. Mac was on his back.

There was too much gas in the room to risk standing up. For a few tense moments neither of them did anything. They just waited to see if the gas would get low enough to touch them. It stopped two feet above the ground just as they'd hoped. Two feet wasn't much space. Mac took shallow breaths. He didn't want to take too deep a breath in case that made his chest rise just enough to touch the gas.

They were on opposite sides of the room, but Raymond had the advantage. He had rolled to the side with the wrench. Mac was truly starting to hate that wrench. Raymond gripped it in his hand as he crawled to make an attack.

Mac knew he had one weapon, one advantage that he'd rather not use, but Raymond was forcing his hand. Raymond swung the wrench and hit Mac in the chest. Mac reacted with a punch to the face that didn't stop Raymond. He swung the wrench again, aiming for Mac's head. Mac rolled away just in time, but Raymond was relentless. He was a thin punk, but with his life on the line, he fought big. His teeth were clenched together and his eyes were full of hate. He would not stop until he got what he wanted.

"Stop! Let's talk about this!" said Mac.

Mac kicked the wrench from Raymond's hand, but that didn't deter him. He clawed at the suit, trying to rip it off Mac's body while repeatedly hitting Mac in the face. Mac had no choice; he had to make his play. He raised a gloved hand up into the gas and grabbed a fistful of it.

"Raymond!" Mac yelled as loud as he could.

Raymond took notice and stopped his assault. Killing Mac in a fit of rage wasn't worth being burned alive. He rolled away from Mac and toward the remaining space suit. Mac shook the gas out of his hand and rubbed the remnants on the floor of the shuttle. It immediately started sizzling. He couldn't imagine the pain he would have inflicted had he been forced to rub that stuff in Raymond's face.

"I'm taking the suit and I'm leaving," Raymond said as he awkwardly struggled into the suit. It was hard to do in only two feet of space. Mac decided to just let him go. It wasn't worth dying over and if he got seriously injured, he wouldn't be able to help Lynn.

"Where are you going to go?" asked Mac.

"I'm going to look for a way out."

"Even with the suit, you won't be able to get out of here fast enough. We don't know how far down we are."

"How is that a worse plan than just trying to get to the other side of the ship? Even if you get to Lynn you won't be able to help her. You know that, right? All you will have accomplished is dying in the same room."

"It's better than dying alone in this cave."

"I don't plan on dying."

Raymond got the suit on and crawled to the door. Mac wasn't sure what to say. *Goodbye? Good luck?* He didn't care if he ever saw him again. Raymond's parting sentiment was heartfelt.

"If I ever see you or Lynn again, I will kill you."

Mac shook his head in amazement. That guy certainly wasn't worried about leaving a bad impression. On the plus side, he was an optimist. He thought that they would actually meet up again. Mac knew that wouldn't happen. Raymond crawled out of sight, destined to die further into the cave.

Mac put the remaining helmet on, rolled out the cargo door, and looked for a way to get to Lynn. The rocky terrain made it hard to crawl out the back, but he made better time when he got around to the shuttle's side. When the shuttle slid into the cave, it cleared its own path so Mac had a stretch of fairly clear ground to follow. The first real test for the suit came when he got near the front of the ship. A boulder, five inches taller than he was and as wide as his outstretched arms, stood between him and the front of the ship. He needed to break through the control room glass to get to Lynn. The gas had already been eating away at it for a while now, so he thought he should be able to break through easily enough.

The boulder stood before him like a mountain, but if it weren't for the gas he could have easily gotten over it. After a few minutes of waiting he realized there was nothing left to do but climb. He took three quick breaths and plotted his course up and over. He needed to do it as fast as he could to minimize his contact with the gas.

He jumped up from where he was lying on the ground. Instantly he was surrounded by the hissing, burning sound that only motivated him to move faster. One hand in front of the other, toes feeling for footholds, pulling himself up and over the boulder. When he got to the top his helmet's visor was already turning dark purple. Instead of climbing down he jumped off and landed with a thud on the ground.

It wasn't enough to just jump out of the gas cloud. He needed to get rid of the gas that was clinging to him. He rolled on the ground, wiped off the remnants with his hands, and then wiped the stuff from his hands onto a cave wall.

It was a terrifying process, and he would have to do it again when he got inside the shuttle. First he had to break the glass. From the outside it looked dark purple, almost black. Mac suspected he could kick it in, but he didn't want to stand up and expose himself to the gas any more than he needed to.

He looked around and found a decent sized rock that he could throw while lying on his back. Hopefully Lynn hadn't figured a way out, or she was about to be attacked by a rock.

The glass broke under the weight of the rock. Mac didn't feel the need to hesitate anymore. He got up quickly and hoisted himself into the shuttle. He quickly, but carefully, took off the space suit before the entire room filled with gas. He was able to do it without burning himself. He took the gloves off last and used them to move the space suit away from the dangerous goods compartment. He couldn't avoid getting bits of gas on the suit when he climbed in the shuttle, and he didn't want to accidentally touch it.

He crawled over to where Lynn was trapped and banged on the door. She screamed in surprise.

"It's me," said Mac.

"How did you get here?"

"I'll tell you when I let you out. You need to get as low to the ground as you can. When I open the door it's going to fill with the purple gas. The gas is lighter than air, so if you lay down on the ground you'll be fine."

"I can't lie down in here."

"Okay, just get as low as you can and roll out."

"Okay."

"Let me know when you're ready."

Mac heard Lynn shifting objects around.

"I'm ready."

Mac put on a glove and reached up into the gas to open the door.

Lynn was low enough, and she rolled out of the compartment quite easily. Once she was out she stayed as low as she could. Her eyes relayed her fear—she was sure she was going to die.

"It's okay," said Mac. "It's not getting any lower."

"Are you sure?"

"Yes."

She waited a few moments, breathing shallowly like Mac had done before. She desperately needed a hug, but that was not the most pressing problem now.

"Well, we're in the same room. Now what?" she asked.

"I have no idea."

"Where's Raymond?"

"He decided to crawl his way out of the cave."

"I heard something. I thought maybe one of you got hurt."

Mac pointed at the blood that had dried under his nose. "One of us did get hurt. He was willing to kill me for the other space suit, so I had to let him take it."

Mac explained what she hadn't been able to see. And that the only space suit they had was ruined by the gas. And that he didn't know how far below the surface they were. And that there was no way to predict how much protection they would need in order to get out of the cave.

"So this is the rock you threw."

"Yes, but…"

She picked it up before Mac could warn her. It must be covered in gas particles.

But it didn't burn her. The gas didn't stick to it.

"The rock didn't get burned," she said.

"You're lucky. If it had, your hands would be toast now."

"I could tell it wasn't burned."

"Are you suggesting we make a rock suit to get out of here?"

"No, but I am a biological engineer. I could try to do something. I'll study this rock with the equipment I saw in the dangerous goods compartment. There has to be something I can do with it."

"What kind of equipment is it?" asked Mac.

"It's basic stuff. I can study small samples, and mix a few things together. I doubt I'll be able to do much, but we have to try something. I'll scan the rock to see what I can learn from it. The equipment doesn't run on the ship's power, so it will still work."

She crawled back to the dangerous goods compartment to get to work. She was lying half in, half out of the compartment while she looked for useful equipment.

Mac was tired. He had used a lot of energy getting Lynn freed. Making sure he was flat on the ground, and that rolling over wouldn't expose his shoulder to the gas, Mac shut his eyes and rested.

Chapter 15
Lynn Rock and Mac Gas

Mac dreamed about his family. They were in Valentin Park, but it wasn't fake monsters they had to worry about. The ground beneath them was opening up and the burning purple gas was surging out. He tried to yell at his family to warn them, but they weren't listening. Their slashed, bleeding corpses were running through the field. They ran straight through the gas and came out the other side as revenants. He didn't want to see this anymore. The scream in his sleep woke him up.

"You okay?" asked Lynn.

"No. I mean, yes. Just a messed-up dream."

Lynn was still partway in the dangerous goods compartment. They couldn't make eye contact, but they didn't need to.

"Despite everything, I still feel like I should say thank you," Lynn said.

"You know it's my fault we ended up here. I'm the one who came to rescue you from Zinger, and I'm the one who told Captain Tompkins to change course. If it weren't for me, they would still be alive."

"I don't blame you for other people's mistakes. If it weren't for you, I would be dead as well."

"If you get to say thank you then I get to say I'm sorry."

"Deal."

"How long was I out for?"

"I'm not really sure. A while. I don't have any way to tell time. And I drifted off for a bit too. I want to show you what I've been working on, but I thought I'd say thank you first—just in case."

Lynn grabbed something, rolled over, and showed it to Mac. She wanted him to look through the microscope, but Mac just asked her to tell him what was on the slides. They would be nothing more than magnified blobs to him.

"This sample is blood. When exposed to the gas, it burns up. This sample is the rock. When it is exposed to the gas, it doesn't burn. I found a small burner among the lab supplies, and I was able to melt down some of the rock."

"What?"

"It doesn't take a lot to melt this stuff down. Plus, I don't think it's really a rock. As far as I can tell, it's organic. It doesn't weigh nearly as much as a normal rock would. Didn't you wonder why you were able to lift and throw something so big?"

"Hadn't thought about it," he said, his masculinity only slightly bruised.

"If this ship were to explode, there would be a puddle of melted rock underneath it. Anyway, I was able to melt a bit of the rock and mix it with a sample of blood. When I exposed that to the gas, the blood survived."

"You want to inject us with melted rock?"

"It's not like a normal Earth rock. It's something we have never seen before."

"If it's not a normal rock, then maybe we should name it," said Mac.

"I'm thinking Lynn Rock."

"Just *Lynn* Rock? What about me?" Mac teased.

"We'll name the mystery gas after you."

"Lynn Rock and Mac Gas?"

She smiled, then got serious. "Injecting ourselves may be the only way to get out of here."

"How much do we have to inject ourselves with?"

"I don't know."

"Is it safe?"

"I don't know."

"How long until it takes effect on us?"

"I don't know."

"We don't have another choice, do we?"

"No," said Lynn. "Unless you want to wait here and see what happens to us."

"How do you know that the liquid rock won't turn back into a solid once it's in our blood stream?"

"I thought about that. When I melted the rock and just left it in a dish, the pool of liquid solidified. But when I poured some into my hand, my body warmth was enough to keep it from solidifying. Once it melts, it's very easy to keep it in liquid form. It's like nothing I've ever seen before."

Lynn rolled over again and grabbed two prepared samples in syringes. She handed one to Mac while she injected herself. He held it up to his eyes and looked at the murky liquid inside. Was it going to kill him or save his life? Was it going to hurt? The liquid inside looked thicker than blood. It wasn't red anymore, yet it wasn't the color of the black rock either. It was closer to the color of the burning gas than anything. That was a good sign, right? Or did that mean that Mac was going to burn from the inside out?

Lynn stood up. The gas swirled around her, but did not burn her. Her skin gave off light—not enough to read by— but any amount of light was abnormal. People aren't supposed to glow. Would she do that forever? None of her clothes were burned either. The glow protected them. The mix of the melted rock with her body looked like a match made in heaven.

"I guess you injected yourself," said Mac.

"Yeah."

"This is the most amazing feeling," Lynn said.

"How does it feel?" asked Mac.

"It feels a little uncomfortable at first—you can tell it makes a difference right away. And then when you stand up and let the gas interact with you, that's when the glowing starts and you really feel the energy."

"Is it reversible?"

"I don't know. You might be able to get a blood transfusion, but I can feel it everywhere now. Not just in my blood. I feel it in my bones, my lungs, my muscles."

What other choice did he have? There was no getting out of there without it, and she wasn't hurt by the gas. *Nothing bad will happen.* He had to keep telling himself that. *Nothing bad will happen.*

He rolled up his sleeve and used it as a tourniquet. The vein in his arm started throbbing. Mac hesitated one more time.

"You sure you don't feel any different?"

"I feel very different, but in a good way."

Mac stuck the needle in and pushed the liquid rock into his veins.

Everything changed.

Just like Lynn said, he started to feel different almost immediately. His whole arm felt like it was vibrating with energy even though it was perfectly still. He could feel the liquid moving up his arm. He felt it go to his heart and then spread throughout his whole body. The feeling was exciting and peaceful at the same time. It was like nothing he had ever felt before. He wasn't even sure how to describe it. His eyes were wide and his mouth hung open in amazement, but this wasn't even the pinnacle.

Remembering what Lynn had told him, he reached up into the gas with his unprotected hand. Instead of burning, it tingled and started glowing, just like Lynn. A light seemed to be emanating from his hand.

"How is this possible?" he asked.

"I don't know," said Lynn. She reached down and pulled Mac all the way into the gas.

Instinctively he held his breath and closed his eyes.

"It's okay," said Lynn.

Mac slowly opened his mouth and let a little of the gas in. It didn't burn going down. When it got into his lungs it felt much more refreshing than normal air would. It was warm and electric. The gas caused a positive reaction everywhere it went into and onto his body, and it gave him more energy than he'd ever felt before.

When he opened his eyes, he realized his vision had improved too. That gave him an adrenaline boost that made him feel like he could take on the world. If an alien army invaded, he was sure that he could take them all on by himself. Not that he thought there was one, but if there were, he could take them.

"Look at my leg," said Lynn.

She rolled up her pant leg, but Mac didn't see anything unusual.

"What am I looking at?"

"My leg was seriously cut during the attack on Northgate. Remember? Now my leg is perfectly healed. It looks like it didn't even happen. I wish I could take some samples with us, but I think what we have in our own bodies will have to be enough," said Lynn. "I don't want to carry anything that will slow me down."

"Let's get out of here," said Mac.

They vaulted out of the shuttle and moved towards what they thought might be the way out. They didn't need a flashlight. As long as there was Mac Gas, they would give off their own light.

The cave floor was level for a few yards until they got to the point where the shuttle had punched through the rocks—the same kind of rocks whose liquid was now flowing through their bodies. Had they been solid rock, the shuttle would have exploded on impact.

They knew they were going in the right direction because they could see a current of gas flowing up into the shaft created by the shuttle's entry. They jumped—higher than either of them had ever jumped, or had thought it possible to jump—and latched onto the side of the shaft. Mac was amazed that, in the absence of footholds or places to grab onto, he could punch into the rock without hurting himself.

Before the injections Mac had undoubtedly been stronger than Lynn, but now they were evenly matched. Neither of them needed footholds; they just punched their way up the shaft. The closer they got to the top, the thicker the gas got. The thicker the gas, the more energy they had and the faster they went. When they got to the top they saw why the gas was pooling.

Where the shuttle punched through the hillside, the entrance had collapsed into itself. The way out was blocked by massive boulders. There were still some spaces in between the rocks for Mac Gas to seep through, but none big enough for Mac and Lynn to squeeze past.

Mac remembered the view of Ronos from the *Terwillegar*, and it didn't include purple gas. If they opened up this passageway, the Mac Gas would stream into the atmosphere and possibly kill everything.

"I don't think we should go out this way," said Mac.

"What? Why? Look, if we pull this boulder out, then the rest will come down and we can keep climbing out."

"What if the gas doesn't stop? What if we end up poisoning the entire planet with this stuff? We would be the only ones left alive, and even then we wouldn't last long with nothing to eat but Mac Gas."

They both froze for a moment, then made eye contact. Neither of them said what they were thinking. Their most recent meal was compliments of the *Terwillegar's* cook, but they didn't feel hungry or thirsty anymore. Another side effect of the Lynn Rock concoction?

Mac tried a different approach to convince Lynn to change course. "If we let this gas out, we won't be able to steal a ship from that base to get out of here."

That was a point that resonated with Lynn. Going out this way meant that she would never get back to her husband again.

"Let's go back. We'll find another way and then come back and block this off better from the outside.

Going down was a lot easier than going up, and going up had been pretty easy. They got to the bottom of the shaft in minutes, doing things that would have broken normal people's arms, legs, and fingers. But they weren't normal people anymore.

"This time let's go against the flow." Mac led the way back to the shuttle.

On the other side of the shuttle, the cave floor was no longer level. It now looked like a real cave. They had to crawl through a crack in the wall that was just big enough for them to pass through. Plum-purple gas, a higher concentration than they had yet encountered, streamed out of the crack. The cramped passageway was the least of their worries.

They popped out the other side and entered a forest of brightly colored stalagmites and stalactites. The color came from the gas, and each spike reacted differently to it. A lot of them had a purple tinge, but others were blue, green, red, or orange.

There was so much gas in there that Mac and Lynn glowed even brighter. This cavern was huge—ten shuttles could fit inside of it. They heard a waterfall in the distance. Mac wanted to see how their bodies reacted with water.

They couldn't see where the water came from, but they made their way to the sizable pool at the waterfall's base. Mac stuck his hand in the pool to see what would happen. The water was cold, and the light coming from his hand was dimmer when it was submerged.

"There's no Mac Gas here," said Lynn. "The mist from the waterfall chases it away."

"We need to see where the water goes. It might be the only safe way out of here."

"Can you swim?" Mac asked.

"Yes, but…" Lynn was looking at a fissure in the floor that all the gas was coming out of. "I want to see where the gas is coming from."

"But we don't know how far down it goes. What if we can't get back up here?"

Lynn looked at him as though he was an idiot. There was no place they couldn't go. The gas gave them that power.

"Okay, we'll go look," said Mac.

When they stuck their heads out over the edge of the hole they glowed even brighter, but they still couldn't see bottom. Lynn didn't wait for Mac; she started her descent.

When they got far enough down that they couldn't see the ledge they started from, they noticed a dull light coming from below. Maybe there were more people down there that had adapted to the gas.

They got to the bottom of the shaft and saw it led to another rocky tunnel with stalagmites and stalactites. It looked like they were walking into the mouth of a giant alligator. The light was coming from the end of the tunnel that displayed a gradient of purple shades. Different shades dominated the pulsing for varying lengths of time.

As Lynn and Mac approached the light's source, they could feel themselves being pulled toward it. A slight pull—not enough to knock them over or force them to walk faster—but a pull nonetheless. More like a subconscious desire to move forward.

When they reached the end of the tunnel, the spectacle before them was as befuddling as anything else that had happened that day. It would have taken their breath away—had they still needed to breathe. One more side effect. The end of the tunnel looked down on a massive cavern. They were gawking at the wreckage of an enormous spaceship in the middle of that cavern. Bigger than the one that attacked Northgate. The biggest ship Mac had ever seen.

The ruined ship filled the goliath cavern and was the same round shape. It looked like a three-story metal plate that could hold enough food to feed thousands of people. Time had taken its toll, and the ship was broken into five uneven slabs. Mac was sure there was a pizza joke in there somewhere, but he couldn't think of it right then.

The strangest thing about the ship was it didn't look like it was designed to carry any people, or aliens, or whatever. There were no passages or hallways inside the ship, just wires and tubes and machinery.

"Mac, what is this thing?"

"I don't know. Looks more like an oversized machine than a spaceship."

The top of the machine was flat except for a small raised platform that, before the damage occurred, sat in the middle of the roof. The platform housed a single red light that pulsed in concert with the pull he and Lynn were feeling. It couldn't be a coincidence.

"That's what pulled the *Terwillegar* here," Mac said. He was guessing, but it was a solid guess.

"It's not the gas source, though," Lynn said.

She was right. The gas was coming from a fissure in the ground where the pull machine had landed and broken apart. They peered down into gap but weren't willing to go any closer to the planet's core. This cavern gave them the creeps. For the first time, they felt like trespassers.

There was nothing natural about this cavern. It was perfectly circular and had neither stalagmites nor stalactites. Rows of symbols had been carved into the walls. They started so high up in the cavern he couldn't see the beginning, and the symbols he could see were in a language he didn't recognize. But all the cave carvings led to the fissure in the ground where the gas was.

This could only lead to one conclusion—the cavern and the machine were man-made.

"But we couldn't see any buildings on the surface other than the military base," said Lynn. "They obviously didn't put this here. Who do you think did?"

"I don't know. Do you still feel it?"

"Yes."

A subtle pull, like a voice in the back of their heads, beckoned them to come closer to the massive machine. This psychological pull was similar to the physical pull that trapped the *Terwillegar.*

"Let's climb down. Let's get a closer look. Maybe there is something we can use to get out of here," said Mac.

"Okay, let's go," said Lynn.

It was hard to tell how far up they were but they were up far enough to look down on the disk-shaped pull machine. Mac knew they were way more powerful and durable than they used to be, but he didn't want to push his luck by jumping down. He stuck with their proven climbing technique and got to the cavern floor by punching handholds and footholds.

Once he landed on the ground he waited for Lynn to land beside him. The ground was not just dirt and rock. There were patterns in the floor as well. Smaller versions of the symbols carved into the walls completely covered the cavern's floor. They were uniform in size; Mac could cover each one with one hand but the symbols weren't anything he recognized. There were different geometric shapes mixed with things that looked like scribbles.

One looked like two slightly overlapping circles, one bigger than the other, with three wavy lines running through both of them. Beside that one was an acute triangle that had a figure carved around it that looked like it was on fire. Every so often there would be something normal like a square, or a hexagon.

Lynn wasn't looking at the floor. She was too distracted by the massive disk that was now looking down on them instead of them looking down on it.

"Mac, how did something that big get down here?"

Mac shifted his gaze to the pull machine. "Beats me. It's as tall as the three-story apartment building my sister used to live in."

As they walked towards it they could no longer see the blinking red light, but its on-and-off glow still illuminated the cavern. A massive split in an outside wall allowed them to see inside the machine. Mac wanted to know what was in there.

He and Lynn walked through the opening and saw miles of wires and tons of metal girders that were covered in a thick layer of dust. The farther they walked the more dust they kicked up. Mac wanted to walk even farther, see more of the machine's interior, but it was getting too dark. The wires had to be relaying power because the pulsing light was still running. But other than that, he didn't see any evidence that the machine was functional.

"I don't see any of the cave symbols on the ship," said Lynn.

"Me either."

They walked back to the outside of the ship and started walking around it. They found some doors but couldn't open them. It was the only evidence they could find that suggested someone used to be inside the machine.

Mac knocked on one of the doors as hard as he could. The sound echoed off the walls. Even with his newfound strength, he didn't leave a dent in the door. They wouldn't be able to force their way in. No one responded to his knocks.

"I hit that as hard as I could, and…nothing," said Mac. "I wonder what happened to make it split into so many pieces."

"I don't know. This place is giving me the creeps," said Lynn. "I don't think we're supposed to be here."

"Do you still feel the pull?" asked Mac.

"Yeah, but that doesn't mean I don't want to get out of here."

"I think we might be able to use something here to get off the planet. Obviously this didn't get burned by the gas like our shuttle did."

"Look at this mess. All it can do is power a big red light and create the pull. Neither of those things is going to help us get off the planet."

"I don't know. I feel something when I'm down here."

"Then we need to go before you start making some real dumb mistakes. You could cross a wire and electrocute yourself. You could crawl in and get trapped. You could force your way through the door and not be able to get back out. How are you going to find your girl when you're down here searching through wreckage?"

She was right. They could spend days searching and still not find what they needed. Combing through the disk was a waste of time for now. It wasn't going anywhere. If they needed to, they could always come back.

As they turned to leave, Mac felt the slightest bit of resistance. They were lucky the pull only kept ships in orbit around the planet and didn't trap people in the cavern.

There was only one other way to get to Ronos' surface and—they hoped—a getaway shuttle.

They hesitated at the edge of the pool, although neither was afraid of water or claustrophobic. They just weren't sure what to expect when they got into the water and their exposure to the Mac Gas was gone.

"How long do you think we'll have to swim?" asked Lynn.

"A long time. Have you noticed that we don't need to breathe anymore?" asked Mac.

"Yeah, I noticed. But will that change when we get in the water?"

"Let's stop talking about it and go test it out."

Mac got in the water. The gas that was already in his system created a slight glow that dimmed a little when he was under water. They were in no rush, so he waited to see if it would diminish to nothing.

"Can I ask you something?"

"Sure," said Lynn.

"Since...potentially...we could both die today...I was wondering if you would like to tell me the truth about Grenor."

"You want to know if Zinger was onto something or if he was just chasing old spacer stories?"

"Yes."

Lynn thought for a moment. "I was born on a secret planet, a planet hidden from other people because of the...potential...that is given to the people who are from there."

"Are you serious?"

"Zinger was onto something, but he wasn't going to get anything out of me. And it's not a special power he could use to control people."

"So you have power?"

"I have access to power. But it's complicated. There are rules I have to follow."

"I don't get it."

"You don't need to," said Lynn. "The power won't help us out of our current situation. But if we do get through this I need you to know... I haven't told anyone outside my family about this. I didn't even tell Scott until after we were married."

"I understand."

"Trusting you with my secret means that you have to follow the same rule."

"Which rule?"

"Don't tell anyone."

"But you told me," said Mac.

"Don't tell anyone you don't love."

Lynn got in the water and walked up to Mac. The water was up to their waists. She put her arms around him and brought him in for a hug.

"I don't mean that I'm in love with you, Mac. I mean I am grateful for what you've done for me. You sacrificed everything for me and expected nothing in return, other than some help to bring the truth to more people. You are an honorable man. Thank you. I count you as a brother now. A big brother?"

"I think you're older than me."

"I've never had a sibling before, older or younger."

Mac lost his entire family in the attack on Northgate. Now he had a sister and brother-in-law. He was determined more than ever to reunite them.

"I still don't feel the need to breathe," said Mac.

"Me either," said Lynn.

"Should we do this?"

"After you, little brother."

Mac stuck his head in the water. They would feel really foolish if there was nowhere to swim to. The light coming off of them had diminished, but with the two of them standing in the pool he could see enough to notice an underwater tunnel at the bottom of the waterfall.

He was trying to see how long he could hold his breath. Without an Imp it was difficult to time but he got bored after several minutes and his lungs never burned. They didn't need to breathe as often as they did before.

"I think we'll be okay," Mac said when he came back up. "There's a tunnel. It's totally immersed, but we can hold our breath for a long time, so it's not a big deal. Follow me."

Mac dove underwater. Lynn followed soon after him.

Chapter 16
Abandon

Lynn tugged on Mac's arm and pointed to the right. He smiled and nodded. They followed a small, slower branch of the underground river and popped out of a lake like a couple of muskrats. As curious as they were about their new surroundings, they lay down and did nothing for a while to slowly allow themselves to adjust to daylight. Mac noticed something puzzling about the area around the lake.

"Look at that, Lynn. The hills just end."

On Ronos' horseshoe-shaped continent, the foothills abruptly gave way to an expansive prairie. It was almost a straight line where the hills were cut off and the prairie started. Mac and Lynn emerged near an imaginary border marveling at this strange geological feature.

"Weird," Lynn replied. "On Earth, the hills would get smaller and smaller before they met prairie."

"Do you think it's natural, or did someone terraform this area?"

"I don't know. Everything about this place is strange."

That remark got Mac thinking about the gas. They needed to stop up the gas leak caused by the shuttle crash. They assumed the gas plume would be easy to see.

"Go figure," Mac said. "It's so flat you could watch your dog run away for three days, but we can't see a tower of purple gas."

They climbed the nearest hill to get a better look. Climbing a soft, grassy foothill was a pleasant change from climbing on rocks and, especially, the rubble that once was Northgate.

When they got to the top they spotted the Mac Gas leak almost immediately. If they hadn't been given this new energy, they wouldn't have bothered covering the distance. But they didn't even hesitate.

They weren't glowing as brightly as they had been, but they still had energy to burn. They ran almost the entire way. The shuttle had smashed into the side of one of the hills. The terrain was rockier here than it was in the areas leading up to it. The first hint that the mountains were emerging.

Mac and Lynn studied the area around the gas leak. The gas was going straight up and dissipating in the air like colorful pollution. They were careful about where they stepped; causing a cave-in would be counterproductive to sealing the hole.

Mac noticed that the grass closest to the gas didn't look any different from the other grass. He scooped a handful of gas onto the grass. He didn't hear any hissing, so he knew it wasn't burning the grass. In fact, now it looked greener and bigger than the grass around it.

"Check this out," said Mac.

"It's making the grass healthier," said Lynn.

"Maybe it only helps organic things."

"We are organic, remember? It still burned us."

"Then maybe it only burns foreign matter. Stuff not from Ronos."

"Do you still think we should plug the leak?"

"I don't think we need to, Lynn."

"Me either."

They turned away from the crash site and realized they were being watched. Dozens of soldiers wearing Earth military uniforms were pointing their weapons at Lynn and Mac. None of them were glowing and they all wore gas masks. Lynn had figured out the secret of surviving the gas in a matter of hours and all she had to work with was a microscope and a small burner. How could these guys not figure it out?

"What are the chances we're laser-proof?" Mac whispered to Lynn.

"Let's not find out."

A shuttle did a fly-by. The soldiers were here to take them away, but were giving the gas leak a wide birth. They weren't careful enough. A gust of wind blew purple fumes at some of the soldiers. They started screaming and running, bumping into their comrades, and creating a chaotic scene. It was the perfect distraction for Mac and Lynn to make their escape. They ran faster than any of the soldiers could. There was no way they would be caught. As they ran, they planned what they'd do when they got to the base. They wouldn't have much time now that their existence was known.

"I need to find Janelle before we leave this place. I have to know for sure why her name was on that list," said Mac as they blazed over the foothills towards the base. "But we aren't going to have much time. You know how to fly, right?"

"Yes."

"Then you go get one of the shuttles ready."

They stopped outside the base near some trees. The base was the size of a large village; the airfield Lynn needed to get to was on the far side. The only building segregated from the rest was a large building a half mile away. That's where Mac would start his search.

"Take the shuttle furthest away," said Mac.

"Okay."

"And don't leave without me."

Lynn gave him a sideways look. "Why would I leave without you?"

"Just making sure."

Mac lurked in shadows, dispatched two guards, borrowed a gun, climbed a rickety fire escape, and kicked down a door. He had found the lab. He was looking down on it from an observation platform on the second level. Only one man was working, but three others were strapped onto tables. Two of them looked like they had already expired. They had burn marks all over them. The third person wasn't awake, but Mac could see his chest rising and falling with each labored breath. He wasn't long for this world and each moment he was forced to cling to life was torture.

Elsewhere in the lab were several biohazard containers. Mac couldn't see inside them, but he guessed they were full of gas. They wouldn't be able to hold the gas for long unless it was diluted or a very small specimen. Half the lab looked like a hospital and the other half looked like a mechanic's shop. It was easy to see they were trying to weaponize the gas.

That's probably why they hadn't figured out that there was a way to survive the gas. The Lynn Rock wasn't plentiful enough for them to notice, and they were too busy trying to figure out a way to use the gas as a weapon to worry about how to survive the gas. They thought it was unbeatable. Lynn found a way to survive the gas because she was motivated to live. Focusing on destruction was costing the military time, money, and lives.

Mac found the stairs quickly and then the door to the lab. It was locked. He kicked it open and pointed his gun at the man in the lab coat.

"Where is she?" asked Mac.

"Who?" said the lab man, raising his hands into the air.

"Janelle Stewart. I need you to tell me where she is."

"I don't know anyone by that name."

Mac pointed at the only living test subject left, "You're experimenting on humans?"

"Yes."

"Did you experiment on a girl named Janelle Stewart?"

Mac brought the gun sights up to his eye so that he could make a clean shot. If this man tortured Janelle then he would die.

"What are you doing? You can't kill me."

"Tell me where she is."

The man looked frightened and frustrated, "I don't know. How many times do I have to tell you? There aren't many people on this planet, and I know all of them. There is no one here named Janelle Stewart, so just put the gun down and let's be calm about all this, okay?"

Mac took a shot at the man, deliberately missing him by inches.

"I know she is here," said Mac.

"Let me show you," said the man.

"What?"

"I'm trying to send you the information on our Imp network, but you aren't accepting it."

"I don't have an Imp."

"Can I use the computer terminal without you killing me? I'll show you everyone who is on the planet right now. Your friend isn't here."

"Okay, but keep your hands in sight," said Mac.

The researcher walked over to a computer terminal and punched in his user name and password. Once he did that, Mac didn't need him anymore. The gun he had stolen was on its lowest setting, so Mac didn't feel bad when he shot the man in the back. He slumped to the floor, and Mac stepped around him to use the terminal to search for any references to Janelle Stewart.

A video popped up on the screen.

Mac pressed play. There was a girl, who Mac recognized immediately, walking down a hallway. She was wearing the same clothes she had on the day she was taken. It didn't look like she had changed at all. That was almost five years ago, and she hadn't aged a day.

Janelle was walking down the hallway. Then she stopped. It looked like she was trying to turn around, but she couldn't get her body to work. She ended up running into the wall and falling on the floor. The video ended, but another one started.

This was an interrogation.

"What is your name?" asked the interrogator. His back was to the camera but he sounded uncomfortably familiar.

She didn't answer.

"My name is Major Raymond Tysons. I'm here to get some answers from you. Let's start with your name."

She didn't answer. She didn't even acknowledge that there was anyone in the room. She wasn't even blinking. Raymond leaned forward and snapped his fingers in front of her face. No response.

Mac knew what was coming. He had been interrogated by Raymond before.

Raymond reached across the table and punched Janelle in the face. Her head snapped back and came forward to rest on the table. She let out a quiet moan, but other than that there was no answer.

"You were on the ship that destroyed the *Capilano,* weren't you?"

Raymond stood up and walked around to her.

"There is nothing my superiors can learn without your talking, and they've given me license to do whatever I want."

He grabbed a fistful of her hair and slammed her face into the table a couple more times. Then he pulled her back so he could look into her eyes. He didn't say anything at first. He was caught off guard by the fact that there was no blood coming out of Janelle's nose.

Raymond noticed something abnormal happening to her face. He reached out and touched her. Mac could actually see his finger go through her nose. She was becoming...cloudy? That didn't make sense.

Mac paused the video and zoomed in on Janelle's face. Everything else in the room was in perfect focus, but her face was cloudy. As if part of her face was missing and the remaining pieces were trying to build something that still resembled her. Zoomed in, Mac could see Raymond's fingers going into Janelle's head like she wasn't even there.

Mac pressed play again. Raymond spoke.

"How?" Raymond asked.

Then he drew his hand back again and slapped her as hard as he could. The chair she was sitting on fell over and she fell to the floor beside the table. Mac could still see her, or at least what was left of her. She had no face. Raymond started kicking her and every time he kicked her another piece of her would disappear.

He took out his gun and shot her. There were no burn marks left behind. The laser was just absorbed into her body. At this point the kicks Raymond was delivering weren't making a connection. Janelle was breaking apart and coming back together randomly, but every time she came back together she looked less and less like a solid mass.

What was going on?

Finally she broke apart and did not come back together. Her name was on the list because they were trying to make a weapon that would destroy her. They thought she was an alien now. She was on a list of future victims. Was the girl that Mac's father found the real Janelle or an alien that looked like Janelle?

Either way, she wasn't here. And now they were trapped.

Or were they?

Mac did some more searching on the terminal and found out there was a way to escape the pull. A narrow corridor of space unaffected by the pull led away from the planet. That's how they got personnel to and from the base. If Janelle wasn't here, then it was time to go.

Mac wasn't sure the video proved they were under an alien attack. It did prove that something the antipode of normal was going on. Unless an invading army of aliens that were non-verbal, cloudy, human clones existed, Mac still wasn't prepared to believe the war was real. He needed more facts.

Lynn would already be at the ship to take them off Ronos. Mac quickly searched the computer for more information. While he searched, he heard a moan from behind him. Lab coat dude was waking up. Mac let him.

When he saw Mac using the computer terminal, he said, "Hey. You can't …."

Mac didn't feel like reasoning with the man anymore. He turned the gun up to full power, pointed it at the toxic containers in the room, and pulled the trigger.

"What are you doing? That gas will kill both of us. It burns through everyone."

"Not everyone," said Mac.

The man ran out of the room too soon to see the gas interact with Mac and add to his glow.

Hours had passed since Mac and Lynn left the cave, but their shuttle was still there, sizzling away as the gas swirled around it. The entire thing was a purple so dark it was almost black. The shuttle's structure struggled to stay together and hold everything up. But it wouldn't last forever. It couldn't last forever. The gas was relentless. Eventually the shuttle collapsed on itself until its interior was as badly burned as its exterior. Within minutes the gas punctured the fuel cell and launched it straight up into the air.

The gas reacted with the fuel, creating a shock wave that tore the ship apart and scattered some nearby rocks and boulders as far as a mile away. Milliseconds after the shock wave, an explosion threw up a giant fire ball. The remnants of the shuttle were destroyed immediately.

Just as Lynn had predicted, the explosion transformed the immediate area instantly and irreversibly. All the Lynn Rock melted into a big pool of liquefied rock.

The explosion reached the surface and tore a hole ten times bigger than the original crash created. Ten times as much gas gushed from Ronos' core.

Until now, a gas leak like that was unheard of on Ronos. To do their experiments, scientists harvested gas from a fissure near the military base that emitted only a puff of gas every ten minutes. The cloud was thin, but early explorers of the planet had still been burned by it.

This hole in the ground could not be plugged. This was not something that could be undone. The cloud expanded faster and faster. Nothing could stop it.

Mac felt the earth shake, but he didn't know what it meant. He walked outside to see what was going on. When he saw the giant cloud of gas he realized his time for poking around was coming to an end. He started running.

"Hey!"

It was the man in the lab coat. Mac saw him out of the corner of his eye, but didn't stop to chat. He needed to meet up with Lynn at the ship. He hoped she was able to get it started. The cloud was moving fast; they didn't have time to waste.

The lab coat guy didn't want to talk. He had gone for a protective suit and a weapon. He pointed the gun at Mac and pulled the trigger.

The impact of the laser spun Mac around and threw him to the ground. He looked at his shoulder. The burn on the front wasn't that big, so he imagined it took up a larger portion of his back. It smoked. The smell of his flesh burning was disgusting. The skin around the burn mark wasn't glowing as much as the rest of his body, but the gas did have healing qualities to it.

Mac was lucky he had just been exposed to the gas in the lab. The gas still in his system sensed the injury and set about to fix him. The burn had started out dull, but now it was glowing brighter than anything else on Mac.

It still hurt. He lay down on the ground while the guy in the lab coat walked up to him.

"You aren't going anywhere," he said. "If you aren't affected by the gas, then we need to do some testing on you."

"I think you have bigger things to worry about than me," said Mac.

"There is nothing more important than the survival of the human race."

"How about your own immediate survival?"

The lab coat guy just laughed thinking it was an empty threat meant to alarm him. Had he really not seen the giant purple cloud bearing down on the base?

Mac pointed toward the cloud, "I'm pretty sure I'll survive that, but I think you might get burned. I promise you, you do not want that to happen."

The scientist turned and started running for the airfield. He didn't need the situation explained to him. The planet was full of the toxic gas. It was going to destroy all foreign materials, be they skin and bones or shuttles.

The burn from the laser blast was completely healed, and Mac still had some glow left in him. He was going to need to use that to beat everyone to the airfield. It was a good thing he had Lynn waiting for him.

Mac passed the man in the lab coat easily. Other soldiers were running and Mac passed them as well. He got to the airfield just as the cloud got to the other side of the base. This cloud was dense. As it descended on the buildings, they were destroyed after only a few moments. They collapsed on themselves and then the rubble was burned away. The ashes mixed in the cloud, making it dark and easier to see.

The ship Mac had told Lynn to steal was the one farthest away from the base. He had suggested it in anticipation of a situation just like this. Everyone was running for the closest ship, which was also the biggest, leaving the farthest one wide open for them.

The ship was dead quiet. The engines weren't on and the ramp wasn't even down. Mac had a funny feeling, but he hoped that Lynn was just trying not to show their hand. When Mac boarded all she had to do was push a button and they'd be off.

He used the hand crank to manually lower the ramp so he could get in the ship. He punched the button to raise the ramp and headed to the command deck. There was no one there.

He locked the ship's doors so that no one could get inside. Panicked soldiers swarmed the landing field. Behind them, the all-encompassing purple gas cloud ate up every building it touched. It wouldn't be long before it got to the ships. Lynn had ten minutes to get there or he was going to have to leave without her. He had to protect this ship or neither of them would be able to leave.

The other small ship raced down the runway but didn't get high enough fast enough. It skimmed the gas cloud, lost control and smashed into the ground in a giant fire ball. The big ship was just starting to take off as the cloud got to the airfield. The biggest escape vessel, a ship holding hundreds of soldiers, was too big and too slow to outrun the cloud. The gas swallowed it and spat out another fireball.

The ship crashed to the ground as Mac took off in his ship. There was still a chance for Lynn as long as there was still a ship to escape with. He saw her emerge from the rubble of a building. Amid all that gas she glowed as bright as a neon sign. She wouldn't be able to hear him but he yelled at her to hurry up. Mac kept the ship low to the ground and lowered the ramp again. The expanding cloud was relentless. He kept having to move farther and farther away from Lynn.

"Run!" he yelled.

She couldn't hear him, but she saw the ramp and started running anyway. Being caught in the gas worked to her advantage. It prevented her from being permanently injured when the building she'd been in collapsed, and it gave her incredible strength and speed. Lynn was running past the burning wreckage of the big ship when the gas burned through its multiple fuel cells. A high concentration of gas generated a massive explosion. Mac had to back away. The blast tossed Lynn backwards, farther away from the shuttle. It would have killed a normal person, but Lynn flew through the air uninjured. Mac hoped she would remain that way when she plummeted to the ground, but he couldn't see her anymore.

The cloud expansion was accelerating. Mac was flying the ship backwards at an alarming speed. The explosion had acted like a catalyst for the gas. It made it stronger and faster, like it was a living thing now and eager to expand as far as it could, as fast as it could.

Where was Lynn? Mac searched where the base used to be, but he couldn't see a glowing confirmation of her existence. He couldn't leave her behind, but there was no way that he would be able to steer the shuttle into the gas to look for her. Once he was in there it would cling to the outside of the hull and wiping it off with his hands wasn't feasible. Then he remembered the one thing that the gas didn't react to. Water. He could search in the cloud for Lynn, pick her up and make a run for the ocean to wash the gas particles off and prevent them from destroying the ship. He figured he could last a few minutes at best. This was his only chance; he had to take it.

Mac changed directions and flew into the cloud. The hissing was louder than he had ever heard it before. He realized he didn't have a lot of time before the gas ate down to his fuel cell and blew him up. He might survive being in the middle of the gas, but he didn't want to risk being inside the ship when it exploded.

Warning buzzers competed with the hissing sound, and emergency lights flashed crimson. He searched the ground for a glowing body but didn't see one. The ship was being destroyed—he couldn't stay any longer.

Just as he was leaving, he thought he caught sight of a glow in his peripheral vision, but he couldn't turn around now. He needed to get to some water. The glow was moving with him. It was Lynn! If she could follow him to the water then she could escape with him.

He flew as fast as he could out of the cloud, but that didn't stop all the hissing. Something important must have been damaged; it was getting harder to control the ship. On the horizon Mac could see the ocean.

He eased the ship down and submerged it. Submerging himself in the calming blue ocean was such a relief. The hissing stopped, but Mac swore he heard water sloshing. Was the hull compromised? He wouldn't be able to stay under for long. And he wouldn't be able to wait for Lynn. She needed to be here now. He looked for her glow. The ship was right by the coast. If she was on the shoreline, he would be able to see her. The blue around him was replaced by the menacing purple. Not because the gas was mixing with the water, but because it was now spreading out over the ocean.

He wouldn't be able to surface here. He couldn't risk exposing himself to the gas anymore. He allowed the ship to be swept out to sea and farther away from Lynn. There was no other option. *I'm sorry, Lynn. I'll find Scott. Let him know what happened to you.* Mac covered his eyes with his hands. He could only afford a few seconds to grieve—he had to focus on getting off the planet.

When Mac could see blue again, he took the ship to the surface and into the sky. The shore was so far away he couldn't see it. There was no way for Mac to signal Lynn, to say he was sorry for leaving her behind. There was no way to save her. He had no choice but to leave it all behind him and move on.

Mac was trapped in orbit and trapped in his own thoughts. The pull was still there. He knew there was a corridor of space that the pull didn't affect, but he didn't know where it was. While he searched, he kept an eye on the planet.

The entire horseshoe continent that they had crashed into was now covered in the gas. It was taking a bit longer for the gas to cross over the ocean but, the water wouldn't be a safe place for long. An entire continent was overtaken by the gas. In time, the rest of the world would be too.

Mac's thoughts returned to Lynn. *She's down there somewhere. But how much longer can she survive by herself? How could I leave her behind? It's not like she was already dead. There has to be a way to rescue her.* Mac just needed a ship that wouldn't get burned by the gas. He would come back for her. Sooner, rather than later. As soon as he had some answers.

By the time he found the corridor—it was just a matter of flying away and getting pulled back over and over again until he found it—the entire planet was covered in gas. As far as he knew there were only two people that could survive in that environment: him and Lynn.

But he was wrong about that.

Chapter 17
Leader

The damage done to the ship Mac had stolen, the *Duggan*, was greater than he originally thought. The speed gauge moved like a windshield wiper because the ship kept speeding up and slowing down. The engine was damaged but he didn't know how to fix it without doing a spacewalk and he couldn't see a suit.

The trajectory of the ship wasn't taking him anywhere near Earth. Mac didn't want to go there with a stolen military ship, but he'd need to get there eventually. The corridor was leading him further away from Earth and he was too afraid to leave the safety of the corridor because he wasn't sure how long the pull lasted. He didn't want to get sucked back to Ronos and waste more time.

The events at Ronos left him completely exhausted. He put the ship on auto-pilot and fell asleep in the captain's chair. It wasn't very comfortable, but he didn't want to leave the command deck. He thought about just sprawling out on the floor, but it wasn't clean enough to rest his face on.

When he woke up several hours later, he realized the navigation computer wasn't working anymore. He had no idea where in space he was. He looked around for some kind of reference point but it was a useless exercise. There were a million stars, and Mac had no idea which was which.

The *Duggan* was still on the same course away from Ronos, so Mac knew he was further from Earth than he wanted to be. He had been traveling this same path for hours and was surely out of range of Ronos' pull. He felt it was safe to veer off, but wondered if it was really a good idea. Without a nav computer there was no way he could get back to Earth safely. He didn't even know which way it was.

He used his sensors to look at where he was in space. Maybe there would be something that stood out—a passing ship or colonized planet. Wishful thinking. He knew there weren't any colonies this far out. The best he could hope for was another secret military base. And that was a long shot.

The sensors beeped and displayed information. The screen flickered as it listed the data for Mac to read. How long were the sensors going to last? What about the life support? Even if he knew where Earth was, he didn't think the *Duggan* would make it there.

He read quickly. There was something going on further out, signs of ships in the middle of nowhere. Mac changed course and headed in that direction.

The sensors kept feeding him information. There were two ships, but they weren't fighting each other. The smaller one had docked with the larger one, most likely to transport goods. Maybe they were pirates or smugglers. He didn't care. He'd rather they were smugglers than military, but smugglers didn't usually stray this far away from civilization.

The smaller ship left. Mac followed it as best he could and remembered its path. He might need to follow it later. But first he was going back to check out the large stationary ship.

When he got closer he realized what it was. It was an alien ship. It was the same one that took Janelle all those years ago. He continued moving towards it. The alien ship didn't acknowledge his presence. It appeared derelict.

Mac felt rejuvenated. This could be the proof he needed. If this was an alien ship, and the war was real, he would be under attack him by now. Even if it was a military ship made to look like an alien ship, there would have been some kind of communication attempted already. He was dying to know to whom it really belonged.

Mac asked for permission to dock. If it was a military ship then Mac's stolen military ship should have no problem communicating with it. The ship responded, and its lower docking doors opened. The doors were adjacent to the laser cannons that Mac was now convinced had leveled an entire city—an alien ship wouldn't respond to his request to dock. This was one human-operated military ship talking to another. They had taken Janelle and done experiments on her. They changed her. What was that video he had seen on Ronos? Zinger finding a new way to kill more people? Why take her and not him? Why pretend to be aliens?

Mac guided his broken ship inside. There were no other ships in the docking bay and no people walking around. No one came to greet him. He walked down the ramp, and as he walked beside his ship he noticed a jagged, elongated hull breach. Mac could see the *Duggan's* interior from outside the ship! That by itself wasn't amazing. What was amazing was that Mac had survived in the shuttle for hours with no atmosphere. Injecting himself with the liquid rock had changed him more than he knew. He could survive without air and heat. How did he not notice this? Then he scolded himself, remembering that he didn't need to breathe when he and Lynn had swum out of the cave system on Ronos.

He decided he would explore his newfound abilities later. First he needed to find out where he was. The outside of this ship looked alien, but the inside was obviously developed by a human. It was easy for him to figure out where in the ship he was and where to go. The elevator had Earth Common words in it. That was all the evidence that he needed. This was the ship that had destroyed Northgate, and it was built by the military.

It wasn't just about finding out where he was anymore. He was inside the evidence he needed to prove to all the worlds that Earth's military was behind the deaths of millions of innocent citizens. He needed to hijack this ship, use its communications to send a message to Jace and the only man in Passage with an Imp, and then figure out a way to break the news.

Mac took a moment to slow down the barrage of thoughts and emotions roiling around inside him. His family was killed by Zinger. Everyone on Earth and its colonies was being lied to. The military couldn't be trusted. Mac had no idea how he was going to overcome all of this. It was overwhelming and for a moment there was panic and he stumbled. Unable to mentally process the truth he had just learned and the responsibility he had now taken on himself. After a couple deep breaths he started moving again and forced aside all thoughts of doubt. He laughed. *I think I just surged myself. The Luddite way.* He reminded himself that he was more than able to bring an end to all of this and that he wasn't alone. He had allies and he would get more as soon as the news about the fake war broke. There was still hope for him and the rest of humanity. Now that his surge of emotions was over he started to develop a plan. There was no way he could just fly this thing back to Earth. Someone would shoot him out of the sky. He'd do some exploring on the ship and think of something better.

He got to the command deck. It was the biggest command deck he had ever seen. There were computer terminals for three dozen people, three control consoles instead of one. Mac went to the one that was much bigger than the other two. This ship was half the size of Northgate, so the size of the command deck shouldn't have surprised him. He was surprised there were no windows. The engineers had installed giant displays on all the walls.

He brought up information from the nav computer. He was shocked at how far from Earth he was. He was on the very edge of explored space right now. There weren't many people who had been this far out before.

More information was coming to the control console. A ship was approaching. It wasn't human, at least according to the control console. Did that mean it really wasn't human or that, like the ship he was on, it was pretending to be alien? The approaching ship had a similar design to the one Mac was in.

A message appeared on all the screens. It was a countdown to *Operation: Capilano's Revenge*. Mac recognized the name, but he couldn't quite place it.

The countdown started at three minutes.

At two minutes, Mac remembered where he had heard it.

Raymond had asked Janelle about *Capilano* when he was interrogating her. The *Capilano* was a military station destroyed by the aliens.

Everything coalesced at that moment. The war was real. The ship in front of him really was an alien ship and there really was a war. What Zinger had told him was true. There was a war, but the average citizen had forgotten about it. It was happening so far away that they weren't directly affected by it, so they weren't supporting the war effort like they should have been. Zinger had destroyed Northgate using a look-a-like alien ship to unite the people and to remind everyone that was in on the conspiracy where the real power was and what he was willing to do to win. Now he was using the fake alien ship as bate to destroy a real alien ship. Even though Mac now believed him, he still thought Zinger was an insane, bloodthirsty animal for killing millions of his own people.

Mac was pretty sure that this seemingly disabled ship was about to explode and take the alien ship out with it. He needed to get out of there—the countdown was at one minute. He hit the button to open the docking bay doors and ran for the elevator.

Sixty seconds wasn't enough time to get back to the *Duggan* and fly out of there, but he had a plan. It might kill him, but he had to know the truth. The elevator doors opened. Through the open doors at the far end of the docking bay he saw the alien ship. A force field prevented all the atmosphere from leaving the docking bay, but Mac knew he could just run through it. The *Duggan* had a hull breach the entire time Mac had been in space. That meant Mac could survive space all on his own.

As he ran for the door, the ship he was on started shuddering. Leaping through the force field and into space, he couldn't help but hold his breath. The same phenomena occurred in space as they did underwater—he didn't feel the cold, and he didn't need to breathe.

The fake alien ship exploded, propelling Mac forward. The aliens must have noticed something was up, or they thought a human jumping out into space was cause for a full retreat, because their ship moved away quickly.

Their ship retreated far enough to avoid critical damage, but the explosion did eat at one side of the ship. Mac avoided the explosion's destructive path and was now floating uselessly in space. He didn't think the alien ship sustained enough damage to disable it, but it wasn't moving away. It just drifted lazily like him. And then Mac realized why.

A bright light shone on him. This was the second time in his life that had happened. The first time had been when Janelle was taken. Now it was his turn. The light carried him up into the ship, a place she never returned from.

The light was blinding. The sensation of floating in space stopped, and Mac knew he was being pulled into the ship. The light turned off and he fell. Not far. He couldn't see how it happened, but the floor had formed below him. After the camera-flash effect wore off he could see that he was in a small, well-lit room. A smooth gray box with bare walls and no windows, no doors, no light switch, no buttons—nothing at all. He was in a flawless prison. Mac ran his hands over the walls—there had to be a way to open an imbedded door or...something...but he had no luck. He sat with his back to a wall and sighed. All he could do was wait.

Suddenly a wall opened up and several life forms entered the room. Mac rubbed his eyes; he wasn't dreaming. There were humans of every color wearing casual clothes. Everyone was stone faced, but no one said a word. They were accompanied by unusual bipeds with leathery skin and big eyes. The tallest of them was still a foot shorter than the shortest human. They had woolly clothes on as if they were trying to keep warm. Next came three robotic-looking things. They moved silently—no beeps or mechanical whirring, no clanking metal noises. Their skin, or exoskeleton, or whatever they called it, was metallic yet flexible. As more people came into the room the walls expanded to accommodate the growing number of occupants. It was not meant to stay one size. The room just got bigger and bigger as needed. Mac stood in the center of it and the random creatures gathered around him.

Mac noticed an animal too, a four-legged furry creature whose tongue constantly rolled out onto the floor and then back into its mouth. It looked like a thin, sick version of an Earth dog with a disturbingly long tongue.

Mac didn't know what to say. Part of his plan was to get on the alien spaceship, but now that he was here he wasn't sure what to do. Everyone was gawking at him. The dog creature looked like it was trying to smile. Why was everyone looking at him with eager eyes? What did they want from him?

"Hello," said Mac.

Their demeanor changed at the sound of his voice. They looked at one another and then everyone left except for three humans.

One was a burly black man wearing a shirt that could barely contain all his muscles. One was a petite, brunette woman in her forties. She was wearing a plain blue dress and too much makeup. The last person was a white man in a military uniform. At six feet two inches, he still wasn't as tall as the black guy. He was thin, and his baggy uniform looked as though it was two sizes too big for him.

They looked intently at Mac, who stood still and didn't speak. They stared at him for minutes before looking at each other. Mac's best guess was that they had thought he was a friend, but when he spoke they realized he was an enemy.

They were communicating somehow, but Mac wasn't hearing anything. The big black guy was in the middle. He kept turning his head to look at the people on either side of him. The look on his face indicated he was having a spirited discussion with the older lady. She kept rolling her eyes and looking past the black man to communicate with the too-thin military man. Apparently they could not reach an agreement.

Mac wondered if it was possible for him to send messages. He looked intently at the man in the middle and thought the same thing over and over. *My name is Mac. What's yours? My name is Mac. What's yours?* After the hundredth time Mac sent this message, they all stopped communicating with each other and looked at him. He got really excited and wanted to talk but was afraid of what their reaction might be.

The big black guy looked quizzically at Mac, but Mac still couldn't hear his thoughts.

Mac tried sending a new message. *I can't hear you. What is your name?* The man got closer to Mac, but still there was no communication. The big guy was in his face and then Mac heard a message in his head.

We are who we are.

The look on Mac's face told them he got the message. This didn't make the aliens happy. They looked even more confused.

Do all of your people have this ability? asked the big black man.

Haven't you tried this with other people?

Yes.

And it's never worked?

Never.

Then I guess I am special.

The big black man smiled. He continued to talk as he slowly moved away from Mac. Now that the connection was established, they would test its range.

Let me know when you stop hearing me.

I still hear you.

Were you born with these abilities?

No.

When did you get them?

A few days ago.

The black man was taking small steps backwards and as he did the connection got weaker and weaker. The voice in Mac's head got quieter. He had to really listen if he wanted to hear what was being said to him.

It's getting hard to hear you.

But you still can?

Yes.

How did you get your abilities?

Can I ask you a question before I answer that one?

Yes.

Have your people ever attacked Earth?

No.

Why are you fighting us?

Because you are getting in the way of our purpose.

Your purpose?

The military man looked at the big black man and said something to him. Mac still couldn't hear Baggy Pants, but

CATALYST

he sensed he was issuing a reprimand. The big black man was in line with the rest of them now.

We do not talk of these things with you, said the big black man.

Am I your prisoner?

Yes.

The woman looked at Mac like she was saying something to him, but he couldn't hear her. She looked at the big black man to pass the message along.

Come with us. Our leader will want to talk to you.

They turned toward the solid wall behind them. It opened up without them touching it. Must be more mind games. Mac wondered if he could do something like that. They walked into a long hallway crowded with people walking back and forth. At first people would stop and stare at Mac. They wanted to know what was up with the new guy, but Mac couldn't answer them.

The people wandering the halls of the ship were as diverse as the people who had come in the room to look at him when he first got there. He noticed something else that was tripping him out. There were doubles of people. He walked by another big black guy just like the one he was already following. They were even wearing the same clothes. He saw three more of the older ladies and two of the military man. What was going on?

The people got tired of trying to communicate with Mac and moved on. Either that or they got a reprimand from one of the three people he was with. He couldn't hear any conversation. All he could hear were footsteps. It was strange, disturbing even, to see all these people and not hear anyone talking.

The people walked in both directions. Every once in a while one of them would stop, a door would open in the wall in front of them and they would go inside. *There must not be any real doors in this ship,* Mac thought to himself.

Then he wondered if anyone could hear him talking to himself.

They walked until the crowd thinned out and he was told to stop. Mac looked around for something that indicated they were near a door, but this part of the hallway looked exactly the same as all the other sections. The signals must have all been in their heads. Mac immediately got rid of the idea of breaking out. There was no way he would be able to get anywhere unless he figured out how to open doors with his mind.

The room they went into was the strangest thing Mac had seen on the ship. In the middle of the room there were three columns of triangular prisms, stretching from floor to ceiling. They each had a red surface that faced the middle of the triangle created by the three pillars.

The floor and walls were still gray. These guys had no imagination.

When all four of them were in the room, the door closed and the room adjusted its size so that they could all fit comfortably. Then red areas of the rectangular prisms lit up and started pulsating with power.

It was a familiar feeling. The pillars were still warming up, but the more powerful they got the more obvious it became to Mac about what was going on. Tiny particles were moving toward the center of the room. Individual particles were too small to be seen with the naked eye, but when they moved in groups they formed a visible air current. The room was full of them and they were all being pulled to the center of the pillars. The cloud was densest there.

The pull was exactly the same feeling Mac experienced on Ronos when he and Lynn stood on the ledge overlooking the machine that trapped the *Terwillegar*. That sensation, plus his ability to talk to the aliens because of the Lynn Rock injection, made Mac think that Ronos was the aliens' ultimate destination. That had to be a clue as to what they called "their purpose."

The particles formed a human being, or at least a creature in human form. Whatever it was had two arms, two legs, and one head. At that point it still wasn't dense enough to be solid.

The pillars had warmed up all the way now and were pulsating more rapidly. With every pulse the being in the middle of the pillars became more and more solid. It also became more and more familiar to Mac.

Three more pulses and there was no denying who Mac was looking at. It was Janelle. The same girl from the video he had seen on Ronos. The same girl who had been taken from him that night years before. She hadn't changed in the least, and she was still wearing the same clothes. Mac had to resist the urge to run out and touch her. He didn't know why or how they did this, but he knew it couldn't be the real Janelle Stewart.

Janelle opened her eyes and looked at Mac. For a precious moment it looked like she recognized him. Was it possible? Then she looked away to the other people that were in the room. They communicated, but Mac didn't know what they were saying. Then he heard a feminine voice in his head. It wasn't Janelle's voice, but the alien that looked like her was staring at him. That confirmed for him that Janelle wasn't in the room. This was just someone pretending to be her.

They tell me that you can understand me. Is this true?

Yes, said Mac in his head.

Mac was surprised that he could communicate. They were across the room from each other. The big black man had to stand nose to nose to establish a connection with Mac, but that was not the case with the Janelle impostor. She must have gained more power or experience than the others. That's why she was the leader.

I feel a strong connection to you. I have met several humans before, but never one like you.

I'm told I am special.

It's more than that. I can see that you are more than human now, but there is something I feel coming from my human emulator. It's...familiarity. Do you recognize me?

Yes. I was there when you took her.

Not me. I didn't take her. I'm just using her, like so many others are. An emulator like her is sought after. Only the important ones get to use her.

She briefly broke apart and swirled about the room. The pulsing from the pillars became intense and she was brought back together. Mac recalled seeing similar transformations in the video he's seen on Ronos.

Are you dying? asked Mac.

We can't die. We can only move on.

That wasn't good news.

Move on to where?

To the place that made you special.

Ronos.

And you want me to take you there? asked Mac.

No. We know where it is. We have felt its pull for millennia. We have been journeying to it all this time.

This is all your people? You fit on one ship.

We lead the people. We are without number. Our ships will flood your space.

She looked away from Mac and communicated with the other three people in the room. They left. The room got smaller. Now that he knew they couldn't be killed, he understood why she wasn't afraid to be alone with him. He supposed she just wanted some privacy.

While the people were leaving the room she broke apart and had to come back together. He wondered if it wasn't so much that they couldn't die, but that they would reach a certain point when they couldn't come back together. She probably couldn't last long as a solid substance like the others, and she obviously needed help to take form.

When she came back together Mac couldn't help but take a few steps toward her. It looked just like Janelle. Just like he remembered. All this time he had conserved her image and everything else he could remember about her. He didn't want to forget.

Where is she? asked Mac.

Who?

"Janelle. Where is Janelle?"

Mac said the words out loud and a transformation occurred in the alien. Her eyes got wide, she stumbled forward, and then fell to her knees.

"Mac." Her voice was raspy and buzzed when the particles didn't stay completely solid. But it was her voice. Not the voice that had spoken to him in his head. It was the voice of the girl he had kissed. The girl he'd spent years searching for. He had found her. Kind of.

"Where are you?" Mac asked.

He rushed forward to embrace her, but as soon he touched her she broke apart and he had to wait for her to take form again. Inside the triangle, the pulsing created an unsettling feeling, like his insides were being pulled together. Immediately he stepped away.

"I don't have long," Janelle said when she took form again. "This alien is very old and weak. That's why I can take control. But they don't know I can do this. Someone is probably already on their way."

'Where is your real body?" asked Mac. "I'll come get you."

"You can't. I'm not on your ship."

"I can still come find you."

"No! Listen to me. You have something more important to worry about," said Janelle. "These things must not get to where they are going. You have to stop them."

"Why? I don't understand."

"All you've seen is one ship, but my real body is back with the fleet. The ships in the fleet number in the millions, maybe hundreds of millions. They'll say they won't hurt you, but it's a lie. They will go right through the humans to get what they want. They've done it to countless civilizations before us. They use us to create prototypes—emulators—that they can produce copies of. Then they use the copies to help them get to their destination."

"I know where they are going."

"Then you have to stop them from getting there."

"How do I kill them?"

"You can't kill them, not them exactly. I'm not even sure how they're alive. But you can kill their emulator bodies. Start by destroying the particle organizers in this room. "

"But...I've finally found you. I can't just leave."

"There are more important things than you and me. First, stop them. Then come for me."

She started convulsing. As she convulsed she got fuzzy. The little pieces of her were breaking apart and she was screaming. He could hear it with his ears and in his head. Janelle was losing control again.

"I'm sorry," said Mac. "I'm sorry it took so long to find you. I'm sorry they took you and not me."

"There is still a chance... Please..."

But then she was gone. Her impostor stood up straight, and looking at Mac with death in her eyes, said, *How did you do that?*

"I don't know."

You can't win. We are too many. There is nothing you can do to stop us, let alone escape.

Mac refused to use their way to communicate.

"That doesn't mean I'm going to stop trying."

He brought his leg back and then put his foot through one of the pillars. Fake Janelle screamed in his head and then vanished into dusty existence. He felt buzzing all around him and his vision got murky. Was she trying to attack him? It wasn't working.

The pillar snapped in half. The top half fell onto one of the other pillars and he destroyed the last one easily. Then all the buzzing stopped. The weak alien couldn't hold herself together without help. She dispersed into nothing. Existing only in millions of invisible parts, unable to do anything but exist.

Chapter 18
Swarm

Mac searched through the broken pieces of pillar for a suitable weapon. Janelle had said all he needed to do was kill the emulator bodies. He found a long piece with a sharp end he could use for stabbing. He gripped the blunt end and made a few practice thrusts. Now that he was ready to take on a ship full of aliens, he realized he still didn't know how to open a door. He wasn't even sure he knew which wall he had walked through before.

Willing to try anything, he walked up to one of the four walls and thought orders at it.

Open.

Nothing.

Open.

Nothing.

Please open.

Nothing.

Open Sesame?

Nothing. Mac was almost glad that last one hadn't worked.

He didn't give up. It took a while to connect with the big black man, but he did. Mac moved closer to the wall and thought the same thing over and over. *Open. Open.* He didn't worry about how long it was taking or about someone coming into the room to see how things were going. All he did was focus his energy on trying to open a door.

And then it happened. The door opened into the familiar crowded hallway. The military man was waiting for him. Or at least one of the military men was. There was no way to tell if it was the same guy.

Whoever he was, he looked over Mac's shoulder and saw the destroyed pillars. Mac used this as an opportunity to strike. He stabbed with his jagged piece of thick glass. It slid easily into the man's stomach. Too easily. The man just looked at Mac and smiled. He stepped away and the glass slid out of him. The hole it had made in his torso was there for only a second before it disappeared. The alien and his emulator were unhurt.

Mac attacked again. This time he sliced at the head in an attempt to disconnect it from the neck. The glass slid through harmlessly. The military man smiled and then vanished in a cloud of particles. The alien was doing the same thing that the fake Janelle had tried: turning into a cloud and flying through Mac's body. Maybe it hurt other humans, but it did nothing to Mac. It didn't even tickle him. He looked human so they were trying to kill him like a human and it wasn't working.

He could feel the alien rushing into his esophagus in an effort to cut off the airway, but Mac didn't breathe anymore so it did nothing. He decided to let the alien keep trying as he ran down the hallway to find a way out.

The hallway was still packed with people. Everyone stared at him as he ran. It was another thing he noticed about these aliens; no one was ever in a hurry to get anywhere. Some people turned and followed him, but no one chased after him except for the cloud of the military guy that was trying to attack him.

The hallway ended. Mac looked at it and thought, *open*, over and over again, but nothing happened. It was because he couldn't focus. When he looked back the way he had come he saw that everyone was looking at him. Everyone in the hallway as far back as he could see. Maybe they were trying to communicate with him, but that was pointless. Then Mac heard the voice of the big black man from before.

There is no escape.

There were five of those big black guys, and no way to tell which one it came from. They were all looking at him intently. Mac was worried and chilled at the same time. He was sure that one-on-one the aliens couldn't hurt him, but he wasn't sure what would happen if all the people in the hallway charged at him.

And that's exactly what happened.

The beings furthest away started first. They transformed into a particle cloud and then shot toward Mac. Everyone they passed changed into a cloud and soon there were no solid beings left. The aliens all left their simulated solid state to charge at the interloper.

Mac was consumed by his attackers. They had complete control over him. Hundreds of them were flying in and out of his body, trying to tear him apart from the inside out. When that didn't work they had to settle for lifting him off the ground and slamming him into walls.

The air was so thick with them that Mac couldn't see anything. They were tossing him around so much that he couldn't even tell which way was up. When they slammed him into things he only had one clear thought. *It doesn't hurt.* The aliens could do nothing to hurt him.

What happened next was so fast and unexpected that Mac wasn't sure it was really happening.

The wall at the end of the hall exploded. The force of the explosion momentarily freed him from the misty onslaught. The cloud was thrown down the hall by the shockwave. Some of the aliens returned to their solid state to prevent their essence from getting too far away.

The explosion caused an opening at the end of the hall. Soldiers streamed through the hole. Human soldiers. The military was making an attack. They stormed in, firing their lasers at anything that moved. Mac was in the line of fire. He got on the floor and shouted.

"Don't shoot! Don't shoot! I'm human! I'm one of you!"

One soldier kicked him over and pointed a gun in his face.

"Don't shoot!" said Mac.

"I'm not going to shoot. We need to get you out of here."

"I'm a soldier."

"Doesn't matter. Come with me before a swarm gets you."

Screams echoed down the hallway as soldiers writhed on the ground. All the aliens returned to their cloud forms—what the soldiers called "swarms"—and attacked. The human soldiers were being torn apart. The attacks that hadn't worked on Mac were easily subduing the soldiers.

They fired their weapons, but to no avail. What good were lasers as weapons? There was no way they could destroy enough of the swarm's little buzzing particles to do any damage. They couldn't even say with certainty that the parts they were hitting were actually being destroyed. It was a hopeless endeavor. Soldiers that weren't being torn apart were being physically carried further into the ship. Doors opened and men disappeared, screaming.

There was one positive. The lasers were destroying the ship. They cut through the walls so easily that there was no need to be able to communicate with the ship through your mind.

"Use your grenades!" yelled one lieutenant before a swarm descended on him and tore him to bits.

Three soldiers threw grenades.

"Come on," said the soldier that had come to Mac. He grabbed Mac by the arm and pulled him to his feet just as the grenades went off. The force of the grenades scattered the clouds. There was at least one soldier who was fooled into thinking that it worked.

"We did it!"

He was the first one to die when the clouds came back together. The gun he had been holding clattered to the floor and slid to Mac's feet. Mac pulled out of the grip of his rescuer. He picked up the gun and started running and shooting at the wall.

"Where are you going?" asked a soldier.

"Get everyone back on the ship! There's nothing you guys can do," said Mac.

He kept opening up rooms with the gun. Most of them just had more swarms inside. They attacked as soon as they saw him, but couldn't harm him. The soldiers saw the attacks and didn't know what to think of it.

Mac didn't know where the emulators were, but he had to find out. If it was the only way to defeat the alien swarms, then he had to figure it out before he left the ship. And he had to do it quickly or there would be no soldiers left. Their lives were now in his hands.

Fortunately multiple swarms were following him. That would relieve the soldiers a bit. Hopefully they had better weapons besides lasers and grenades.

Halfway down the hallway, Mac found stairs leading down. The cloud started attacking him even more intensely so he knew there was something important down there. The intensity of the attack did nothing to stop him. If anything, it motivated him to move faster. He jumped down the stairs. At the bottom he shot out the wall, revealing a bigger room inside. Instantly he knew he was where he wanted to be.

Dozens of bodies were suspended in the air. They were all floating above a bright blue light that pulsed slowly. Above them was a display, but the language was one he did not recognize.

From up the stairs Mac could hear more explosions and more screaming. Things didn't sound like they were going well. Mac walked up to the first human body he could find. It was the big black man. He was wearing the same clothes as all the other ones. Was this just another alien? He reached to touch the body floating in the air. It didn't feel like the other aliens. It felt like real flesh and blood. Was this an actual person? Was he alive?

When he walked on to the blue area on the floor, his body lifted off the ground just like all the others. He was still able to put his fingers against the man's neck to feel for a pulse. There was none. These people weren't alive.

But Janelle had talked to him, and she had been emulated. He guessed that the beings in this room were emulators—copies of the real people. Janelle and the others must still be alive somewhere else. At least he hoped so.

One shot with his gun was enough to completely blow apart the man floating in the air. A second shot at the blue light below him destroyed the suspension and brought Mac back to ground level.

Even with just the big black man's emulator gone, Mac could feel a difference in the swarm that was buzzing around him. There must have been a few of his clones in there that, having lost their base, drifted into nothing. They couldn't even stay in cloud form without an emulator.

It was a free-for-all now. Mac ran around the room shooting each of the free-floating bodies. There was a shout of victory from above each time he did. Some soldiers had gathered at the top of the stairs to cheer him on. There were dozens of emulators but his weapon was more than capable of taking care of them. The cloud around him thinned out and eventually disappeared.

Just as he took care of the last one—the sick-looking dog with a too long tongue—the soldiers started coming down the stairs. They had to know by now that he wasn't one of the bad guys, but that didn't stop the lead soldier from pointing his gun at Mac and yelling orders.

"Put down the gun and put your hands in the air!"

Mac did as he was told. It didn't matter. He was going to the same place they were anyway. Besides, this was just a soldier following orders. Mac had no reason to assume the worst of him.

They grabbed his gun and bound his hands. There were two soldiers on either side of him as he was led up the stairs and down the hallway. Nothing remained of the swarms. When Mac destroyed the emulators, everything disappeared. The bloody remains of human soldiers were the only things left in the hallway. Some soldiers were not disfigured. These must have been the ones that died from obstructed windpipes. Others had more horrific deaths—the enemy tore them apart from the inside out.

Soldiers were busy collecting the remains of their fallen comrades. Others were trying to figure out a way to fly the ship so they could take it to Earth.

"The only way to open one of the doors is to shoot it open. We are going to have to just tow it back."

"That will take forever."

"We can't go fast or it'll break off."

"We'll reinforce it."

"Let's just scuttle this one. Send a message."

"You idiot. We need to take it and study it."

"After what happened on Earth, we need a victory."

Mac was on the human ship now. It was strange how similar the two ships were. The aliens and the humans were both using military ships and neither of them put much thought into making them look nice. The alien's ship was the same dull, metallic gray throughout. The only other color he saw was the red on the pillars and the bright blue light under the emulators. The human's military ships displayed a little creativity. They had different shades of gray and much more lighting. Also, the maroon and dark blue military crest was painted onto the wall every so often. As Mac was escorted through the ship he noticed the hallways just had metal tiles, but some of the rooms were painted the same dark blue that was in the military crest.

He wondered which capital ship he was on, who the captain was. He hoped it was someone sympathetic to his cause—he was a deserter, after all. Mac didn't like his chances of getting off easy.

Mac wondered how much information these front-line soldiers were given. Did they know the truth about what happened back on Earth? Did they even have an inkling? Some of them had to know something was up. They used the fake alien ship as a trap. Where did they think it came from? Did they think its only purpose was what they were told? These men were fighting for the right reasons and they were fighting the right people, unlike Zinger, who chose to blow up an entire city to unite humanity. Mac had a good feeling about these front-line soldiers.

"How long have you been out here?" asked Mac.

"Three years," said one of his escorts.

"Did you hear about Northgate?"

"Yes."

"Did you hear who did it?"

"What are you talking about? Is there doubt about who did it?"

Another soldier piped up, "No talking to the prisoner until the general talks to him."

"Zinger is here?" asked Mac.

"*General* Zinger will talk to you via vid link."

"I don't have an Imp."

"Then we'll set up a terminal."

Mac hoped they would stick around to hear the conversation—Zinger wasn't calling just to catch up. They were about to get a new perspective on the orders they were following. They walked Mac to a large room with a computer terminal. The three men then stood behind the computer terminal with their guns pointed at him. Standard procedure.

"He's going to say something that you guys aren't going to believe," said Mac.

"What?"

"I'm going to tell him the room is empty, and then we are going to talk about things that will be hard to accept, but it's information you *need* to hear."

The three soldiers looked at each other. No one was sure what to say.

The vid link opened up. Zinger's massive form was sitting behind a polished desk in a lavishly decorated room. His back-up office, apparently. The general didn't look so hot. His face was blotchy and his left arm was bandaged. His left eye was bloodshot. Whatever safety measures he had initiated saved him from perishing as his yacht crashed into the ocean, but he didn't get away completely unscathed. The fact that he was still alive was impressive.

"Hey, Zinger. Where are you? That can't be the office on your yacht."

"I was monitoring the video feed coming from my soldiers during the attack on the alien ship." Zinger indicated the wall of screens behind him. Mac looked to see if the feed of the three soldiers in the room was up there too, but he couldn't see it.

"Did you think I died on Ronos with the rest of them?"

"Ronos?"

"We went there. Right after we sunk your yacht. We found your base and we destroyed it. By accident, of course, but we still destroyed it."

"Of course," Zinger leaned back in his seat. "Is that where you gained your new abilities? Did you find something on Ronos that made you invincible to alien attacks?"

"That's not all I found there," said Mac.

He thought back to the cave. To the large broken disk that was the source of the pull. It was alien technology, and it was where the alien menace meant to go. Janelle had said not to let them get there, that they would kill everyone.

"Where is Lynn, by the way? I haven't seen her yet," asked Zinger.

Lynn. Trapped on Ronos. How was Mac going to get her back? There had to be a way to build a ship that could get to her. But all foreign material would get burned by the gas. Maybe a heavily armed shuttle could land there. Mac wasn't sure. If the cloud was still highly concentrated, then nothing could set safely in and out.

Once again, Mac regretted leaving Lynn behind. There had to be more he could do. There had to be something he wasn't thinking of.

Mac.

"What?" asked Mac.

"I asked where Lynn was. She's not dead, is she?" Zinger seemed genuinely concerned.

Mac, can you hear me? It was a voice in his head. It was Lynn's voice.

"Lynn?" asked Mac.

"Yes, Lynn. Where is she?"

Use your mind to communicate with me. Project your thoughts while thinking about me.

It was just like communicating with the swarms.

Lynn? Can you hear me?

Yes.

Are you on this ship?

No, I'm still on Ronos.

Mac was shocked. That was impossible. Talking in your mind was a lot like talking with an Imp, but an Imp couldn't transmit further than from one side of Earth to the other. Lynn was light years away. It wasn't possible.

"What's the matter with you?" asked Zinger.

"She's dead," said Mac.

"What?"

"They are all dead. Lynn, Raymond, everyone posted on Ronos. I was the only one who got away."

I ran into some aliens after I left you. They tried to kill me, but they couldn't. I'm not affected by their attacks but other humans are.

The war is real?

Yes. But I know how to win it. We have to bring people to Ronos. Is there any way to get a ship down there?

I don't know.

Is there a spot where the cloud isn't as thick?

I don't know. I'll have to look around. The gas is lighter than air so the thickest parts are in the upper atmosphere.

We'll think of a way.

"Are you listening to me, Mac Narrad?" asked Zinger.

"No."

"Listen here…"

"I found your ship," Mac said.

"What ship?"

"The ship you used to attack Northgate. Your fake alien ship."

"We were using it to lure other alien ships to it and then blow it up. It didn't work out as well as we'd hoped, so we had to send in the troops as well. That seldom works out for us. Good thing you were there."

"Why did you kill all those people?" asked Mac.

"In Northgate? Had to be done. People were losing focus on what really mattered. The war was not being supported."

"That's not the way to gain support. There were better options."

"Do you think killing millions of people was my first choice? Do you really think I wanted to do that? We had to put up the information barrier between the front and the rest of the galaxy because when the swarms took our soldiers they learned everything the soldiers knew. We had to control our intelligence, so no reporters were allowed at the front. We didn't issue updates on the war because that information would be intercepted by the enemy."

"You could have faked it," said Mac.

"Don't be an idiot. Of course we faked it. We filmed fake battles and sent vid feeds to the media, but people still didn't care. Beyond moral support we needed supplies, fuel, spare parts, food, ammunition—you name it—on the front line, but no one cared because we couldn't tell them what was happening. People stopped living like there was a war going on. The only thing we could do was bring the war to them, and that left us with two choices. We could either let the enemy through the line or we could do it ourselves. We made the right choice. It was our only choice," said Zinger.

"Your weapons don't even work against the swarms. They can walk right through you at any point," said Mac.

"You're wrong again. Our weapons have minimal effect on the actual aliens, but we've been blowing their ships to pieces for years. They keep coming, and we keep fighting. We have no other choice. Plus, now we have you. You can get to them without being hurt. We can use that."

"I'm not fighting for you."

"Then fight for the survival of the human race," Zinger said.

"Not like this, and not for you. I'm not going to sacrifice people for a plan that can't work. You can't hold them off forever. There are more coming and more behind them. They will overwhelm us and kill us all."

Mac remembered what Janelle had said about there being millions of them.

"That's why we need you," said Zinger. "Don't act like you're so much better than me. We both made the same choices to get here. We've lied, cheated, murdered, and stolen to get here. Are you telling me Raymond died of natural causes? I have money on you as his cause of death."

"Raymond was a serial screw-up. His choices killed him."

"Justification. I also killed millions of people for good reason. My work on Northgate will help us win this war more than your killing Raymond will. You think you have some kind of moral high ground, but the truth is that you are so high on yourself and your morals that you don't understand we have to do everything we can to win this war. What's moral about sitting back and expediting the extinction of the human race? The attack on Northgate was absolutely necessary."

"You're wrong," said Mac.

"No. And it's only a matter of time before you realize that. This isn't the front line! This is a trap we set up away from the front line. If you want to see the real war, I'll gladly take you there. Then you'll see the destruction, how fast we're losing ground. One hour on the front line and you will see the wisdom of my decisions. You'll throw your morals right out the window and do everything you can to stop the invasion."

"If we have to lose our humanity to win this war, then we've already lost."

Zinger rolled his eyes. "This is the only way."

"No. I have a plan," said Mac.

"Didn't you hear what I said? I'm ordering this ship to go to the front line. Then you will see the truth, the reality of the situation. There can be no peaceful end to this conflict. While you are fighting for us on the front, I'll be at Ronos trying to figure out how to become invincible like you. We will go easy on you at your court martial if you'll tell me how you made yourself immune to the enemy's attacks."

Mac no longer gasped or felt as though ice flowed through his veins when he heard something disturbing. The

Lynn Rock had also turned him into the ultimate bluffer. When he heard Zinger talk about military personnel going to Ronos to turn themselves into weapons, Mac instantly knew that was a bad idea, and for several reasons. First, the changes were likely permanent and they affected every part of his body. Mac wasn't convinced he would ever be normal again.

That led to the second reason: unlimited power. Mac gained abilities that far exceeded his imagination. He shuddered at the thought of Zinger and his goons having the same powers. They would win the war, but they would simply replace the alien swarms with corrupt superpowers. Raymond with the power of Ronos would be more devastating than a billion aliens. He'd be unstoppable. Even his superiors would be unable to convince him to behave himself.

Zinger would get to Ronos before Mac could. He was closer and knew its exact location. At least the general didn't know how to get past the gas. That was the only thing Mac had going for him.

"You can't be trusted with that information," said Mac.

"You're placing your morals above everything else. It's people like you that will cause us to lose this war."

Zinger finished talking and then switched off the link.

I have a feeling I'm about to be thrown in the brig. We can talk more when I'm alone, said Mac.

Gotcha, said Lynn.

When he was alone he would ask Lynn where she learned to mind speak and then he would ask what kept her from keeping to the plan on Ronos. What was she doing instead of prepping the ship like she was supposed to?

Mac looked up at the three soldiers that Zinger didn't know were in the room. None of them had their guns aimed at him anymore.

"Please tell me that one of you is the captain."

"No," said the one in the middle. "But I did record that entire conversation."

All three of them were getting instructions over their Imps.

"We've changed course. Some soldiers are being left on the swarm ship to see if they can salvage anything. The rest of us are to prepare to defend the front line. General Zinger has more pull than General Roy."

"Told you," said one of the other soldiers.

Mac didn't know who General Roy was. Since he'd never heard of him, he was probably the ranking officer at the front. Mac didn't know any of the top people out here. It was all part of the secret.

"What are you supposed to do with me?" Mac asked.

"We are supposed to leave you here as a prisoner," said the shortest of the three.

"But we can't do that." said the guy in the middle.

"Why?" asked Mac.

"Because we are going to the front line. Chances are we'll die. Don't look at me like that. You know it's true. The best chance we have is to have you there fighting with us. We'll find you a uniform so you fit in."

"I don't have an Imp," said Mac.

"We'll fill you in," the soldier put out his hand. "My name is Nelson, this is Ryan, and this is Cliff. Until we have time to pass this message along, we'll protect you. But right now this message will just freak everyone out when we need to be focused on fighting."

"How long are we going to be at the front?"

"We won't know until we get there."

"But we might not be there for the entire campaign. After what Zinger said, I think he just wants you to get a sense of it," said Cliff.

Ryan said, "Let's hope that's all Zinger wants. I've heard about people getting sent to the front line just to get them out of the General's hair."

"Possible, but either way, Mac needs a uniform so he won't stick out. Then we'll go see what's what," said Nelson.

Nelson came back a few minutes later, alone. The fatigues he brought with him were close enough to Mac's size that no one would notice. Eventually someone would come to the room to talk to the prisoner, but they would have to worry about that later.

"What's your assignment in the upcoming battle?" asked Mac.

"I'm a gunner, but I'm going to try to shuttle you to a swarm ship. You are your own weapon. If they can't hurt you, then we need you over there to destroy their ships."

"Is your captain going to be okay with that?"

"No."

"What if we talked with him? Showed him what we knew?

"We will, but now is not the time. When we're at the front, the captain won't have time to listen to us. We need to focus on surviving so we can have that conversation."

Nelson led Mac to a wide walkway. He walked fast, and Mac had to really move to keep up. There was a general feeling of tension coming from everyone they passed. All the soldiers had stone faces and they moved quickly to where they were supposed to be.

"I don't need you to come with me," said Mac.

"I'll fly the shuttle. It's no big deal. Are you a pilot?" said Nelson.

"Yes, but that's not the point. You just need to point me to the nearest exit and I'll be fine."

"What?"

"Just trust me."

Chapter 19
There Will Be More

Dozens of soldiers jogged to the weapons station, a two-level room with one floor-to-ceiling window. On both levels, individual weapons stations formed a row the length of the window. Mac and Nelson stopped at a weapons station halfway across the room on the upper level.

The station was designed for one person, so Mac stood by while Nelson operated it. The controls only responded to the touch of the person standing on the weapons pad. Standing on the pad enabled Nelson's Imp to access the ship's weapons systems. The Imp's heads-up display interacted with the see-through touch screen. In battle, he used the Imp targeting system and fired by touching the screen.

Mac had been trained to use these kinds of weapons but had never had a chance to use one in an actual battle before. There weren't many capital ships on the Earth side of the war. At least fifty soldiers fired from the weapons pads in this room. Hundreds more were manned all over the ship.

"These pads weren't here before. When the war started we didn't realize that throwing soldiers at the enemy wasn't going to accomplish anything. Before you came along there was no way we could hurt them. They mowed us down every time," said Nelson.

"I didn't actually kill any of them, I just took away the bodies they were using," said Mac.

"That sounds a lot like killing them to me."

"If you guys know you can't kill them, why did you storm that last ship? Didn't you know you were just going there to die?"

"Yeah, we did. The military gave us new weapons, but none except the most naive thought they would work. We had them go first, of course."

"Why were you sent there? Why even try?"

"They wanted a swarm ship so that they could set another trap. We have never caught one of their ships before. Catching one meant we could learn more about them. We never would have learned how to defeat them without you."

Mac would let him know later that destroying the emulators didn't mean the aliens were dead. They were made up of billions of little particles. Even now the swarms were still on the ship they had caught. They were just all broken up and spread out.

"We're almost there," said Nelson. "Can you see them?"

Nelson obviously had some visual enhancements with his Imp's targeting system. All Mac could see were distant flashes. The battle must have already started.

The closer they got the more Mac realized it wasn't like any battle he had seen before. At least twelve beetle-shaped alien ships were in a single file formation.

"Good, not as many as I thought," said Nelson. "We have as many ships as they have. We're usually outnumbered two to one."

The human capital ships were shaped like footballs, but their surfaces were far from smooth. A command deck protruded from the top of each ship, and weapons ports formed a dotted line all way round the long oval vessels. The main docking bay was underneath the ship, near the back. Adjacent to them were the smaller airlock doors for shuttle docking.

The military concentrated its attack on the front beetle ship. Lasers rained down on it, blackening its gray shell. Just when Mac was sure the ship couldn't take much more of a beating, thin metal arms came out of the beetle ship and reached for its attackers.

All twelve of the ships broke from their single file position, deployed similar arms and reached for the nearest military ship. No weapons were ever fired from the alien ships.

"Is this how they attack?" asked Mac.

"Yeah. These are the only types of ships we've seen in five years of war, and this is how they attack."

"They never fire any shots?"

"Never. They just…collect us."

Mac's confusion was short-lived. He watched the first beetle latch onto a capital ship and pull it up until the beetle appeared to be resting on top of it. More arms came down to crack the ship open. Lights shone down and soldiers got sucked out of the ship.

Collectors was an appropriate name for the beetle ships; they needed more fodder for the emulators. Three more collector ships latched onto capital ships.

"I heard we could destroy their ships," said Mac. "It looks like we're getting owned out there."

"Our ships stop functioning as soon as we get under their control. There is something in those arms and lights that jams our technology. We have to take them out before they get to us or…"

BOOM! The first capital ship that had been collected exploded, sacrificing everyone on board in order to destroy the beetle. Its shell split in two, and bodies blasted through space. Mac wondered if the swarms could survive space like he could.

"If the ships stop working, how do you rig them to blow up after they get caught?"

"We have a shuttle hovering in the docking bay. As long as it's not touching anything, it's not affected. When we get caught, the shuttle fires at an explosives cache, destroying the ship."

"All of our ships have this?"

"Yes."

"If we get caught, I can save us. Can you message the docking bay soldiers and tell them to hold off? Do you have any pull?" asked Mac.

"We were already planning on stopping our ship from self-destructing, but only if you can make sure we don't get collected. Cliff is one of the guys in the shuttle. He is supposed to take care of that. Are you sure you can do your part?" asked Nelson.

"Yes."

The ship Mac was on, the *Skyrattler*, was now in range to fire its weapons. Nelson's hands flew across the display in front of him as he struck out at one of the alien ships that hadn't yet attached itself to a military ship. Two others were destroyed when the human's ships blew themselves up.

Mac figured the aliens were not the best fighters. If they had anything resembling a real weapon, humans would be totally at their mercy. The barrage of laser fire from the *Skyrattler* didn't seem to be doing much damage to their hull.

"Try aiming for the arms!" said Mac.

"What do you think I'm doing?"

There was no way for Mac to be able to tell which laser blasts were Nelson's. More soldiers focused their fire power away from the hull and on the collector's arms. One arm broke off from the beetle they were attacking. It must have been an important one, because the aliens stopped their ship and started moving backwards. The captain ordered them to pursue and destroy. The *Skyrattler* descended to attack the ship's belly. That was the collector ships' weak spot. Relative weak spot. They still couldn't destroy any of the collectors without sacrificing a capital ship of their own.

More arms shot out to catch them. Skinny and constantly moving, the arms were difficult targets. Nelson and his crewmates responded to the challenge and destroyed two more arms.

"We aren't going to make it," said Nelson.

"What are you talking about? How many arms do they have?"

"It's not an arm thing. It's a light thing. Once we get pulled in by the light, all ship functions will shut down. I've already sent a message to Cliff to ignore the self-destruct order. Whatever your plan is, you better get ready to jump over there and take care of things."

"Where is the closest airlock?"

"Go through the door at the end of the walkway, past the escape pods. Good luck."

"Thanks."

Mac started running down the walkway. Some crew members sneered and shouted insults at Mac for running for the escape pods. They thought he was abandoning ship. *You're part right. But I'm going to the enemy. I'm not running for it.* As he ran past the escape pods he noticed some had already been deployed. He even saw a terrified young soldier climb inside one of them and take off.

Mac got to the airlock. He opened the first door and waited for it to close all the way. A long hiss confirmed the seal was made. Mac cussed when he looked out the window—he was on the wrong side of the ship. He got a firm grip on a handhold before he hit the button to open the door. It wouldn't do any good to get sucked out into space flying in the wrong direction.

The door opened. Mac should have felt the air burn in his lungs or the freezing cold of space. He felt neither.

The outside of the ship was knobby and made for easy climbing. The only things he really had to look out for were the laser cannons. He pulled himself around the curve of the ship until he saw the beetle ship looming above him. Its arms whipped around in space, trying to get close to the ship. They made an electric humming noise that complemented the faint white noise always present in the emptiness of space. The humming was interrupted by the concussion of the laser cannons, the high-pitched tones of the lasers traveling through space, and the thundering explosions as they hit their target.

One arm waited for a pause in between laser rounds and then struck fast, slamming into the *Skyrattler*. The end of the arm looked like a mechanical hand with only three fingers. Each finger was twice the size of Mac. When it slammed into the ship, its prongs were so heavy and had so much power behind them that they easily punched through the hull. The prongs spread out inside the ship so that when the arm retracted it wouldn't slip through the hole.

When the arm breached the hull, Mac almost lost his grip. The worst thing he could imagine was floating out into space. Now that he didn't need to eat, drink, or breathe to survive, he feared he would just float through space forever.

Lights flickered to life on the underbelly of the collector ship. The lights made Mac's hair stand straight up, just like when Janelle had been taken. The light and arms worked together to bring the ship in.

Soldiers aimed laser blasts at the arm holding them captive, but by the time they broke that arm three others had punched through. The *Skyrattler* was close enough to the light for it to drain them of all power. The laser blasts stopped. They were completely defenseless.

Mac let go of his ship. The light caught him immediately and pulled him toward the aliens. As he floated up he passed two thin metal arms heading down. They had laser cutters that started burning through the hull of the *Skyrattler*. Just as Mac got up to the ship, the *Skyrattler*'s hull opened and crew members were collected.

He got inside the ship, but kept moving up. The room he entered was huge. It looked like an enormous, bottomless swimming pool with no water in it. It was nothing like the perfectly smooth room he had been pulled into last time. It must have been because this was where prisoners were gathered. Last time he was pulled in they thought he was one of them. Dozens of aliens, standing behind a railing around the opening, watched him. Mac had seen so many duplicates on the last ship that he expected to see at least one version of the big black man he had seen before, but no. These were all new emulator bodies, and most of them wore Earth military uniforms.

There was no way for Mac to get to the edge of the large, open area he was floating in the middle of. He knew speaking would give him away, so he used mind speak instead.

Help me! Pull me in!

No one did anything right away.

I'm one of you.

One of the military men looked at Mac.

How did you get on that ship?

I was captured.

I do not recognize your emulator.

It's new. I don't like it, but there was an emergency. My old one was destroyed, and this was the closest one I could use.

That must have been an acceptable excuse. The military man looked up at the ceiling and an arm came down, grabbed Mac around the waist and moved him out of the light and to where he could stand near the railing.

Thank you, said Mac.

Everyone was turning their attention back to the middle of the room. Soldiers were floating out there now. They were yelling at their captors. There must have been some force field keeping the atmosphere in the room despite the fact that the floor led out to space. Mac let them float. They would be safe there—as long as Cliff didn't blow up the *Skyrattler.*

Mac wasn't sure how to leave this room. He needed to go find the emulators. That was the only way he could take over the ship, but he didn't want to reveal himself as an impostor. This ship was exactly like the other alien ship that Mac was just on. The walls were smooth, and no doors could be seen. He needed to see someone use a door before he could start racing through the ship.

Some of the soldiers carried weapons, but none of them worked while the abduction lights were on. Soldiers pointed and cursed at the aliens, but the guns did nothing.

"Mac!"

Who was calling his name?

It was Nelson. He had been collected, and he brought a gun with him. He threw it towards Mac. It didn't follow the arc he expected it to because the light kept everything level. The gun slid along an invisible line until it got to within a foot of the edge. Then it stopped. There was an invisible barrier there as we'll. Otherwise, when the room was filled with the *Skyrattler*'s entire crew, men would be able to climb out.

The barrier did not stop Mac from reaching out and grabbing the gun. His cover was about to be blown. It was a good thing none of the aliens could hurt him.

But the real threat wasn't going to come from the aliens.

Cliff waited with another gunner, Rory, in the docking bay. He was even younger than Cliff, who was only nineteen. Always eager to do as he was told, Rory had his hand on the fire button, ready to carry out the order he was expecting.

"You do realize that this is a suicide mission," said Cliff.

"I know."

271

"If you push that button before we are supposed to, you will kill all of us for no reason other than you were too puppy-dog excited to sit back, relax, and wait for the order to kill ourselves."

"Oh, right."

Rory leaned back. But he didn't stop looking at the fire button. In front of the attack shuttle that Cliff was flying, containers filled with explosives were stacked from floor to ceiling.

The shuttle itself, a HAAS3, was hovering in the docking bay waiting for its signal. Soon the collector ship would envelop them in an energy-sucking light. All the power would go out in the *Skyrattler*, and that's when Rory was supposed to make the shot.

The shuttle wouldn't be affected because it wasn't touching the ship. Only things that touched the ship or the light coming from the collector ship got the power sucked out of them. Floating in the docking bay avoided both of these conditions. Cliff's job was to make sure the shuttle stayed where it was supposed to. The shuttle wasn't affected by outside influences. If the *Skyrattler* was flying close to the speed of light, the shuttle wouldn't have to go the speed of light while flying inside of it. He just had to keep it off the ground and away from the walls.

The ship started shaking. Cliff adjusted to keep from making contact. He didn't do it fast enough and bumped the wall.

"You're the one that needs to concentrate," said Rory. "If the power had gone out just now, the swarms would get us all."

"You worry about your button. I'll worry about the ship."

The lights started flickering as the *Skyrattler* shuddered even more.

"Here we go," said Rory. His hand hovered again.

Cliff knew what he needed to do. There was only one sure way to make sure no one pressed any of the buttons. Seeing no point in being discreet, he put the ship down.

"What are you doing?" said Rory.

The lights went out just then. The ambient light from the windows and docking bay door allowed Cliff to see the outline of the explosive containers and the shocked looked on Rory's face. The shuttle was completely dead, just like the rest of the ship.

"Why did you do that?" asked Rory.

"You have to trust me."

"What?"

"The man we found on the swarm ship, do you remember him?" asked Cliff.

"Yeah, what does he have to do with anything?"

"He has a better perspective on this war than anyone else. He knows how to save us without blowing ourselves up."

"He told you this?"

"The swarms can't hurt him. He's going to go over there to kill them all."

Rory shook his head. As he got up and headed for the door, he drew his gun. He intended to take care of things himself.

"Wait!" Cliff jumped up just as Rory fired.

The laser hit Cliff in the leg and sent him to the floor. Rory was shaking. He knew what his orders were. Blow up the ship. It didn't matter if he had to kill Cliff to do it. They were all going to be dead soon anyway. Rory got out of the shuttle and walked toward the munitions cache.

Cliff was still in the shuttle. He pulled himself up on his good leg and hobbled after Rory. If he couldn't prevent the explosion then he at least needed to delay it as long as possible.

"I'm not asking you to disobey orders. I'm asking you to wait. Give him some time," said Cliff.

"This is standard procedure. We have to follow procedure."

"You're following it blind! There is a better way."

"This is the only way we can avoid being their slaves and kill them at the same time."

Rory raised his gun to shoot at the containers. Cliff knew they didn't have to sacrifice ship and crew, but he couldn't persuade Rory to stand down. Cliff's hand shook as he squeezed the trigger and shot Rory in the back. He lurched forward and slammed to the floor. Cliff was shaking so hard he accidentally fired another blast. This one hit the explosives.

As soon as Mac reached for the gun, every alien in the collecting room turned to look at him. The ruse was over. They all turned into attack clouds and rushed at Mac. Nothing hurt him, just like before, but he still had to see to know where he was going.

He shot at the wall and a door opened into a hallway. He ran through it and pulled away from the swarm, but as soon as he slowed down they were all over him. He fired again at the wall and opened up a small room.

He found the emulator room just as the *Skyrattler* exploded. The explosion was so close to the collector ship that he was thrown into the ceiling and slam-dunked to the floor. But unknown to Mac, the delay Cliff created was enough time for the collector ship to pull away to avoid catastrophic damage that would kill the *Skyrattler* crew that had already been collected. When Mac stood up he had trouble keeping his balance.

He had been surrounded by a cloud of pointlessly attacking swarms ever since he picked up the gun Nelson had thrown to him. When the *Skyrattler* broke apart, the attacks stopped. The clouds flowed out of the room heading for some unknown haven. Mac didn't know where they were going but he knew they weren't going to get there. He started destroying the emulators.

After they were all destroyed he had to find a way to save the people who had been abducted—if they were still alive. Mac didn't want to waste time running to see if they were. Instead he went to the wall and thought over and over in his mind: *Communications. Communications.*

He kept his eyes closed and hoped that when he opened them he would see the communications console emerge from the wall the same way doors magically appeared. That's how everything seemed to work on these ships. When he opened his eyes, nothing had changed.

He closed his eyes again and pictured the computer console in his mind. He pictured the buttons he would push when it formed, and who he would call and what he would say. All the while saying over and over in his mind: *Communications, communications, communications.*

This time when he opened his eyes the console was there. He punched the buttons just as he had been thinking. Using the screen, he called out to the nearest capital ship.

"This is Mac Narrad. I was on the *Skyrattler*. Our ship was destroyed, but we have taken the enemy ship. I need help rescuing the crew. They are in the collecting area where the lights came out of. I don't know if they are still alive."

"Mac Narrad, this is the *Bear's Paw,* are you saying you figured out how to use the alien's communications systems?"

"Yes. We need your help."

"We see that and are en route with support shuttles."

That probably meant people were starting to drift out into space. Mac hoped that at least Nelson was okay. He would need some allies when this was all over. The *Bear's Paw* shuttles flew to the collection room's opening.

Just like he did with the communications terminal, Mac thought over and over again about accessing a computer terminal so he could see what was going on out there. He tried picturing it in his head, but what came out of the wall wasn't exactly what he had pictured. Instead, a control pad and a split screen appeared. The screen showed a live feed of the battle on one half and sensor readouts on the other half.

The good news was that the humans were winning the fight—the aliens were retreating. The bad news was that they were literally trading ship for ship. The humans couldn't destroy collector ships without destroying their own ships in the process.

Another readout tracked the currents of aliens who were in swarm form. Some were stationary. Their clouds were drifting further and further apart because they had no emulator to cling to. The space around the destroyed collector ships was full of swarms that weren't dead, but they weren't alive either. They were waiting for someone to put them back together.

Four collector ships were intact, but there was a mass exodus of swarms from three of them to the one farthest from the conflict. Mac watched their retreat on the readout, but the alien clouds couldn't be seen with the naked eye. The human's warships were uselessly attacking empty collector ships.

The last ship was making a slow retreat. It waited while aliens swarming around it tried to get in. Once the surrounding space cleared up, Mac heard a voice in his head. A female voice, similar to the one that came from Janelle's emulator. But he knew it couldn't be her, because she was in a billion little particles light years away. Yet they sounded almost the same.

We see you, Mac Narrad.

Mac didn't know how to respond. He didn't even know who was talking to him. Would it work if he pictured Janelle?

You cannot stop us. The battle may be lost, but you have yet to see the full extent of our power, the voice said again.

I know how to stop you, said Mac. He didn't picture Janelle; he just projected his thoughts outward and hoped that whoever was talking to him would pick it up. *I took out two ships all by myself. There is only one of me right now, but there will be more. How do you expect to get through someone you can't even hurt?*

There is potential for you that you do not understand. Come with us now and we will show it to you. We will teach you how to best use your new abilities.

I think I can figure it out for myself.

What about her? The one you call Janelle. Do you ever want to see her again?

Mac hesitated. What if there was a way to get her back? He could go with the aliens, get Janelle, and *then* come back and tell people about Ronos.

How do I get her back? asked Mac.

Come with us. We will take you to her.

How do I get to you?

Jump out of that ship. We'll come get you.

In and out. Mac could be in and out before anything went wrong. He could save Janelle. That had been his goal all along, hadn't it? That's why he had joined the military. That's why he got an Imp. That's why he survived and his whole family died. That's why he was here on the edge of space fighting alien invaders. If he could get her back it would make everything worth it.

Then Lynn started talking to him mentally.

Mac! I need your help! I need you to come back here right now!

Her frantic plea came out of nowhere and freaked him out.

What's wrong? asked Mac.

It's Raymond. I don't know how, but he's still alive.

What?

I can't get away from him. He always knows where I am. It feels like I've been running for hours.

Mac knew that he couldn't go for Janelle yet. Lynn needed him right away; Janelle would have to wait just a little longer. Soon, just not soon enough for Mac, they would be back together. First he needed to save Lynn from Raymond and then win this war. He had no idea how he was going to do any of this. How was Raymond still alive? How was Mac going to get back to Ronos to save Lynn? Getting to Ronos was only a small part of the problem. Zinger and his army of followers would already be there trying to solve the mystery of where Mac got his powers. How was he going to use the Lynn Rock to change enough people to win the war with Zinger snooping around? He wouldn't let uncertainty undermine his determination. He hadn't battled this far just to give up on everything. His family was dead. They were murdered. Zinger had to be stopped. The war had to be won.

Don't worry about it, Mac said to the alien, *I'll just come get her some other time.*

There won't be another time.

The last collector ship vanished into hyperspace, going back the way it had come. The alien voice in Mac's head went away. He hoped he hadn't made a huge mistake.

I'm on my way, Lynn, said Mac.

There was no response.

Lynn?

Nothing.

She was gone.

Mac had lost them both.

TO BE CONTINUED…

What I Know

I need to tell my readers some of the things I know. The list of things I know isn't very long but it still has some important stuff on it. Like how I know that the paninis at the Italian Market in Edmonton are the best sandwiches I have ever had, that I'm lucky to be married to someone as amazing as my wife and that I am truly in love with her, that Joseph Smith was a prophet of God, that the Book of Mormon is a true book, and that Jesus Christ is the Savior of the world, I know that this book would not have been possible to do on my own.

Yes. There is only one name on the cover, and yes, that is my name. But I know that it wouldn't have ever been written if I didn't have the early support of my parents. Those poor guys had to read my first attempts at prose. I'm sure it was a struggle but they told me I was good and should keep writing. It did wonders for an aspiring author's ego. I know I wouldn't be a writer without my parents.

I also know that this book would have been delayed by several years if I had to work normal working hours at a day job. So, without Rod Kay, who let me set my own hours, thus allowing me to write the entire first draft of Catalyst for NaNoWriMo 2010, Glenn Penman, who trained me in the art of tank car loading, and Shane Trewin, who hired me despite the fact I had no experience with tank cars or trains in general, this book would not be in your hands right now. I know that I am very lucky to have the job that I do.

I also know that I am lucky to have the friends I do. Without my friends to use as a test audience I would have had to spend even more money on editors. If that happened, my wife and I would have had to survive off of noodles, water, and the kindness of strangers. I know I couldn't have done it without my test readers. I love you guys.

Speaking of editors, I know this book would have been much harder to read if I didn't have Rhonda Skinner edit it for me. She worked hard on this book and it shows. It wouldn't have been the same without her. Thank you!

I know that one of the hardest choices I had to make for this book was choosing which cover to use. The talented Chris Pratt gave me two choices and I wanted to use them both. It was a hard choice but there's not much to complain about when you're choosing from two awesome covers. It's not like there was a wrong choice because they were both better than I could imagine.

I've said it already but I also know that I couldn't have done this without my wife. She keeps me motivated and passionate about writing. She inspires me to be better in every aspect of my life.

The last thing I know is that there is an audience out there looking for exciting, well written, professionally edited, entertainment that can be enjoyed by everyone. I wrote this book for those people. Mostly because I'm one of those people. I have already told everyone I know about this book and I hope you do the same thing. I know that the best way to reach as many people as possible is for the readers to go out and spread this book like wildfire. Remember, only tell people who like to be entertained about this book. No one else.

If they like book one then tell them book two is going to blow their minds because it only gets bigger and better from here. What happened to Lynn? What secrets is Jace hiding? Who is the only man in Passage with an Imp? How is Mac going to stop the invaders from reaching Ronos? What happens when they reach Ronos? How will he make Zinger pay for what he did?

I've read book two and I know most of these questions will be answered and it will not be easy going for any of the characters. Especially Mac and Lynn.

About the Author

Tyler Rudd Hall is a member of the Church of Jesus Christ of Latter-day Saints. He grew up in the small farming community of Rosemary, Alberta. Because of this he had to use his imagination and VHS copies of *Star Wars* to keep himself entertained. After graduating from Rosemary High School he went into the Professional Writing program at McEwan University in Edmonton, Alberta. There he met his beautiful and talented wife who was enrolled in the same program. Both of them are now recent graduates and pursuing their professional writing goals in Edmonton.

Find more books by Tyler Rudd Hall on
goodreads.com/tylerruddhall

Manufactured by Amazon.ca
Acheson, AB

14235733R00160